I remember shouts, people crying, some screaming, and the frantic starting of engines. Sounded like the gunning of engines at the Indy 500. I don't even remember who grabbed my hand and pulled me out from under the tent where I'd been standing with one of the volunteers. I do remember being shoved, buffeted, and pummeled on all sides, but eventually making it to the area roped off for the parked vehicles.

Someone was holding tight to my hand, squeezing it so hard that I thought the bones would crack. I looked up.

"Mal!"

I clung to him for a moment. Only a moment. It was all the time that he would allow for us. It wasn't enough. Not nearly enough! At the same time, it was too much. I could feel his heart beating, even through his coat. It was beating fast. Fast enough to burst. I could feel him squeeze me for just a second and whisper a few words in my ear. Words that would only come out in the worst of times. Words that I'm certain that he would never have allowed himself to say otherwise.

"I love you, Jess Ramsay."

Too much and not enough. I'd waited for so long to hear those words. Over a year. The last time he'd said them didn't count. Maybe this time didn't count, either. Fear did strange things to a person. Maybe, if we survived this, he'd wish that he'd never said those words to me . . .

BOOK YOUR PLACE ON OUR WEBSITE AND MAKE THE ARABESQUE ROMANCE CONNECTION!

We've created a customized website just for our very special Arabesque readers, where you can get the inside scoop on everything that's going on with Arabesque romance novels.

When you come online, you'll have the exciting opportunity to:

- View covers of upcoming books

- Learn about our future publishing schedule (listed by publication month and author)

- Find out when your favorite authors will be visiting a city near you

- Search for and order backlist books

- Check out author bios and background information

- Send e-mail to your favorite authors

- Join us in weekly chats with authors, readers and other guests

- Get writing guidelines

- AND MUCH MORE!

Visit our website at
http://www.arabesquebooks.com

Love
Runs Deep

Geri
Guillaume

BET Publications, LLC
http://www.bet.com
http://www.arabesquebooks.com

ARABESQUE BOOKS are published by

BET Publications, LLC
c/o BET BOOKS
One BET Plaza
1900 W Place NE
Washington, DC 20018-1211

All Kensington Titles, Imprints, and Distributed Lines are available at special quantity discounts for bulk purchases for sales promotions, premiums, fund-raising, and educational or institutional use. Special book excerpts or customized printings can also be created to fit specific needs. For details, write or phone the office of the Kensington special sales manager: Kensington Publishing Corp., 850 Third Avenue, New York, NY 10022, attn: Special Sales Department, Phone: 1-800-221-2647.

First Printing: August 2005

10 9 8 7 6 5 4 3 2 1

Printed in the United States of America

Acknowledgements

This novel is dedicated to the memory of my mother, Mary Ann Williams—the epitome of the modern educator. A true gentlewoman.

I'd also like to thank my Aunt Elaine and Aunt Ann for their strength and support during our time of sweet sorrow and perfect praise.

For my brother Malcolm and sisters Donna and Kendra, thank you for encouraging me to continue doing what Mama would have wanted me to. For my husband, Robert, thank you for always being there for me. For Grandma Winnie Bell—her love and devotion is a model for us all. For my father, Don, and all of his support.

And to my extended family at the Integrity Group, the Livingstons, and my host of nieces, nephews, cousins, uncles, and aunts in Jackson, thank you. Thank you all.

Chapter One

Jess

The weather forecast last Friday had predicted light rain through the weekend. How are you gonna call this light rain? Light rain doesn't creep up past your back porch, seep under your door, and puddle ankle deep on the brand-new wood laminate floor that I'd just put in. Brand spanking new. I'd just installed it myself last month.

Six A.M. on a Monday morning, and what am I doing? Mopping up light rain, that's what. Instead of getting ready for work, I'm bending over a mop bucket, wondering if I should have my head examined.

The first thing I did when I finished laying the last laminate plank was rush out and buy one of those cute little mops—one of those Swiffers that squirts a jet of cleaning liquid at the push of a button. I'd seen a commercial for one on one of those decorate-your-house-for-under-a-hundred-dollars shows.

I took one look at the private lake forming in my kitchen and knew that Swiffer wasn't going to cut it. Not this time.

Guess it's back to "ol' faithful"—the mop I'd gotten from my job. Mr. Victor, the school custodian, didn't need it anymore. He was going to throw it out. But when I told him that I was moving into my new place, the first home that I'd purchased on my own, that mop was his housewarming gift to me.

At first, I thought he had a screw loose, giving me that smelly, beat-up-looking thing. That mop had certainly seen better days. It was as old as Mr. Victor. The wooden handle was cracked, and if you weren't careful, it could give you splinters. Half of the cotton strings were gone. And the metal base that barely held the remaining strings in place scraped more of my floor than it cleaned. The first time I used "ol' faithful" on my original orange and brown, hole-filled, bubble gum–stained linoleum floor, I thought I'd have the health inspector after me.

I must have soaked that mop for two hours in a concoction of bleach, Pine Sol, and ammonia before I felt it was safe enough to use. Almost passed out from the fumes. The disgusting thing was probably more trouble than it was worth. I should have just bought a new one. But I had just put down every last dime on closing costs for my house. I was broke. Flat broke. Couldn't even afford to buy a cheap mop at the dollar store. You know it's bad when you can't even afford to buy a new mop. Couldn't afford a broom for the first two weeks I lived here, either. When the floor got really dusty, I just dragged out a box fan and blew the more noticeable trash out the door.

Now, I was thankful that old Mr. Victor hadn't thrown out "ol' faithful." After tossing my soaked bunny slippers into the washing machine, rolling up my cotton pajama bottoms to my knees, and flipping the circuit breakers to kill the electricity to the kitchen appliances, I reached back into the utility closet and dug around for the mop and bucket.

The mop wasn't pretty. Still, it got the job done. Even with most of the strands missing, soaking wet, it still felt heavy to me. And the longer I pushed it across the floor, the heavier it seemed to get. But I was thankful to have it. With the huge plastic yellow bucket on wheels marked PROPERTY OF COLE ELEMENTARY in fading black letters on the side, I used both to slowly reduce the lake in my kitchen to a couple of puddles.

It was hard work and it gave me a deeper appreciation for Mr. Victor's stamina. I only had a kitchen to cover. He had an entire school—two floors of classrooms, a cafeteria, a gym, a music hall, and various administrative offices. Every morning, starting about four A.M., you could find him patiently swabbing the corridors. Always a pleasant word. Always a toothless smile for those tracking over his freshly mopped floor. How he did it, day after day, year after year, I don't know. I was nothing but scowls and curses as I imitated his routine. Back and forth. Back and forth. Lift the mop into the bucket, push on the handle to squeeze out the excess water, then attack the floor again.

At first I'd opened the back door, thinking that I could push most of the water back outside. No chance of that. The water that had covered my porch had receded somewhat, but it was now pooling in my driveway. It had already reached midway up my tires. My car is midsize, just a step up from an economy car. Not the kind of car that can go sloshing through the rain and the mud like in those sexy SUV commercials. If I go plowing through a river, I'd be one of those people with a flooded engine, calling for a tow truck.

If the rain keeps coming down like it is, the water in my kitchen is going to be the least of my worries.

Another hour or so of this and the water will be back in my house before the floor has dried. It might creep up past the kitchen and soak my carpet and Oriental-style throw rugs.

"*Damn!*"

Hindsight is twenty-twenty. No wonder I slept so well last night. Rainwater falling against my window pane soothed me like a lullaby. Maybe I dreamt. But I don't remember any dreams. I was sleeping hard, the kind of deep sleep that leaves pillow-crease lines on your face.

The alarm went off at five-thirty that morning as usual. I guess I was well-rested, because I didn't even bother hitting the snooze button like I usually do. Especially on Mondays. I always hit the snooze button on Monday mornings. Without even thinking, my hand reaches out and slams on the snooze bar like swatting at an annoying fly. I usually hit the bar two or three times, giving me almost twenty extra minutes of not-quite-restfulness. Not as satisfying as a deep sleep, I admit. But any extra minutes lying in bed makes me think that my weekends have lasted just a wee bit longer.

Not this Monday. This morning I sat right up, swung my legs off the edge of the bed, and into my waiting bunny slippers. I was awake, but not completely alert. My brain wouldn't really start firing on all cylinders until I had that first cup of morning coffee.

Nothing like stepping into a puddle of ice-cold water to get those brain synapses firing. Coffee or no coffee, I was awake. After half an hour of mopping and wringing, I was tired again even before the day began.

When the floor was just about done, I straightened up my body—one hand on the mop handle, the other rubbing the kinks out of the small of my back. I was sweating. Beads of perspiration gathered on my forehead, plastering my auburn-tinted hair against my forehead.

I really have to start increasing my workouts. Cleaning my house shouldn't be this hard. I licked my dry lips and debated turning the electricity back on. I could really go for some freshly brewed coffee right now. I have a Gevalia coffee brewer. And fresh gourmet coffee was delivered to my doorstep whenever I wanted it.

"Except for when water in your house threatens to electrocute you," I reminded myself.

I reached into the fridge, settling for orange juice instead. In my current state of mind, I didn't even pour it into a glass. Just tilted the carton to my lips and gulped down several swallows.

I didn't stop guzzling, even when the phone rang. I tiptoed across the floor, glancing back over my shoulder to see if I'd left any tracks. Hard to tell in the dark since I'd cut the electricity to the kitchen. I swallowed the last of the juice as I reached for the receiver.

"Jessica?"

A concerned voice on the other line made me put down the carton and wipe my mouth with the back of my hand. Mama! How did she always know to call when I was doing something she would consider less than appropriate? Her impeccable timing was the very same reason I stopped walking around the house in the nude. It was the reason she stopped coming by unannounced, too.

I still remember the look on her face when she walked in without knocking, without calling out to let me know she was inside, and caught me, naked as the day I was born, cooking a Saturday morning breakfast.

It's my house. I should be able to walk around with nary a stitch on if I want to. Still, I keep several robes stashed in different corners of the house for those unexpected visits.

"Yes, Mama."

"Are you watching the news, Jess? Have you heard the latest weather report?"

"You mean the one that promised light rain?"

My tone was openly sarcastic as I stared warily at the floor, trying to detect evidence of warping or staining. I walked back over the kitchen, dragging my feet across the floor. I'd laid the floor myself, taking advantage of all of the home improvement shows that I'd watched. The flooring-supply store assured me when I'd selected the brand that it could withstand almost anything, and would look beautiful for years to come. I wonder if he'd make the same promise if he knew about the downpour now?

"Light rain? Jess, what in the world are you talking about?"

"What are you talking about, Mama?"

Sometimes, it took us a while before we were able to get on the same page. I think it has something to do with the way we only half-listen to each other.

"I'm talking about the news. Haven't you been following it?"

"Ummm . . . not really," I confessed. "I've been watching a lot of old movies this weekend."

Seems like I've been watching a lot of old movies lately. Romantic ones. Comedies. And tearjerkers. Just me, my collection of remote controls, and—if I make a run to the grocery store—a tub of kettle corn and a couple of pints of butter pecan ice cream. Last night, I'd boo-hoo-hooed over a double tearjerker. *Mahogany* and *Imitation of Life*. I'd fallen asleep to the mournful wailing of Mahalia Jackson, singing the dirge "Trouble of the World" in that heart-wrenching funeral scene.

"Jess, turn on the television," Mama orders. "Turn it on right now. Honey, we're under a flash flood watch now. That tropical storm in the Gulf of Mexico has been moving toward us since Friday night."

"What tropical storm? You mean that front that was supposed to miss us and take an easterly turn? That's what had been predicted last week."

I took the cordless phone with me, cradling it between my ear and shoulder, and moved from the kitchen, through the breakfast area, and back upstairs. The open area at the top of the stairs was the unofficial game room-slash-office-slash-exercise room-slash-media room. I picked up the remote from the plush chocolate-brown sectional couch and pointed it at the flat-screen television. I had to surf through several movie channels before finally landing on a local news station.

The reporter was standing in front of a map showing several counties and the inches of rainfall received over the past twelve hours. Our own Codell County, Mississippi was highlighted in bright red on the map, indicating an increased likelihood of flooding. We didn't have a television station of our own. All of the local channels were either from Jackson or from Natchez. This particular newscast was out of Jackson.

"Eight inches," I murmured, and gave a low whistle under my breath. "I'm not surprised. Half of that water wound up in my kitchen."

"You've got water coming into your house?"

"Uh-huh."

"Oh, Jessica! Your new floor," Mama said, in a kind of way that made me believe that there was something I did to cause the flooding. Like I'd done something bone-headed like leave the water running all night. Sometimes my toilet runs long after I flush; jiggling the handle fixes that. Just as soon as I watch another home improvement show on plumbing or log on to the Internet and pull up that Do-It-Yourself Network, I am gonna fix that, too.

Mama didn't hide the fact that she didn't want me to

buy this house. She said that it wasn't a good deal. I dis-
agreed. The price, the location, and the square footage
were simply perfect. And I was out of Mama's house—
which is where I really wanted to be. That's what made it
most attractive.

A thirty-two-year-old, able-bodied, educated, self-
sufficient woman has no business living at home with
her parents. I'd been saying that ever since I was eighteen. But it took me this long to save up the money to
really get out on my own.

I tried apartment living for a while. I'd shared a really
nice two-bedroom garage apartment with my girlfriend
Shelby. But it seemed as though I was just throwing my
money down a hole. The folks who owned the garage
apartment were Shelby's cousins. Though they'd cut
Shelby a break on the rent, I still had to pay up. After a
few months of that, I told Shelby that things weren't
turning out like I expected. I wasn't feeling that I-was-
the-only-one-who-had-to-pay arrangement. It just wasn't
working for me.

So, when I was twenty-four, I moved back in with
Mama. Six months and I was going to be out of there, I
told myself. Eight months at the latest. Took me eight
years. Not because I'm lazy. That wasn't it at all. Stuff
happens. And when it does, you put your life on hold.

We all had to sacrifice after Daddy had a stroke. Mama
came out of retirement and went back to work. I put off
my dreams of owning my own home. Private in-home
care was so incredibly expensive. Each time we had to
pick up the cost of Daddy's medication and examina-
tions and the part not covered by his medical insurance.
After a while I tried not to see it as one more piece of furniture or one more unnecessary knickknack that my
house wouldn't have.

Any money they could have given me to help me out

with the down payment for the house was spent taking care of him. Thank the Lord Daddy's better now, and can get along without being watched twenty-four hours a day. But when somebody's that sick for that long, the recovery is more than just physical. It's financial. With everyone pitching in, including my younger brother, James, we managed to pull through.

Eight years of scrimping and saving. But I did it. I was in my own home now. Flaws and all. Better late than never.

"I got most of it all up, Mama," I protested, trying to impress her with my housekeeping skills.

"Did you go over it with a big, soft drying towel?"

"Mama, I know you didn't call me this early in the morning to talk about housekeeping, did you?"

Next thing you know, she was going to ask me whether I was washing behind my ears or wearing clean underwear every day. For the record, I do. To both.

"No . . . no, I didn't. I called to tell you, in case you haven't heard, no school today, Jess. I've got a telephone interview with the television station at seven o'clock and one with the radio station at seven-thirty to confirm that the district is canceling school for today. I'm going on early. I don't want anyone trying to make it in. It's just too nasty out there."

Mama was the principal of the elementary school where I worked as a third grade teacher. Another reason to get out from under her roof. We were with each other all day at work and all day at home, too. I love my mother. Cherish her. But we had gotten on each other's last nerve a long time ago. We're just too much alike, as Mama was often quick to say when I did something she didn't approve of. "There's only one woman living in this house, Jessica Ramsay, and that's me."

"No school. I can practically hear the collective

cheering of every student in Codell County." I laughed. "All two hundred and fifteen of them."

There were only two schools in Codell County, a combination elementary and middle school and a high school. We weren't really a county, as I often had to explain to new parents who had moved to our town and were looking into education options for their kids. Codell County was the town name—named so in honor of its founder, whose name was Codell County. Honest. If I'm lying I'm dying. Codell and his wife, Rachel, started out with a modest general store in 1905. Now, a hundred years later, we had two general stores, a bank, a post office, and fast-food restaurants to suit almost every taste.

"Call it an early Christmas present," Mama said sarcastically.

"Christmas? It's not even Halloween yet, Mama."

Halloween was two weeks away. As bad as this weather was becoming, we were all getting a little frightened early this year.

"We've still got temperatures in the seventies. That's why this weather is so crazy. Hot one day. Cold the next. No wonder we're all walking around here with the flu."

"Is the bus running?" I meant the school bus. We didn't have public transportation yet. Well, there was Bull Pearson's tractor, but that didn't count. He'd just as soon spit on you as give you a lift if you and he happened to be out on the road at the same time. Just because you could find him at almost any time of day or night running that old John Deere up the road, it didn't count as town transportation.

"Yes, it's running. Miss Willis called me this morning around five A.M. and told me that she'll take anyone who wants to go to the high school as long as the roads are passable. The Red Cross has set up a shelter there in anticipation of more bad weather."

"Is it that bad out there, Mama?"

I turned up the volume so that I could hear what was going on. An on-the-scene reporter, in head-to-toe rain gear, was standing in front of the high school turned shelter interviewing our Chief of Police, Malcolm Loring.

"Mama, do you—" I started to say, but she shushed me.

"Quiet, Jess. That's Mal on TV."

"I know who that is, Mama," I said testily.

I'd only known Malcolm Loring since we were in grade school. He was three grades ahead of me. Would've been four, but he got held back in the first grade. He might have been held back in the second grade, too, if it weren't for Mama. The boy wasn't stupid. But he was so quiet and reserved, he hardly ever opened his mouth to speak. The school principal at the time and the counselor thought he was just plain slow, and would have put him in the special education class, if it weren't for Mama. Working with him, she brought him out of his shell and showed everyone his full potential. Not many of the teachers in Codell County had heard of dyslexia back then, which Mal had.

I remembered staying in Mama's classroom, long after school had let out, reading my story books or drawing on the chalkboard while Mama and Mal patiently went over his schoolwork. Actually, Mama was patient. Mal was frustrated, angry that it took him longer than other kids to grasp the concepts. He was frustrated, and I was bored. Used to throw chalk at him when Mama wasn't looking, just to see that look on his face when I popped him.

He had that same look on his face now—like he'd rather be anywhere but there.

"Well, let's find out what he has to say, honey."

She had her TV on the same station. Her volume was so loud, I could hear Mal on Mama's television and mine.

He stood with his hands thrust deep into his pockets,

head lowered, speaking into the microphone held just under his nose. With his hat pulled low over his eyes, I could barely see his face. I think his posture was as much to keep the cameras away as it was to keep his face from being pelted by the rain.

Mal never really was comfortable in the spotlight. How he worked up the nerve to apply for the chief of police position, I don't think I'll ever know. The boy used to get sick standing up in the church choir before every solo performance. And he was asked to sing a lot. If I had a voice like that, I wouldn't be ashamed of it. Soft and mellow. When he really got to blowin', it made all the ladies lose their religion, hollering and carrying on so.

There he was, looking all official in his black rain slicker with "Police" in bright yellow letters across his back. Mal was a soft-spoken man. Barely raised his voice. But something about him made you listen. I was listening now, as he was urging anyone living in low-lying areas to move to higher ground while the roads were still passable.

That would be me he was talking to. I could almost hear him tack "Jess" at the end of every sentence.

I was living in what was called a flood-control zone. Which meant my section of town was developed specifically to hold the flood waters if the river overflowed its banks. We had two levees, Bramfort and Fulsome, that acted as another line of defense for the heavier-populated areas of the county. My house and a few others in the area were smack-dab in the middle of the flood plain. Another reason for Mama to remind me why I shouldn't have bought this house.

I'd taken a gamble. Yes, it rained a lot here. And yes, the river always rose some. That much was to be expected. But I was assured that the likelihood of the flood overrunning the levees was once in every hundred years or so. As much as I wanted to live forever, I figured I would have moved at least a couple of times in that length of time, or be buried in the same ground the waters would wash over. So, I signed the papers, comfortable in the fact that it I wouldn't have to worry. I'd done it and nothing could be done now but wait out the weather.

"Why don't you pack some things, Jess, come on over here?" Mama suggested.

"I don't know, Mama. Maybe I should—"

"Should what?!" Mama cut me off. "Wait until you're stranded and Mal has to come and get you?"

Ooohhhh, her tone cut me like a knife. She'll never let me forget the time I snuck out of the house, drove that clunker car that she told my daddy not to buy for me, and wound up stranded with a flat tire on some back road looking for a party one of my girlfriends had gotten a flyer about. I was seventeen years old then. I was too scared to walk to a neighbor, almost five miles down the road, to call home to let Mama know where I was. And I was too goofy to look into the trunk of the car for the jack and the spare to try to figure out how to change the tire.

Three o'clock in the morning, Mama discovered I was gone and called the police to hunt me down. Mal was the one who'd come out to get me and my three girlfriends, whom I'd picked up along the way. He never let me forget that stupid stunt either—which is one of the many reasons why I can't stand his officious ass. He's thirty-six years old. Too old to be bringing up a mess out of our past.

I doubt if he would come after me. Because sometimes, Mal can't stand me either. I am the only one that could make Mal raise his voice. My own special talent for getting on his nerves.

"All right, Mama. Just let me clean up, throw some things in a bag, and I'll be over in about an hour."

"Do you want me to come and get you, Jess? That old car of yours, I worry about you driving it in this weather."

Another one of my special buys that Mama advised me against purchasing.

"Nuh-uh. I'll be just fine. You go on and conduct your interviews, Mama. I'll be there as soon as I can."

Chapter Two

Mal

I can't be every where at once, even if I wanted to be. What do they think I am? A jackrabbit hopping back and forth across the county? Talking to reporters first thing this morning. Into the station by seven. Back out to the high school by eight to make sure those folks from the Red Cross have everything they needed.

Man, I hate this freakin' rain. Hate that I have to be out here. What am I doing out here? Talking to these idiot reporters who're just looking to make a name for themselves on the national news by chasing every mud puddle that looks like a potential human-interest grabber.

If I could have pushed this public-service announcement detail to one of my officers, I would have. The reporter wouldn't hear of it. She had to convince me that the story would have more emotional impact coming from me, the so-called authority figure in town, rather than from a junior officer.

"I'm standing here with Chief of Police Malcolm Loring of the Codell County police department. Chief, can you tell us what we can expect over the next few hours if this weather continues?"

Clearing my throat, I tried to sound . . . impactful.

"Well . . . uh . . . Our office has been in contact with meteorologists from your news station. According to the national weather service, more rain is to be expected."

"Do you think the river will reach flood stage? And if so, when?"

"Of course there's always that possibility," I said carefully.

We are living along a river. What else could you expect it to do but flood when you get this much rain in such a short period of time? I didn't want to panic anyone and make them do anything foolish, however. There were a few odd-balls in our town who would want to take their boats out onto the river, just brag about having gone down the river when she was at her most dangerous. Just like those folks who flock to the Gulf of Mexico when there's a hurricane brewing, just to be able to say that they'd ridden it out.

"But I don't have any information on that at this time," I continued. "Because of the downpours, there has been some localized street flooding, however. The list of road closings should be appearing on the screen now."

The production assistant, who was holding up the cue cards for the reporter, gave me the thumb's up sign letting me know that the street closing information was being broadcast as I'd said.

"If there is major flooding, does Codell County have an emergency plan?"

"We're asking that anyone living in low lying areas to move to higher ground. Right now, this is strictly a precautionary measure. We're calling for a voluntary evacuation. The high school is open and the folks from the Red Cross have set up a shelter. Anybody who needs assistance should call the Red Cross or the Codell County police department directly. We'll help you. I'm reminding everyone that unless it's a real emergency, please leave the 9-1-1 lines open."

"Thank you, Chief. If there is flooding, we'll be here, live on the scene, bringing you up-to-the-minute reports on weather conditions as they happen. This is Janay Russell, Channel Five news."

Sometimes these reporters make me sick. It's ridiculous what they'll try to sell as news. Whoops, there goes another tree branch floating by. Better get a camera shot of that. Look, there's a car with water almost up to its hood. Let's see if we can get a shot of some poor soul stuck on his roof with water pouring into his house. That oughta tug a few heartstrings on the evening news.

While I'm standing out here mugging for the camera, with rain dripping all down my collar, making me miserable, I could be out there doing my job. They don't need me to stand here and tell them that it's raining outside. What I need to be doing is getting out there and helping those who can't do anything about the rain for themselves.

Back at the station, Walker told me that all of the phone lines were lit, folks calling in to report high water sightings. I'm trying to do my job, give that professional but compassionate air. But all the time I'm thinking that if you've got half a brain and you know the water is coming up faster than you can bail it out, then heaven help you if you don't have sense enough to get out of the way.

And that's exactly what I told Ms. Ramsay when she called me on my cell phone complaining about her daughter Jess again. What did she expect me to do? Drop everything and rush out there because that mule-headed daughter of hers won't listen?

She didn't listen to me when I told her not to buy that cracker-box house right there in the middle of a flood-control zone. Why should she start listening to me now? She *never* listens to me. Not when it matters. I can't make her go if she doesn't want to. And I don't want to hear her mouth if I show up at her doorstep. I don't have time for that crap. Other folks need my help a lot more than she does.

Who am I kidding? I know I'm gonna go. I'm going right over there. You know why? Because I'm the biggest idiot of them all. I can't say no to Ms. Ramsay—just because she was my second grade teacher. Saying no to her is like saying no to God. You don't do it. You just don't do it. All she's gotta do is remind me of how she used to stay extra hours after school helping me with my schoolwork so I could pass to the third grade.

So, against my better judgment, what am I doing? As soon as the reporter moves on, searching for someone else to interview, I climbed into my Jeep four-by-four, cranked up the engine, and called in to the station to let them know I'd be making rounds. I wasn't fooling anybody. They all knew where I was going—and why.

Damn that Jess Ramsay and her stubbornness. Damn her straight to hell. And me along with her for not sending one of my officers out there to get her instead of me. That would have been the prudent thing to do. Send Walker or Edmonds or Myles. Yeah, Myles Overton would've been a better choice. I think he's got a thing for her. He tries to hide it, but I can tell. If I'd asked him to go, he would have been out there before I could finish getting the words out of my mouth. Stroke of genius, sending Myles. But I'm not feeling too smart these days.

I felt even more foolish when I pulled up into her drive, stepping out into water almost six inches deep, and sloshed up to her front porch. The rain was steadily coming down. When I looked up, I got a face full of it. Clouds as black as my mood hung thick and low. Seemed to park themselves right over Jess's house. An omen if ever I saw one.

I rang the doorbell once, then twice. No answer. So I pulled out my Mag-Lite flashlight and banged on the screen door.

"Police department. Open up!" I called out first, letting her know that this was an official visit. No answer. Where was she? Could she have taken off already? I walked to the end of the porch and peered around the corner. Her car was still there, so I went back to the door.

"Jess? Are you home? Open up, now. I don't have all day now, woman."

She hated when I called her woman. Said it sounded like something out of a Tarzan movie. Me, Tarzan. You, Jane. Me, cop. You, woman. I think she hated it because it made it sound like I was claiming her as *my* woman. Which I wasn't, because she wasn't. Everybody in Codell County knew that she wasn't my woman.

A moment later, the door swung wide open. Jess was standing there in a black T-shirt and bleach-stain-splattered jeans rolled up to her knees. She was breathing hard. Sweat popped out of her forehead. She'd pulled her hair back into a ponytail, but it wasn't holding. It was too thick, too frizzy. Half of it hung in straggly strands down her neck. When she looked at me, her hazel brown eyes narrowed to slits. She was pissed about something. Her hair, maybe. I know for a fact that she'd just had it done. I saw her at Marissa's House of Curlz just the other day when I was cruising up and down the streets on my usual meet-and-greet runs.

With a house full of sisters, the first thing I learned growing up was you didn't mess with a black woman after she had her hair done. I learned that lesson when I was nine years old. I'll never forget it. It was Good Friday, and I'd chunked a water balloon at my sister's head. I didn't think she'd ever stop screaming at me. Oh, she stopped all through Sunday service and the Easter egg hunt, but after that it was on again.

Or maybe Jess was upset about the rain. From the look of her back porch, a good amount of it must have gotten inside. The porch was covered with dirt and leaves. A water line stained the paint along the wall.

"What do you want, Mal?" she snapped at me. "I'm busy."

It wasn't what I wanted, but what her mother wanted. I tried not to sound irritated at her. I didn't *have* to be here.

"Your mama sent me out here after you, Jess."

Jess blew out a frustrated breath. Irritation drew tight lines around her mouth when she turned her lips down in a frown.

"What's wrong with that old woman? I told her I'd be out there as soon as I could."

"Nothing's wrong with her." I had to jump to Ms. Ramsay's defense. "She's worried about you. Can't a body show some concern for you every now and then without you getting an attitude?"

That seemed to settle her down, though not by much. She took a deep breath, relaxing her shoulders as she leaned against the door. "As you can see, Malcolm Loring, I'm fine."

Of course she was fine. That was Jess's problem. She was always fine. Just fine. Nobody could ever do anything for her because she was always fine. If she stood right in front of you and spontaneously burst into flames, and you asked her how she was doing, her answer would still be the same. Fine. Just fine.

Crossing my arms across my chest, I took a step back away from her. "So, what do you want me to tell your mama when she calls me again? You know she's gonna call."

Jess shrugged, then swiped at her neck. "Tell her . . ."

Whatever it was she was about to say, she thought better of it. Her voice softened as she completed her sentence. "Tell her that I'll be there as soon as I can, Mal."

"You plan on going to her place?"

"That's what she wants."

"Not now you're not. Fulsome Road is completely underwater. You can't get to her that way. Only way to her now is by boat."

She looked at me, wondering if I was being sarcastic. Maybe part of me was. I wasn't too happy being out here in the first place, and then she kept me out here, talking on her front porch like I was trying to sell her something that she had no interest in buying.

"What are you going to do, Jess? You can't stay here."

"I can't leave," she insisted.

"Why not?" I demanded.

She shook her head, pressing her lips together.

"Jess," I prompted.

"Because I can't move my couch."

"What did you say?" Her answer made absolutely no sense to me. Then again, half the time I talk to her, I can't seem to figure her out. Lord knows, I should have given up a long time ago. Life is too short to put up with small aggravations. And Jess was no small aggravation.

"My couch," she repeated. "It's too heavy. I've been spending half the morning trying to get my furniture up to the second floor, trying to salvage as much as I can before the water gets in again, but I can't! The couch is too heavy."

"Leave it," I said shortly. I didn't sound too sympathetic then. I didn't apologize for that either. A couch could be replaced. Human life couldn't. Right now, while I stood out here, jerking around with Jess Ramsay, somebody else out there was stranded, possibly needing my help.

"Forget the couch," I told her, being careful with my

choice of words. *Forget* wasn't really the word on the tip of my tongue. But if I started cussing at her, it would only make things worse. She'd dig her heels in on principle alone.

Jess knew I wasn't playing around. Over the years, I'd called her many names, but stupid wasn't one of them. She was sharp, all right. It was as if she'd read my mind. She shot back with the same obscenity I'd omitted as she swung the door closed. *"Forget* you, Mal!" Or something like that.

"You get on about your business, law man. And let me take care of mine."

I yanked on the screen door, putting my foot into the entry before she completely closed the door on me. Jess leaned against the door, pushing her weight against it. Neither her strength nor her vehemence surprised me. At five-foot-six and a healthy one hundred and thirty-five pounds, Jess took good care of herself. I wasn't here to play tug-of-war with her. I shoved back, sending her a few steps back into her entryway.

"Let's go, Jess. I'm giving you three minutes to pack a bag. Then I'm taking you to the shelter, whether you're ready to go or not."

"I just finished refurbishing my last piece of furniture, Mal. Took me a week to strip off the layers of paint. You think I'm going to watch it float away?" She backed against a tall mahogany entry table and clung to it as if it were a lifeline.

"You've got homeowner's insurance, don't you? Flood insurance?" I asked her.

"Who's going to sell me flood insurance knowing that I'm living in an area prone to flooding?" she scoffed.

She pointed a recriminating finger at me. "And I don't want to hear any mess about you and Mama telling me not to buy this house, either. The deal is done, and I'm living with it."

"I wasn't going to say a word."

It was a big, fat lie. I hardly ever passed up an opportunity to remind her about the advice that she chose to ignore. This time I didn't. I guess it was because I couldn't ignore the look on her face. Jess Ramsay may get on my nerves, but the fact remains that we're friends. And friends don't let each other down.

"How much?" I asked.

"How much what?" Jess didn't follow me. I don't blame her for being confused. I was confused myself. Was I about to offer to help her move her furniture?

"How much stuff have you got left to move?" I heard myself asking her as I shrugged out of my rain slicker, took off my hat, and hung them, dripping wet, on the coat tree in the hall. I unbuckled my gun belt, carefully wrapping it up and laying it on her precious table.

I ignored the look she gave me, the look that threatened to hurt me for tracking more water and mud into her house.

"You could have left that outside," she said, nodding toward the gun.

She didn't like me bringing my gun into her house either—a .32-caliber Glock. She wasn't exactly afraid of it. I'd taught her a long time ago not to be afraid of it. I taught her how to load and unload it, how to check the chamber for rounds, and where the safeties were. Her uneasiness sprang from her innate maternal instinct. To hear her tell it, one of these days, she was going to have kids. And when that happened, she didn't want them anywhere near any guns.

"If I have to walk out that door to go put it up, Jess, I'm taking you with me, whether you're packed or not," I warned her. "Now, what else have you got to move?"

"Not much," she said. "My couch, two more tables. Oh, yeah, there's my Oriental area rug. Everything else I've either stacked up or moved to another room."

"C'mon," I said, brushing past her. She didn't have to lead the way. I could find my way through this place in the dark. In fact, the last time I was here, it was dark . . . very dark . . . a two-o'clock-in-the-morning kinda dark.

"You take that end." I nodded toward her overstuffed couch as I moved to the opposite end.

She'd thrown a fitted slipcover over it since the last time I was here, but I still recognized the shape of it, despite the cream-colored chenille covering. When my fingers grasped the underside, getting ready to lift, I remembered the feel of her sofa. Rough. Kinda scratchy. Obviously worn in some spots. But the last time I saw this sofa, the last time I felt it, I wasn't thinking about Jess's décor. The last time I was here, I was thinking how I was going to keep us both from rolling off of it.

At that moment, I didn't see us standing on either side of the couch, but falling on top of it . . . me on top of her, she on top of me. But that was a year ago. And some memories were meant to fade—fade as dimly as the original floral patterns of this old couch.

Jess bent down, too, her chin almost touching the arm cushion. She peered across the couch at me to let me know that she was ready to lift.

"On three," she directed. But then, something came over her. Her expression changed. She kinda lowered her eyes, avoided my gaze. And that's when I knew. I knew she was remembering about that night, too.

I didn't give her a chance to get uncomfortable.

"One," I counted for her, bringing her attention back to what we were supposed to be doing . . . and not what we weren't supposed to be doing the last time we faced each other across this couch.

"Two," she continued, sounding grateful that I had the good grace not to mention it.

"Three!" we said in unison, as we both bent from the knees and lifted the couch waist high.

"Which way?" I asked, starting to take a step back.

"To the right," she directed. "No, my right." She then grinned at me when we started to walk in opposite directions. "Toward the stairs. Watch out for that step up."

"I know, I know . . . You don't have to remind me."

And she didn't. I was lifting my left foot up even as she gave me the warning. I'd been mindful of that step that led into her sunken living room ever since that night I showed up here at two o'clock in the morning. That was a year ago. What was I doing here then? Only the devil could tell. Too much liquor and not a lick of good sense.

The only thing going for me was that I wasn't driving that night, but had Gabriel, the bartender and owner of Gabe's, drop me off. I'm not proud to admit that I was stinking drunk. Tore up from the floor up, as they say. So drunk that I didn't even know what I was doing. Or saying.

I thought I was telling him to take me home. Or at the very least to my lady's house. To Shelby's. But Gabe didn't do that. He brought me here to Jess's instead. I don't know how long I had been at Gabe's. I know Gabe finally cut me off, poured out the last of my shot glass down the drain, and poured me into the backseat of his sixty-eight ragtop deuce and a quarter. He told me later that he'd kept the top down, hoping the fresh air would clear my head and to give me a quick out in case I got carsick.

He'd dropped me right off at Jess's front porch. It must have been the racket of my falling down and smashing into her wicker porch furniture that woke her up. Or maybe it was me shouting her name.

Then again, it could have been the singing. It was either let me in or be subjected to another mangled chorus of

Special Delivery's "I Destroy Your Love." My memories are fuzzy on some of the details of that night. An entire bottle of Jack Daniel's will do that to you.

Some things I can't forget. Like tripping over that ugly hook rug, the one she put down as kind of a warning track right before that step down into her living room once she let me inside. She wouldn't get rid of that thing because I'd made it for her in the one class I'd never admit to taking in high school. When most of my friends were taking metal shop, I wound up in home economics so that it wouldn't conflict with my job as a clerk at the police station.

At two in the morning, when you're stinking drunk, that first step down into her living room could be a real bitch. It would have been better for us if Jess had been one, too. Pitching a hissy fit for me dragging her out of bed. But she didn't.

I remember sprawling, face first, at her feet, staring blearily into the eyes of her ridiculous bunny slippers and wondering why Jess's natural light brown, almond-shaped eyes were suddenly big and black and plastic and falling out. It never occurred to me that the pink fur that I'd reached out to stroke was not a strange mutation of Jess's normal mocha skin.

Instead of cursing me as I writhed on the floor for a while, she sat with me for a while. We didn't talk much at first. There wasn't much to say. I had no excuse for the way I was acting. I shouldn't have been there. I knew it, and she knew it. I had a lady. And Jess had a man.

Now that I think back on it, I think it was the news that Jess finally had somebody, a somebody that wasn't me, that sent me diving to the bottom of that bottle. I'm not normally a drinking man. A beer every now and then. Seeing Jess with what's-his-name changed that. Call me a selfish S-O-B. But as long as I had Shelby and Jess had no one, everything was all right in my world.

Whether I liked it or not, we're connected, Jess and me. I don't know how she took it when I upset that delicate balance between us by hooking up with her friend Shelby. But I didn't take it well when she showed up that night at Gabe's with what's-his-name hanging all over her. Nope. I didn't take it well at all. I guess I handled it just as well as I handled my liquor.

I went into her house, fully expecting for what's-his-name to still be there. But that didn't stop me from going. And it didn't stop me from reaching out for her when she confessed that he had been there, but was gone. I should have turned around, right then and there. I should have left her, even when she reminded me that Shelby was probably at home waiting for me. But I didn't. Like I said, I'm a selfish S-O-B. I wanted it all. I had Shelby, but I wanted Jess, too. *God how I wanted her!*

I think I told her that night, too, but she acted like she didn't hear me or didn't understand me. Natural mistake. I must have been slurring pretty badly by then. How could I make her understand?

Some feelings go beyond words. When she helped me from the floor, and onto her couch, my intentions became perfectly clear. Can't mistake the intentions of a man when he puts one hand on your breast and the other down your pajama pants. Crude, but effective. One minute she was laughing, straining, struggling to keep my sorry, drunk tail from falling down again, the next we're on her couch—face to face—staring at each other as awkwardly as we are now.

The only thing stopping a repeat of that night's performance is the fact that I am stone-cold sober. And, I knew that if I dropped this couch and reached out for her again, I'd probably wind up dropping the damned thing on my foot.

Chapter Three

Jess

"Four more steps to your right. Easy . . . easy, now. Lift up on your end. Don't drop it, Mal."

"I've got it. You just make sure you hold up your end, Jess. Don't drop this thing on my foot."

I was huffing and puffing, trying not to let my end fall. It irked my nerves that Mal didn't sound winded at all as we climbed the stairs. Over the edge of the couch, I peeked at him as he lifted his end of the couch over the stair banister to keep from scratching the wood. He made it look so easy.

I couldn't help but notice how his biceps kinda bulged as he lifted it almost chest level, straining his uniform shirt. The uniform was ugly and brown. But it didn't hide how the man was cut. He must be working out more than usual. I didn't remember him looking so *ummm-ummm-ummm* damn fine.

I didn't expect for Mal to show up on my doorstep this morning. Mama, maybe. Because she'd been calling me every fifteen minutes wondering when I was coming over. And every time she called, I always put her off. Secretly, I was hoping that the rain would let up, the water would recede, and I could get through the week without having to move in with her again. I dreaded that, if even for a while.

She didn't show up. Instead, she'd sent Malcolm Loring, and I didn't know which was worse. To say that me and Mal have issues would be a gross understatement. Oh, we're fine as long as we're on neutral territory. We can almost be friendly.

And whenever Mal and Shelby and me were all in the same place at the same time, we were just a barrel of yucks. Shelby's my girl. In fact, Shelby and Mal wouldn't even be together if it wasn't for me.

She'd just moved to Codell County my senior year in high school and didn't have very many friends. The other girls didn't trust her. She'd alienated all of the smart girls by acing every exam and homework assignment. Killed the grading curve every time. And she didn't even have to study hard. She'd knocked the girl who would have been valedictorian right out of the box and into the second-place salutatorian spot, a consolation prize.

She'd ticked off all of the athletic girls, too. Instead of joining the cheerleading squad, she went straight for the tennis team. Codell County High School had an awesome tennis team! We swept the state championships almost every year. If you wanted a sports scholarship, and you went to Codell County High, tennis was the way to go.

When Tamara Jennings, the star of our high school's doubles tennis team, broke her ankle just before the championship tournament, Shelby jumped in, snatching up the trophy, the scholarship, and, as rumor had it, Tamara's steady boyfriend of four years.

That was Shelby. Ruthlessly ambitious. Once she set her mind to something, nothing was going to stop her. She'd had all of the pretty girls in high school out to get her as well. Shelby is a natural beauty. Hailing from Barbados, her ebony skin, wide dark eyes, and long natural braids decorated with shells and beads brought to mind sultry sunny days and balmy island nights.

No, Shelby didn't have very many girlfriends. Shelby had plenty of guy friends, though. She made those kinds of friends very quickly—which was another reason why I started to hang around her. She was a virtual guy magnet—a very valuable asset to have when you're at a party. Especially the kinds of parties that I liked going to. The kinds where I didn't know very many people, and they didn't know me. I was totally free to be me when I got out of Codell County to find a party. I got out as often as I could. I had Shelby with me the night I crept out of the house.

I was so looking forward to hanging with her and picking up her throwaways. I wasn't ashamed to admit it. Nobody but the finest hotties ever approached Shelby. The shy, quiet, studious types never stood a chance with her. The muscle-flexing athletes, the pretty-boy models, and the daddy's-money boys with plenty of cash to flash, they all flocked to her. And since I was there, they all assumed that girls of a feather flocked together. I wasn't as devastatingly gorgeous as Shelby. But once I got one or two of them talking to me, I could hold my own.

Before we set out, we had our game plan all worked out. Shelby would lure them over. She had first pick, cutting those from the herd that she preferred. Me and Nikki took care of any ones who remained. It was perfect. So perfect. The only thing standing in the way of a night of total hottiness was a flat tire and a six-foot-one solid wall of meanness. *Mal.*

Once Mal caught up to us, Shelby took one look at him, looking tall and mean and authoritative in his uniform, and there was no stopping her. She had to have him.

When we got back to school on Monday, it was all she could talk about. Nagged me to death until I reluctantly agreed to arrange for us all to meet up again. After that, Shelby and me were inseparable. She knew that me and Mal were tight. Wherever I was, he was.

I can't put my finger on the exact moment when my twosome became a threesome, with Shelby as the third wheel. But I can remember to the day when we were whittled down to a twosome once again. Only, that twosome didn't include me. It was Shelby and Mal.

He was cramming for some sort of certification at the police academy at the Mississippi Delta Community College. So I'd gone to his house to cook a few meals and tidy up. Not out of the goodness of my heart, but out of the emptiness of my wallet. I was saving up for a new set of tires, and Mal was paying me a few extra dollars to do light housekeeping duties.

Mama would have been so proud of my efforts. I wasn't just pushing dirt around, sweeping it under rugs. I was lifting rugs and moving furniture to get at that dirt. That's when I found them . . . a pair of Shelby's panties stuck under Mal's bed. I knew they were hers. Not because I go rifling through her underwear drawer, but because she admitted they were hers when I confronted her about it at school.

I'd never told Mal about what I'd found. I figured, if he wanted me to know what he and Shelby were doing, he would have told me. If Shelby was his choice, well, as his best friend, what could I do but be happy for them?

Right now, I don't know whether to be glad that he's here helping me or mad enough to grind glass between my teeth because Mama sent him over here like she did when I was a kid. I was a grown woman! I'm not too happy that Mama thought that it was necessary to send Mal after me. She knows that Mal hasn't set foot on my doorstep in over a year. She doesn't know why . . . and I'll never tell her. She thinks this man walks on water. Won't listen to a word that might suggest otherwise.

I know for a fact that Mal's a man like any other. A man with his own strengths—like the ability to lift a four-cushion couch up a flight of stairs, for all intents and purposes, on his own. I was barely holding on as we climbed the stairs, more like guiding him along and warning him where the tight corners were.

He's also got his weaknesses. This is the same man who had me on this very same couch, stroking me like I'd never been touched before. Not even my date for that evening had put his hands on me like that. Mal had me even though he had a lady—my girl Shelby.

Mal's weakness was, strangely enough, also his greatest strength. Even drunk, he knew exactly what he was doing. He knew where to touch me to make me squirm, make me moan. Made me forget myself. Forgot all about my girl. He put one hand on my breast, and it was, *Shelby who?*

The man who, time and time again, had gotten under my skin was suddenly all over my skin that night. Large hands covering me, every inch of exposed flesh. I knew it was wrong. Oh, so wrong. But heaven help me, he was good. I didn't know the man had it in him. And that night, I would have given almost anything to have him in me.

He knew it, too. He knew when he touched me between my thighs and felt the shudder that rippled through me that he could have me. I moaned, long and loud, and he gave me a smile. Made me mad . . . that little smile . . . that a man gets on his face when he knows that he's found that spot that makes your back arch and your toes curl.

We were seconds away from making the biggest mistake of our lives. His poor judgment came from a bottle.

I didn't have any such excuse. I was just out of my head with need.

One thing about living under Mama's roof, you didn't get very many opportunities for late-night tune-ups like that. Not without her raising her eyebrows at you and giving you that silent, disapproving treatment.

That night, I was in my own house, on my own couch, with a man who wasn't mine. Liquor and lust—a dangerous combination. I don't know what snapped me out of it. I guess the promise of pleasure Mal was offering couldn't stack up to the guilt I'd feel after it was all said and done. Guilt for taking advantage of him when he was obviously not in his right mind . . . and guilt knowing that I'd have to face Shelby. Me and Shelby have a lot in common. But going behind her back isn't one of them. I'd never do that to her.

There was no way I could keep something like that from her. I'd have to tell her. Even if I tried to keep it from her, sooner or later, she'd start to pick up on my guilty vibe. She'd know that I was avoiding her. I swear, that girl could sniff out sex. She'd smell it on me. Smell it on the couch when she came over. That's one of the reasons why I had it cleaned and covered. To this day, I think I can still smell him all over it. Which is another reason why he gets on my nerves. Even though he hasn't been in my house in a year, he's *always* here.

"What else?" Mal asked as he set the sofa down and straightened up.

"A couple of end tables and a rug. That's about it," I said, folding my arms across my chest, trying to avoid his gaze. I couldn't look at him right now.

As he turned and headed back down the stairs, the radio clipped to his belt chirped. I could hear a tiny voice, a crackle of static. Mal glanced down, twisted a tiny button to adjust the volume. I felt a tiny pang of guilt—

a much-watered-down version of the way I felt the last time he was here. He shouldn't be here with me now.

He was halfway down the stairs before I called out to him, leaning over the rail. "Mal?"

"Yeah?"

He looked up me, and I lost my train of thought. Sometimes, I can't stand it when he looks at me. He has the most piercing eyes, deep and dark, and sometimes filled with a kind of sadness that makes me want to reach out to him, gather him into my arms, and soothe away whatever is troubling him.

"Uh . . . thanks. You know, for helping me. I know there's other stuff you need to be doing."

"You're right," he retorted, making me almost wish that I'd held onto my gratitude.

"Don't let the door hit you on the way out," I said, dismissing him, waving my hand toward the door.

He shook his head. "Not without you, Jess. You can't stay here."

"I'll be—"

"If you say 'just fine,' I'm gonna push you down these stairs," he threatened. He pointed back toward my bedroom. "You go on and pack your bag, now. I'll get the rest of your furniture up here."

"Fine," I said in a huffy tone.

"And Jess?"

"Huh?"

"Better pack enough for two or three days," he cautioned.

I lost my irritation as fear took its place. "Do you think it's gonna get that bad, Mal?"

When he scowled, something in the pit of my stomach went cold and tight. He didn't have to say anything. The look on his face said it all. Mal didn't exaggerate. He was trying to prepare me for the worst.

I didn't want to believe it. This was my home. My very first home. I couldn't lose it. Not like this. If the water didn't completely wash it away, the foundation would probably be weakened beyond what I could pay to repair. The collateral damage from debris smashing into it, and the toxic mold would probably make it unlivable. I couldn't help it. I felt tears stinging my eyes.

"Go on, Jess," he urged softly.

Nodding, I stepped away from the banister and turned back toward my room. I could hear the scrape of furniture across my floor as he pulled the tables closer to the stairs.

Rummaging through the closet, I pushed back hanging clothes and boxes of stuff I no longer wore and found a small suitcase. It was the kind you see in all the airports these days, with wheels and a retractable handle. I'd bought this one at a garage sale for ten bucks. I couldn't pass it up. It had a lovely tapestry pattern with roses and winding vines stitched with gold thread.

I ran my fingers over it. The last time I'd used it, a group of us had gotten together and chartered a bus to a Biloxi resort for an entire weekend of being treated like riverboat royalty. Free food. Cheap slot machines. Plenty of drinks with more fruit and decoration than alcohol. Shelby had gotten upset because Mal had been called back to work . . . something about a workers' strike. I'd lost all of my money on the first night, so he gave me his credit card with the promise that I wouldn't charge it to the max and I wouldn't tell Shelby. I didn't learn until later when I accidentally let the fact slip out that Mal had never given her access to any of his accounts, even after all that time they'd been together.

"You almost done, Jess?" Mal shouted from the stairs.

"Almost!"

Moving quickly to cover the fact that I hadn't started packing, I tossed in a couple pairs of jeans, several

T-shirts, and, to make my mama proud, plenty of clean underwear. I also grabbed some thick socks and an extra pair of tennis shoes.

From the bathroom, I collected all of the toiletries I thought I'd need for an extended stay and tossed them into a large plastic zipper-topped bag. Toothpaste, shampoo, deodorant, even a disposable shaver. I left most of the makeup where it was. Who was I gonna impress at the shelter anyway?

By the time I added a couple of magazines that I was reading and another thick book for good measure, Mal had already carried up the two end tables and was rolling up the rug.

I pulled on a pair of clean socks and dug out a pair of boots. Unrolling my jeans over them, I straightened up from the bed as Mal appeared in my doorway. He was brushing at the dust that coated his uniform, dust that had fallen out of my rug. He patted himself, then gave a mock cough when a noticeable puff of dust wafted into the air.

"Not one word," I warned him. "Not one word about my housekeeping skills."

"Or lack thereof," he retorted.

"Forget you!" I shouted at him, picking up the other boot that I hadn't put on my foot yet and hurling it at his head.

Mal ducked, letting it sail past his head and clunk on the opposite wall.

"Feel better?" he asked, lifting an eyebrow.

"Not really. If we're gonna get out of here, let's do this," I said, sighing with resignation.

Stepping into the hall, Mal reached down and collected my boot. For a minute, I thought he was going to throw it back at me. But he didn't. He brought it to me instead. Walked right up to me, almost inches away from me, and handed it to me.

I sat down on the bed, not taking my eyes from him, as I pulled on the other boot. Mal didn't sit down next to me. It seemed to me that he was doing everything he could to avoid touching my bed. Not an easy task. I have a huge, king-size bed, with a wrought iron headboard and footboard.

Mal walked around to the opposite side of the room and picked up my travel bag. He zipped it shut and pulled up the handle.

I stamped my foot on the floor a couple of times, settling my foot more comfortably in my boot. After that, I stood and smoothed my hand over the bed, plumped up the pillows. I was stalling, and I knew it. I didn't want to go.

Mal didn't try to hide his impatience, but started to drag the bag on its wheels across the floor.

"Let's go, Jess," he said, jerking his thumb toward the door.

"I'm going, I'm going," I muttered, looking around me one last time. Mal waited, giving me my moment. He looked around, too.

"You know," he said softly, "I've never been up here. Not since you got it all decorated."

"I know."

The few times he was there, it was right after I'd closed on the house. I hadn't begun to move in any of my things. And the last time he was there, a year ago, he never made it up the stairs. I wouldn't let him. If I had, I knew the night would have ended much differently than it had.

He sounded mildly amused, sounded condescending as he said, "Look at you, all color coordinated with pillows and curtains and rugs and every*thang*."

I bit my lip, trying not to cry. Was it all going to be here by the time I got back?

When he saw the look on my face, he dropped the teasing and placed his hand comfortingly on my shoulder. As he squeezed, I closed my eyes, and swayed toward him. I didn't mean to. I couldn't help it. I need to draw from his strength and his calm assurance. I leaned my forehead against his chest. Briefly, almost too quickly to tell if it had happened or not, I felt his hand slide from my shoulder to the small of my back, patting me.

"You did a good job, Jess. It looks . . . looks really nice. Especially the damask duvet," he said awkwardly.

I looked up at him and grinned. A compliment? Coming from Mal Loring? Could have knocked me over with a feather.

"Looks like you were paying attention in Miss Hallet's home economics class," I teased.

"If you tell anyone that I know what a duvet is, you know I'll have to lock you up, don't you . . . put you in jail."

Chapter Four

Mal

I gave Jess as much time as I could, let her say her good-byes to her place in her own way. But now it was time to go. Not just because I had to get back to work, even though I did. When I checked in at the station again, Edmonds told me there was talk going on around town about an emergency-response team forming a sandbagging effort to shore up the levee. Even as I stood in Jess's bedroom and teased her about her decorating efforts, several dump trucks filled with sand and gravel were dumping their loads at several points along the Bramfort and Fulsome road levees.

I had to go. Edmonds couldn't go and assist the ERT. He was on his way to the high school to coordinate the evacuees starting to arrive there. And Walker was staying close to the station, monitoring calls. Roderick had his hands full patrolling the darkened streets where half of the shop owners had already boarded up in anticipation of either flooding or looting.

That left me and Myles to get out there. I was anxious to go, not only because it was my duty to go where I felt

I was most needed. I had to leave because being in Jess's bedroom was making me nervous. More than nervous. Sweat was pouring down my back. Sweat that had nothing to do with the several pieces of furniture I'd just hauled up the stairs.

When she'd leaned against me, I experienced a full-frontal assault of my senses. I tried not to notice how her skin had a lightly floral scent. I heard her sigh, a mournfully pathetic sound filled with regret and resignation. I felt her mouth trembling against my chest as she held back her tears. I did what I could to console her . . . that is, did what was safe. I didn't want to put Jess in the awkward position of having to slap my face if my hand strayed too close to that delicious derriere of hers.

My mind flashed back to the time I had to chastise my male officers for secretly conducting a "best booty" contest. In the running were J-Lo, Beyoncé, Lil' Kim, Jess, Shelby, and a little gal who clerks at the combination gas station and convenience store out on the interstate. I collected all the ballots, shredding them in front of the officers at a weekend sensitivity and sexual harassment training session. No one noticed my sleight of hand, where I pocketed the ballot that clearly indicated Jess as the winner.

"All right," she said, pulling the door closed behind her. "I'm ready."

"I'm taking you to the high school. You should be all right there."

"Are you sure you can't get out to Mama's? I don't like the idea of her being out there with Daddy, all by herself, Mal. She's expecting me."

"No can do."

I made it clear that I wasn't going to let her talk me into doing something else as foolish as spending precious time hauling her furniture up a flight of stairs. Enough was enough.

"I'm taking you to the shelter, Jess. I promise, Jess, as soon as I can, I'll see who I can send, make it out that way, and bring your folks into town. They should be all right. Your Mama's house sits pretty high."

She nodded, but I could tell she wasn't all that happy with my answer.

Jess opened her front door, but I held her back from dashing out into the rain. An hour later and it still hadn't let up.

"Wait here," I told her.

I put on my slicker, pulled my hat low over my eyes and dug my keys out of my pocket. Seconds later, I was dashing out from underneath the cover of her front porch and sloshing through several inches of water to get to my Jeep. After I started the engine, I pulled up as close as I could, and leaned over to open the door to make it easier for her to get in.

Jess pulled her jacket closed, ducked her head, and took the stairs two at a time and launched herself inside.

"You know," she said, gasping and swiping at the water streaming down her face, "it would do us both good to invest in a couple of decent umbrellas."

"Just one more thing I need to keep track of," I retorted.

Putting the Jeep in reverse, I rested one arm on the back of the opposite seat as I turned the steering wheel in a slow arc to back out of Jess's driveway. As I pulled out onto the road, I thought about Jess's car, and how low it sat on the ground. Another half hour and she'd have water past the wheel well. Any higher than that and she might as well have the car totaled.

Out of the corner of my eye I watched her expression.

She took a deep breath, kinda sighed through her nose, and turned her face to the window.

"You gonna be all right?" I asked her, squeezing her shoulder. It was a stupid question. But at the moment, I couldn't think of anything else to say.

"You don't really want me to answer that, do you?" she said, turning to face me. Her expression was hard. And there was a slight catch in her voice, like she was going to start crying. That tough act didn't fool me. Jess was scared, scareder than I'd ever seen her.

The only other times I'd seen her cry was at those stupid movies she liked to watch. It didn't bother me then. That was empathetic crying. Crying because she felt someone else's pain. This was different. This was her own pain. I didn't know if I could handle that. She wasn't the type to break down in tears when she was hurting. She'd always struck me as a strong woman. A woman who could take care of herself. And her being a teacher, responsible for the eager, open minds of all of those third graders . . . I didn't think anything could rattle Jess. This weather did. It had her really twisted up inside.

I could understand how she felt, frustrated and fearful. There wasn't a thing we could do about this rain. Just sit back, hunker down, pray for the best and prepare for the worst.

"I'll answer it for you," I started.

"And don't you say I'm gonna be just fine. Just fine," she threatened me.

I had to laugh at that. Now *that* was the Jess I knew. Always with the quick comeback. Even though most of it was just bluster. I needed to see her like that. I needed to see her being strong . . . strong for herself and strong for me. Because I know me. I know that as long as she's in trouble, I'm going to have to be there for her. Whether it's wise or not, whether I want to or not, I'm gonna drop whatever I'm doing to make sure that she's all right. Why I do that to myself, I don't know. Yes, I do. It's because I'm an idiot, that's why.

I gave her shoulder another squeeze. Sort of a squeeze. Actually, it was more like a caress. Much too friendly for the "just friends" we're supposed to be.

Jess told me as much when she did a little shimmy, shrugging me off.

"Both hands on the wheel, law man," she said, pointing at the steering wheel.

I didn't say a word, just looked at her as if she must be crazy if she thought I was gonna try anything with her. Not after that last fiasco.

"And don't you go rolling your eyes at me, Mal Loring," she warned. "Keep those big puppy-dog browns on the road."

She was right. I know she was. I just didn't like being reminded that she was. My hands, my eyes, my mind should have been on the road. It was bad out there. Getting worse. The windshield wipers were on their highest setting. Yet, they could barely keep up with the rain as they flipped back and forth. It was coming down harder now. The wind drove the rain into us at a slant.

"Watch out!" Jess cried out suddenly and clutched my arm when a tree branch slammed against the windshield and got caught in the wiper blades. With the branch covering over half the glass, I was driving blind. I'm not sure how I managed it, working the clutch, brake, and steering wheel to get us to the side of the road with Jess hanging on to me. I guess the rule about keeping her hands on her side of the Jeep didn't apply to her. That was Jess, too. Always changing the rules to suit her.

The Jeep's all-terrain tires hit gravel. That's the only real indicator that I had that I wasn't on the main road anymore. I turned off the wipers, flipped on the flashing hazards, and then stepped outside. The branch was jammed under the blades pretty good, and took a good deal of wrangling (and a fair amount of cursing on my part) to get all of the strips out.

When I stepped back inside, Jess passed me the handset to my radio, "Myles called for you, Mal. He said something about sandbagging the levee?"

"Yeah."

"It's come to that, then?"

"Most likely."

Jess turned her gaze back out to the window. "I want you to take me out there," she ordered.

"What?"

"I said take me out there," she repeated in that crisp, sharp teacher's voice.

"What for?"

"So I can help," she said so matter-of-factly that it almost made the insane sound plausible.

"Jess, I don't think that's a good idea."

"And sitting around at the high school waiting for my house to wash away is? That's not my style, Mal. You know it. Please! If there's anything I can do to stop it, I want to know that I did everything in my power."

"And I have to do everything in my power to keep you out of trouble. I promised your mama. If I take you out there, I wouldn't be doing my job, now, would I?"

"Hey, I'm a tax-paying citizen. And in a moment of insanity I voted for the man who got you your job as police chief. You let me be the one to tell you what your job is."

"I don't come into your classroom and tell you how to teach."

"This conversation is stupid," she said in frustration. "Are you going to take me out there or am I gonna have to get out there and walk?"

"Don't you tempt me, Jess," I warned her.

"Fine!" Jess said, opening the door and leaning out.

I had half a mind to let her go. How far was she gonna get? As she walked past my Jeep, bending her head against the rain, I knew she'd make it to the levee site just to spite me.

"Get back in here," I snapped. "Don't be stupid."

"I'm going, Mal—with or without you."

"Damn it, Jess!"

"Don't damn it me, *damn it*. And don't make me stand out here in the rain when you know you're gonna take me out there."

She was right. She knew she was right. God, how I hated it when she was right.

Muttering, I started the engine again, jerked my head to tell her to get back inside. Then I checked in at the station to let my officers know that I was going to be joining Myles at the levee.

As she climbed inside and buckled her seat belt, Jess didn't even try to hide the grin.

"I can't believe I'm letting you talk me into this."

"You were going anyway," she said stubbornly.

Every bone in my body was telling me to stand just as firm. One thing about me and Jess. No one could call us pushovers. After this, I vowed, me and Jess's mom were finally even. For every favor or kindness she had ever done for me, I'd paid her back in full.

Chapter Five

The River

It is not in my nature to be unkind. Nor is it within me to be forgiving. It is within me to go where I will—to flow over or around, or if necessary, through. It has always been this way, despite all efforts to make it otherwise.

If anyone had bothered to ask, I would have answered. No amount of concrete or steel, machinery or man's effort will change that fact. I am what I am. And today, I am more than I have been in a long, long time.

Chapter Six

Jess

One of these days, Mal isn't going to back down. One of these days, he's gonna decide that caving in to me isn't worth his time. On that day, he'll tell me in no uncertain terms where to go . . . or what I can do to myself. He'll probably use a lot of profanity in the process, too. But today ain't that day.

He didn't say much after I got back into the Jeep. But I could almost hear his thoughts. He was pissed and trying extra hard not to show it. Keeping his hands gripped to the steering wheel, his eyes pinned to the windshield, he acted like I wasn't even there. I could see the muscles working in his jaw as he clenched his teeth. Every now and then, I heard him grind his molars. A sure sign of frustration.

"Are you gonna call your mama or what?" Mal growled at me.

That question came out of nowhere after almost ten minutes of total silence. Not exactly total silence. There was still the sound of the rain and the wind and the *swhoosh-swhoosh-swhoosh* of the windshield wipers. The hum of the tires against the road had almost lulled me back to sleep. After that scare with a tree limb slamming into the Jeep, I was just starting to get calm enough to relax and let Mal drive without my running commentary.

"Are you asking me or telling me?" I wanted to know.

"She's expecting me to bring you to her. I thought she might like to know that you're completely ignoring my advice, and demanding that I take you to a potentially hazardous situation." He couldn't have sounded more sarcastic if I'd paid him.

I reached up, flipped on the overhead dome light, and then rummaged through my bag for my cellular phone. The LED display was showing that I'd missed about ten calls. When I checked, they were all from Mama. A few messages, too. I didn't bother listening to them. They were probably from Mama, too.

Pressing the button to speed dial her number, I put the phone up to my ear and gave Mal a raised-eyebrow look that said, "Satisfied?"

He just grunted in response and turned his attention back to the road.

"Mama?" I spoke into the phone.

She'd picked up after about the eighth or ninth ring. When she did pick up, she yelled so loud, I had to hold the phone away from my ear.

"Jess! Where are you? Don't you know that I've been calling you for half an hour!"

"I'm sorry, Mama. I must have turned off my ringer."

"Where *are* you?" she repeated.

"I'm here with Mal."

"Thank goodness. So he did make it out there?" She calmed down, sounding very much relieved.

"Uh-huh. We're on our way to—"

"You can't get out here, Jess," she interrupted. "Fulsome Road is completely underwater."

"I know. You told me and Mal told me."

"I'm glad you're not trying to come here. Is he taking you to the high school then?"

"Not exactly," I hedged.

"What does that mean?" Her voice went up another notch. She was getting ready to yell again. I could tell.

"Mama, Mal said that he has to make a stop first," I explained carefully.

Mal shook his head quickly back and forth and whispered loudly. "Unh-uh, Jess. Don't you put that on me. This is all on you."

I shushed him, holding the phone with one hand and waving at him with the other as Mama asked suspiciously, "What kind of a stop?"

"Some volunteers are gathering at the access road to the reservoir, along the old levee."

"For what reason?"

"I think they're gonna try to sandbag the levee, Mama," I began.

"Oh, Jessica." She sounded so disappointed. Like the way she sounded when I told her that my kitchen had flooded. "You didn't make him take you out there, did you?"

"What makes you say that?" I tried to put on my most innocent-sounding voice. "You know I can't make Mal do anything he doesn't want to do."

My tone didn't fool Mama. Not one bit.

"Jess, what do you think you're doing?" she said.

"Whatever I can to save my house," I snapped, angry that she'd taken his side over mine.

"Mal should have better sense than to . . ." she began, and then blew out a huffy breath. "You know what? You put him on the phone, Jess. Just put him on the phone right now. I want to talk to him."

I held the phone out to Mal. "She wants to talk to you."

"About what?"

I shrugged my shoulders. But I don't think he bought my innocent act either. Mal did his best to lean away from me.

"I can't talk to her. I'm driving. Tell her that I have to concentrate on the road."

I wasn't going to let him get out of one of Mama's fussings that easily. So, I put the phone up to his ear. "You tell her."

"Ms. Ramsay," he said, using that polite but professional voice he'd developed for the office. I leaned close, too, my cheek almost to his, trying to hear what she was saying to him. But she didn't yell at him like she'd yelled at me. So, I could barely hear her. I caught every other word, however. Something about me and keeping safe, and hunting somebody down if anything happened to me.

With Mal repeating "yes, ma'am" every now and then, and looking at me as if I'd gotten him into trouble, I caught enough of the conversation to get the gist of what she'd told him.

"I won't, Ms. Ramsay. You have my word on that," he said and shifted his eyes briefly to look at me. For a moment, I thought I saw an expression on Mal's face that I wasn't used to seeing. I might have been mistaken. I mean, I couldn't have seen what I thought I had, could I? Was Mal . . . was he . . . afraid?

Nah! It couldn't have been. Mal couldn't have been afraid. Not of a threat from Mama. Mama stood only five-foot-two in heels. She puffed up at me. But when it came to Mal, whatever she threatened him with could only be a bluff.

Then, just like that, the look was gone. A mask of professionalism covered his face. Finally, he leaned his head away from the phone, letting me know the conversation was over.

"Mama?" I spoke into the phone, making sure she hadn't hung up.

"I don't know what you think you're doing, Jessica Ramsay. Whatever it is, I hope it's worth it in the end."

"It's my home, Mama. I'm not going to stand by and let it be washed away. I'm not gonna do it."

"What do you think you're gonna do? Hold back the flood with your bare hands?" she quipped.

"If I have to." I'd said it in all earnestness. If I had to redirect the river with a spoon and a couple of Dixie cups, I was gonna do it.

"Promise me something, honey," she said, sounding resigned and disappointed with me at the same time.

"What is it?" I wasn't going to give her a blanket promise. Not without knowing whether or not she was going to ask the impossible from me.

"Whoever's organizing the volunteers, you listen to them . . . And do what they say."

I know what that meant. That was her way of telling me that I'd better not challenge Mal anymore.

"Of course," I agreed quickly enough. Maybe too quickly. I don't think she believed me.

"I know you, Jess. If and when they tell you to give it up, you drop what you're doing and get out of there. Can you do that?"

"But, Mama—"

"No buts. I mean it. No house is worth your life. Do you understand me, child?"

"I understand," I said, annoyed at her tone. "Don't worry about me, Mama. I'll be fine. What about you? Are you gonna be all right? What about you and Daddy? Do you need anything?"

"We're fine, Jess."

The rattle of window blinds going up let me know that she'd gone to a window. I imagined her standing there, her face turned up to the sky, with eyebrows knitted together, mouth turned down at the corners.

"It's still coming down hard," she continued. "But everything's running off. From what I can see, there is no water standing in the yard. I think we'll be all right."

"Be careful, Mama. You'll call me if you need anything?"

"If you can keep your cell phone turned on." She was scolding me again.

I checked the phone and the battery level. So far, a full charge. I thought back to what I'd thrown in my bag. Had I packed my charger?

"I will," I promised, and then mentally crossed my fingers. I'd keep it on for as long as the battery life lasted. "I've gotta go now, Mama. Gotta save the battery."

"You need to be worried about saving your butt," Mal muttered out of the corner of his mouth.

"I'll leave that worry for you," I shot back.

"That's just great," he said slowly. "One more thing I need to keep track of."

"That's why you're being paid the big bucks, law man."

Reaching out, I tapped his cheek with the palm of my hand. Just a light smack. Some folks would call that a love tap. But we both knew better than that, didn't we.

Chapter Seven

Mal

Pay me the big bucks? Hah! They couldn't pay me enough for the aggravation of Jess Ramsay. I leaned my head away from her, letting her know I didn't appreciate her sarcasm. Actually, what I didn't need was the feel of her soft hand against my face. She was just trying to distract me. It was working, too.

I needed another worry like I needed a hole in my head. Come to think of it, maybe I do need a hole in my head—if that is the only way I can shake out all of the rocks I have rattling around in there. I must have rocks in my head. Why else am I letting Jess talk me out of doing what I know is best?

She was sitting quietly beside me with her arms crossed at her chest, staring straight ahead.

"You know your parents are going to kill me if I let anything happen to you, don't you?" I commented.

"Nothing's going to happen to me, Mal," she said with so much certainty, that for a moment, I wondered if she saw a giant red *S* on my chest. In her own way, she was expressing her faith in my ability to protect her. I wish I had that much confidence in myself.

"Oh yeah? What makes you so sure?"

"Because I know you, Malcolm Loring," she said simply, shrugging her shoulders. "You're going to do your job. No matter what."

She turned her face toward the window again, whispering softly. "No matter who."

I didn't have to ask her what she meant by that. I was the first one to admit that the job came first.

"Are your folks gonna be all right?" I asked. The look on her face when she'd hung up the phone had me concerned. Jess didn't usually chew her nails. She was biting that one thumbnail down to the quick.

"Mama said that there's water in the yard, but it's not staying. It's running off. She said that they'll be okay."

"We could stop by there," I offered. "Just to make sure."

Jess gave me a funny look. "You sure you want to do that, Mal? I thought you were in a hurry to get back to town."

"I am," I admitted. "As long as I'm out here, I can check on your neighbors to make sure they got the evacuation message."

"That's not what I meant, Mal. I meant, you going to see my folks . . . my dad . . . well, that's a . . . uh . . . very brave offer."

Brave. That was an odd choice of words. Until I realized what she was hinting around at.

"You think I'm scared of your father? Just because the last time I stopped by he tried to hit me in the head with his cane? Your mother explained all of that. She said it was a bad reaction to his medication."

"Well . . . That's not entirely true, Mal," she confessed.

"No?" My tone was pure sarcasm. "You don't say."

I smiled at Jess to let her know that I understood. I

knew her father didn't like me. He'd taken an active dislike of me since the day he found out that I wasn't taking Jess to some fancy college cotillion that she'd invited me to. Shelby had invited me first. Jess wound up not going to that dance . . . And Shelby and I wound up with a pregnancy scare. The test came back negative, but that didn't mean I didn't sweat bullets for a few days. I guess it wasn't a good time for either of us.

That was years ago. You'd think that he would have accepted the fact that Jess and me were never going to be anything more than just friends. I'd moved on, and so had she. And so had Ms. Ramsay. Everybody was on the same page. Until about three months ago, I figured out that not only were we not on the same page, Mr. Ramsay was still stuck in an outdated book.

I'd responded to Ms. Ramsay's call about suspicious activity around her property. Strange noises. Things being knocked over. Vandalized. Turned out to be nothing more than a pack of stray dogs roaming the countryside that had gotten through a hole in her fence. It was late, after ten, when she'd called the report in to the station. I took the call, since I was on my way out to Shelby's. I walked around the property, taking note of how many dogs I thought there were and how many breaks in her fence.

I'd like to think that Mr. Ramsay was doing his duty to protect the home by taking a thwack at me, muttering something about a mangy cur. I'm not sure if I like the comparison. Was he trying to call me a dog for abandoning Jess?

Along this road, between Jess's house and the town proper, there were at least five other houses that stood the most chance of being flooded. As long as the roads were passable, I had to do what I could to see that those who could leave would.

"Who should we see first?" she asked enthusiastically.

"The Pearsons."

"Oh," Jess groaned, making a face. "Good luck."

I knew exactly what she meant. Bull Pearson and his wife, Olene, weren't exactly my favorite couple. They were what I call the three *O's*—old, ornery, and completely outcast. They were firm believers in live and let live, as long as no one bothered them, they wouldn't bother anybody. Trouble was, they *were* a bother even when they weren't trying to be.

More than once I've had to go out there, asking them to stop doing what any sane individual wouldn't even consider doing. Stop burning old tires in the dead of summer. The smoke and smell carried beyond their property and created a fire hazard when we were short on rain for the season.

Stop penning fifty dogs up in a three-foot-by-three-foot cage. Their barks and howls of misery could be heard for miles. I'm not convinced that some of those dogs roaming loose on Ms. Ramsay's property didn't belong to the Pearsons.

And please . . . Please stop peppering the cars of solicitors with buckshot. As much as I am tempted to discourage unwanted solicitation at my doorstep, I know better than to fire at them, especially Jehovah's Witnesses. Whether you believed in their take on God's plan or not, you could never be too sure. And firing at them certainly wouldn't win you any points on Judgment Day.

"Mama tells me that Olene's been wanting to put an addition on to their house," Jess said conversationally.

"Yeah, I'd heard that, too. Bull came into the Home Depot, buying up all of the corrugated tin that he could get his hands on."

"Lovely. I can't wait to see how it'll hold up under all of this rain."

"Why paint when you can let natural oxidation add the color for you."

"Natural oxidation?" Jess repeated, raising her eyebrows then punching me playfully on the arm. "Why, Mal! You've been watching the Discovery Channel again. Such a grand concept for a petite brain."

"I'll admit I've been studying up," I replied. "I keep thinking that somehow, if I can grow my brain as big as your mouth, we'll be even."

Jess laughed, but it was an uncomfortable one.

As I checked in with the station, letting them know my location, I turned on my signal, pulled over onto the shoulder before turning up the access road leading to Bull Pearson's house, an old two-story farmhouse painted slate blue and trimmed in dove gray. A screened-in wraparound porch covered the face and sides of the house. Dreamcatchers and wind chimes lined the eaves. A darker gray lattice bordered the lower half of the house, made more attractive by creeping vines of deep purple morning glories.

Normally, I wouldn't care about such detail. But the house had been kept in mint condition when the previous owners lived there. A retired couple out of Minnesota, looking for a warmer climate, had bought the house as a fixer-upper and had kept it up in the twelve years that they'd lived their until their passing. A terrible shame. Carbon monoxide poisoning from a faulty furnace.

The house seemed to have died with them. Its life was smothered by the mounds of trash collected by the Pearsons over the short time they'd lived there. I'd heard the saying, "One man's trash is another man's treasure." I could respect that. All of us were guilty of dumpster diving every now and then, especially if we knew that someone had thrown out a perfectly good something or other. My house had more than one trash-to-treasure find that I'd refurbished and given a second life.

But this odd collection of gutted cars, complete with blown out radial tires, piles of wood stumps so old they were starting to sprout again, washing machines in disrepair, and console televisions with the screen and picture tubes sitting on top of the faux wood grain cabinets could only be of value to Bull Pearson.

As I drew closer to his house, Jess leaned forward in her seat, peering through the windshield. "What in the world is that?"

"Your guess is as good as mine."

I didn't believe it. I was seeing it with my own eyes. But I wasn't believing it. Instead of the gray picket fence that normally fronted the Pearson home, a wall nearly five feet high ran the length of the front face of the house. Walls shouldn't be glinting.

"I guess Olene isn't getting that addition to her house," I mused. Bull Pearson had built a retaining wall out of the tin he'd purchased.

"Do you think this means that he doesn't intend to evacuate?" Jess asked.

"I don't know. A man goes to that much trouble to protect his property, he isn't going to give up so easily."

I pulled up to what used to be the entry to the house. Hard to tell with a tin wall facing me. Tapped my horn once, then twice. All it did was annoy the dogs. I could hear them barking, snarling, giving warning. But no one was coming out.

"How far do you think he's gotten?" Jess asked. "With the wall, that is?"

"Only one way to find out."

I put the Jeep into reverse and started to drive parallel with the wall. I didn't worry about tearing up Bull's lawn. There was none. Anything that had resembled the immaculate yard of days past was gone now.

I drove several feet before the wall took a ninety-degree bend to follow along the left side of the house. Another few yards, another sharp angle, until we were driving along the back side of the house.

"There they are," Jess said, spotting the Pearsons on the far side of the fence.

The back wall was only three-quarters finished. Looked as though Bull had run out of tin. The wall he'd constructed was almost as high as the tin, but made completely of sandbags.

Bull's back was turned to us as he bent over a pile of sand. He slammed a shovel into the pile, scooped out enough to fill half a bag and allowed the sand to slip into the sack held by his wife.

At the sound of my horn, Olene Pearson turned around. She flipped back the brim of her bright yellow rain cap, trying to get a better look at us. Dressed all in yellow rain gear—from her hat, to her slicker, down to her black thigh-high rubber boots—she reminded me of the figure on the Gorton's Fisherman's fishsticks box.

Tapping Bull on the shoulder, she pointed at us and dropped her sack. Bull must've said something to her, something harsh. Olene snatched up the sack, making sure to hold it wide open while Bull filled it, knotted it, and tossed it onto the stack with the others.

"Wait here," I told Jess, cutting off the engine.

"You'll get no argument from me," Jess said emphatically.

I never knew quite what to expect with Bull. Sometimes he could be affable, easygoing. That was usually when it was just the two of us and after he'd been drinking. Sometimes, he'd offer me a beer, too. We'd sit out on his porch and talk a while. Me mostly listening. And then, after I'd said what I'd come out to say, he'd promise to do better.

Other times, if he'd had too many, he could turn just as mean as those dogs he kept penned up. That was the ornery part of him. That side of him came out quicker when he had an audience. Like whenever his wife was around. Either she brought out the meanness in him, or he liked showing how evil he could be whenever he thought he had a captive audience.

Since I had no way of knowing how he was feeling today, I left Jess in the Jeep and went out to talk to him.

"How y'all folks doin?" I hailed him, putting forward my best "Officer Friendly" face. I approached slowly, making no sudden movements. One of Bull's hunting dogs was tethered to the back porch post. It was a big ugly brute that was a cross between a mutt and a mongrel. The tether didn't look all that strong to me. The dog snarled and strained against it, pulling so hard that I thought I heard the post creak.

Bull straightened, wiping the mingling of sweat and rain water from his forehead with his gloved hands. His dark, lean face looked even more haggard. Speckles of mud and sand were splattered in his beard and in his tight, wispy graying hair.

As I approached him, I noted how his shoulders heaved up and down, as if he had trouble catching his breath. He wasn't wearing a rain coat. Instead, he wore a white T-shirt, clinging to his thin frame, dark blue pants barely held up with a pair of faded red paisley suspenders. The black army boots he wore were without the benefit of laces and coated in mud.

"You settle down over there!" Bull shouted, hurling a clod of dirt at the dog. It ducked, anticipating Bull's poor aim.

"Hey, Chief," Olene said, smiling politely. "What brings you out here?"

"What else? The weather," I said, making a point of looking up at the sky. "They say it's supposed to get real bad before it gets better."

"You don't say." Bull grunted in response, put another sack in Olene's hands, and kept shoveling.

"Weather service advises folks that can to move to higher ground. They've opened up the high school for a shelter."

"We didn't see much use for high school when we was of an age to go," Olene laughed. "We ain't gon' bother with it now, Chief."

"That true, Bull?" I prompted. He didn't respond, just kept shoveling.

I tried a different tact, making sure to sound admiring. "You sure did put a lot of work into this wall, Bull."

That got his attention. He stopped shoveling and looked at me. "You not gon' make me tear it down, are you, Chief?"

"No, sir. The way I see it, you're just trying to protect your property. Right?" I said.

"Damn straight," Bull said proudly. "Took me two years to get this place exactly the way I wanted it."

Two years! With as much stuff as he'd collected, you'd think it was a ten-year collection.

"I gotta tell you, Bull, that even with all the back-breaking work you put into it, it may not hold."

Closer to the truth was that that wall probably wouldn't hold. I could tell by the leaning of the support posts that he hadn't dug deep enough for his post holes. As the ground grew more saturated, the heavy untreated two-by-twos would only get heavier, soaking up water like a straw. And once the pressure of high water was on that wall, it was coming down.

"What're you saying, Chief? You saying I don't know how to build worth a damn? Are you sayin' my work's shoddy?"

"Naw . . . That's not what I'm saying at all," I said quickly. "I'm just saying that folks have been building dams and levees and bridges around here for decades. But when the river decides that she's gonna take it all down, it's not gonna matter how much effort you put into it. You don't want to be hanging around here if we lose the levees, Bull. Trust me. If I were you, I'd pack up what you can carry in a couple of suitcases and head for higher ground. The high school has got plenty of room. If your wall is as strong as it looks, and you've done one fine job of it from what I can see, it'll all be here when you get back."

"I ain't goin'," Bull said, true to his stubborn nature. "I know what happens when property is abandoned. Looters and vandals have a field day. I'm staying right here. So help me, Chief, I'm giving you fair warning. Any fool that tries to climb this fence without my permission will either get a butt full of buckshot or a face full of fangs. I'll set my dogs loose in a minute."

"I can appreciate your concern, Bull. It's why I'm out here. Making sure that doesn't happen. Nobody's gonna go looting while I'm around."

He didn't believe me . . . or trust in my ability to protect his place. As long as he had an audience, he had to show me up. I couldn't come on his place and make demands. I paused, then indicated by tilting my head that I wanted to have a private conversation with him.

Bull followed me. When we were out of earshot of his wife, he leaned both forearms on the shovel handle, taking the opportunity to catch his breath. "Say what you came here to say, Chief. "

"I can't make you get out, Bull. I can try. I can raise

Cain, try to take you in by force . . . But you and I both know that ain't no good. It'll just get you into trouble and me into trouble for overstepping my authority since a mandatory evacuation hasn't been called yet. But I'm advising you, man to man, even if you want to stay here, let your wife go. Let Olene go to the shelter."

"I need her here with me. I need her help," Bull protested. "Who else is gon' hold the sacks while I shovel? I can't do all the work around here."

"Bull, if you care anything at all for her and her safety, you'll let her go."

I could see the wheels of consideration turning in Bull's mind. He looked over at Olene, trying on her own to continue to fill the sandbags. Then, he focused on the Jeep.

"Is that Jess Ramsay you got in there with you, Chief?"

The question startled me. I didn't know Bull's eyesight was that good.

"Yeah," I admitted. "That's Jess."

"And she's going to that shelter?"

I nodded. "I'm taking her myself."

Bull sighed. "If it's good enough for your woman, I suppose it's good enough for mine." He shouldered his shovel and hollered across the yard, "Olene! Pack your bag, woman. You're goin' back to school."

"Thanks, Bull. You did the right thing." I took a chance and decided to push my luck with Bull.

"What about your pets?" I said, gesturing toward the pen.

"My what?"

"Your dogs, Bull. What about them?"

"Those ain't pets, Chief. Those are working dogs," Bull said, laughing at me.

"Fine, they're working dogs," I conceded. "Are you gonna leave 'em penned up like that?"

"How else are they gonna let me know when someone's trying to sneak on the property?"

"What if the water rises? You don't want them to drown, do you?"

"Ain't no water's gonna get in here, Chief. Remember? My walls are good and solid. You said so yourself." Bull winked as if he'd gotten one over on me.

He had. Me and my clever mouth! I tried a different tack with him.

"I can have animal control out here in no time. They'll put your dogs up in a real nice shelter where they can be warm and safe and dry. And you won't even have to worry about feeding them."

"I let you take my wife, now. You can't have my dogs, too. I appreciate the offer, Chief, but the dogs are staying."

I glanced over at pen again. The dogs were all yapping and snarling and jumping over each other. To my knowledge, they all looked healthy, well-fed, and tick-free. If they weren't being abused, I couldn't force Bull to give them up.

"Suit yourself," I said, brushing my hands together as if I was washing them of him.

Maybe, if time and weather and luck permitted, I'd swing back by here to see if he was all right. At least I'd gotten him to agree to send Olene on. I felt better knowing that she would be out of harm's way. I took that as a small victory, even if it did mean that I had to misrepresent the truth just a smidgen. Let Bull think that Jess and me were together. What could it hurt?

Chapter Eight

Jess

Oh, God. He's gonna go homicidal on him, I thought as I watched Mal talking with the Pearsons. Bull was yelling at Mal. Yelling at Olene. Yelling at the dogs. Any minute, I expected to him to become totally out of control. Bull. Not Mal.

From what I could see of Mal's expression and body language, he was doing his best to keep the situation from escalating. It surprised me that this should even be considered a situation. Mal was only doing his job. All he wanted to do was make sure that the Pearsons, and stubborn folks like them, weren't a danger to themselves.

I had to admit, and not without a small amount of shame, that that would be folks like me. Of course it was real easy for me to support Mal now, watching him deal with that beer-swilling Bull Pearson. He'd given me a small, firsthand glimpse of the danger he was putting himself in each and every time he went out in his official capacity as chief of police.

When he'd come to my home, asking me to pack up

and leave, I wasn't so amiable. I wasn't looking at him
as a man on the job; he was just Mal. And I'd known Mal
for a long time. Maybe I'd gotten too familiar with him.
I didn't appreciate what it meant for him to put on that
badge. Watching him in action gave me a healthy new respect for the pressures of his job. The unpredictability of
it. Mal didn't know what he could expect when he went
out there to talk to Bull Pearson. He went out there anyway, because it was his job. He cared about his job, of
that I had no doubt . . . And somehow, that translated
into his caring for the people his job put him in contact
with. Whether he liked the people or not, whether they
were his friends or not, he was going to give them the
same level of consideration.

He waited with Bull while Olene went inside and collected some of her belongings. While Olene was inside,
Mal grabbed a shovel, a couple of sandbags, and filled
them. He didn't get back into the Jeep until Olene had
started up the one running vehicle on their property
and started down the road. Bull walked over to the Jeep
with him, leaning on the driver's-side door.

"The Chief's got you out here in this nastiness, Ms.
Ramsay?" Bull said, taking a rag out of his pocket and
swabbing at his face. Didn't do much good. His rag was
sopping wet.

"Crazy business, this weather, isn't it?" I replied, making conversation.

"Makes us all a little crazy and do things contrary to
our nature," Bull remarked. He glanced at Mal—a sly
look that told me that he wasn't necessarily remarking
on the weather. "When it's just us against nature, there's
no telling what it'll bring out of us."

"Bull, you make sure you call me if it looks like you're
getting in over your head. I mean that now." Mal advised,
sounding very official.

"Thanks for all of your help, Chief," Bull said, holding out his gloved hand.

"You can thank me by making sure that you haven't floated away," Mal retorted. He turned the keys in the ignition, starting the engine. "Good luck to you."

"And the same to you," Bull offered. He gave me a wide grin, showing me a row of broken yellow teeth. "You've got a good man, Ms. Ramsay."

I waited until Mal had turned the Jeep around and was heading out to the main road before asking, "What did he mean by that?"

"Huh?" Mal said, pretending as if he hadn't heard me.

"What Bull said. Why would he say what he said . . . about . . . you know . . . about you being my man?"

Mal shrugged. "Who knows how Bull gets ideas in his head . . . especially when he's been drinking."

Normally, that answer would have satisfied me. Not this time. Bull hadn't been drinking. At least not recently. I hadn't smelled alcohol on his breath when he'd leaned into the Jeep. There was no reason for Bull to think that Mal and I were together. We weren't. Mal was with Shelby.

Almost as if I'd conjured Shelby simply by thinking about her, I knew by the road signs that we were coming up on the turn off to her house.

"Have you heard from her?"

"Who?"

Shelby of course. She was on my mind now, now that Bull had pushed my guilty button. I couldn't have folks getting the wrong idea and Mal and me.

"Shelby," I said quietly.

"No, I haven't heard from her." He shrugged. "She might already be at the high school."

"She would have called you, wouldn't she? To tell you where she was?"

It was odd that she hadn't called him. The more I

thought about it, maybe it wasn't so odd. Shelby was my friend. But we hadn't been as close as we once were. I guess I have Mal to thank ... or blame ... for that. She and Mal hang out now and they don't need me as a third wheel.

Still, I called her as often as I thought about her and tried to make time to keep her friendship warm. I was the one reaching out to her lately. Sometimes she returned my phone calls. Sometimes she didn't. I just figured that she and Mal were busy and didn't want to be bothered with me.

"Nope," Mal said curtly. "It's not as if she has a bell around her neck. I don't follow every move she makes. How about you? Why hasn't she called you? I thought you two were supposed to keep tabs on each other."

"We were," I admitted. "But not lately. You ought to know more about that than I do, Mal. She's *your* lady."

Did I sound bitchy when I'd said that? I hoped not. That wasn't the way I felt. And, if there was the remotest possibility of even a miniscule smidgen of jealousy, I didn't want Mal to know it. He'd made his choice. It wasn't me. I had to live with that. I lived with that fact every morning when I rolled out of bed—alone. While I sat down to my single serving of breakfast—alone. While I came home to check my message and found my machine filled with calls from telemarketers. Or even worse. From Mama! And when I sat down on my couch in the evenings, no one to struggle with over the possession of the remote control. No one to share favorite television shows with ... or ... Lord, I had to stop that downward spiral into self-pity. I sounded pathetic.

I pulled out my cell phone.

"What are you doing?" Mal asked.

"Calling her," I replied. "Unlike some people I know,

I like to give them a warning call before I show up at their doorstep."

The phone rang for several times before her answering machine picked up giving the standard message about not being home and leaving a message. Blah. Blah. Blah.

I snapped the phone shut. "She's not answering. Maybe you're right, Mal. Maybe she's already gone."

Mal indicated the street sign. "We're almost there. It wouldn't hurt to check to make sure."

"Yeah, that's what you said about the Pearsons. And it almost got you mauled by that mangy dog of theirs," I replied, smiling sweetly at him.

"Hey, I had it all under control," Mal said confidently.

"I know you did, law man," I said, all kidding aside. When I looked at him, I know hero worship adoration beamed on my face. "I hate to admit it, but I'm proud of you."

Mal cleared his throat uncomfortably. "Well . . . you know . . ."

"I know, I know," I said, giving a long-suffering sigh. "Just doing your job."

It was easier talking to Mal when we didn't talk about feelings. Neutral territory. We had to stay on neutral territory.

I quickly changed the subject. "Speaking of doing your job, what on earth did you say to Bull to make him let Olene go to the shelter?"

"Nothing much. I simply appealed to his good sense."

"Yeah, right."

"You'd be surprised. Beneath the filth and the cussedness beats the tender heart of a man." Mal thumped his fist against his chest. "All I had to do was get him to admit how much he cared for Olene, and he was happy to let her go."

"That was it? You didn't have to threaten to lock him up or shoot him?" I teased.

Mal chuckled softly. "Like Bull said. If you threaten a man's heart and soul, his reason for living, it brings out all kinds of things in his nature."

"I'll have to remember that," I murmured, then scrambled for my phone as it started to ring. The caller ID showed Shelby's number.

"Hey, Shelby."

"Jessica." She was one of the few who called me by my given name. "Did you try to call me?"

"Yes, I did."

"What do you want?"

"I was worried about you, Shel. I hadn't heard from you in a while."

"Oh. Is that all? I'm fine. But I . . . uh . . . Don't have time to chat right now."

"I'm sorry. I didn't mean to bother you. I was concerned. That is, we were," I added, cutting my eyes toward Mal.

"We? Who is 'we'?"

"Me and Mal, that's who. We haven't heard from you and well . . . We thought . . ."

"Is Malcolm there with you now? At your house?" There was an edge to Shelby's voice that concerned me. If it was jealousy, she could squash that. She didn't have any reason to be. I brushed off her edginess and kept up the friendly chatter so that Mal wouldn't sense my misgivings.

"Actually, we're on our way to the high school. The Red Cross has opened it as a shelter. Mama's worried that my house will float away like Noah's ark, so she sent Mal out there to get me. Can you believe the nerve of that woman, Shel? As if Mal didn't have enough to do without running around after me."

"You got that right," Mal muttered. I batted at him, silencing him.

"Where are you now?!" This time there was definitely something odd about Shelby's tone. She was more than irritated at my calling her. She was panicked.

"About two minutes from your house," I confirmed, checking the road signs.

"No, Jessica, don't!" she whispered harshly into the phone. "Don't come here. You turn around right now."

I didn't know if Mal could hear her frantic whisper, so I continued, "Oh, it's no trouble, Shel. It's on the way to the school. Mal's making his rounds anyway."

"I'm serious, Jessica. Don't you dare bring Malcolm here! Do me this one favor and think of a way to keep him away."

That didn't sound like Shelby. Not at all. I wanted to ask her what was going on. I couldn't. It wasn't as if I could ask Mal to plug up his ears. I couldn't even respond to her in a way that wouldn't rouse his suspicions. The only thing I could do was hang up the phone and hope that whatever was making her nervous would work itself out by the time we got there.

"You're welcome," I said weakly, wishing that I'd made that phone call before we'd left Bull Pearson's place.

Don't go to her house? Too late. We were already there, pulling onto her street. I don't know what was going on with that girl. I guess I'd find out soon enough.

Shelby lived in a garage apartment about a quarter of a mile from the main road. The owners of the house were her cousins. What a sweet deal she had going on. They let her live up there practically rent free. Shelby had also convinced them to renovate the place before she moved in. Updated appliances, new carpeting, and fresh paint. Her place looked better than most luxury condos. I wished I could have afforded to live there with her. Maybe it was for the best that we didn't share the space. I don't think I could have remained friends with her if I had to make myself scarce or pull the pillows down over my ears to keep from hearing Shelby and Mal gettin' busy in the bedroom.

Mal pulled into the driveway, directly behind Shelby's silver Ford Focus. Another vehicle, one that I didn't recognize, was parked right next to Shelby's car. Any other day, I would have figured that it belonged to Shelby's cousin. Only, I knew better than that. Shelby's cousin and his wife had four kids all under the age of seven. Their main mode of transportation was a minivan. Unless somebody in that family was going through a midlife crisis, that motorcycle parked in the driveway didn't belong to anyone I knew. I knew it. And, heaven help Shelby, Mal knew it, too.

He cut off the engine, yet didn't get out right away. He sat there, hands on the steering wheel, looking at that bike. Looking up at Shelby's door. Then back at the bike again.

After five minutes of his sitting there, neither one of us saying a word, I offered, "Do . . . Do you want me to go up?"

He held up his hand. "I'll go."

"I'd better go with you," I said quickly, unbuckling my seatbelt.

"Why?"

I fumbled for the right thing to say. "Because . . . She might need my help."

"I doubt it," Mal said tightly. "Looks like she's got plenty of help already."

"I'm going just the same," I said firmly.

"Suit yourself."

He got out, slamming the door behind him. I slammed

the door, too, talking loudly as we started up the stairs. Mal went first. I followed behind him, making sure my footsteps fell heavily on the creaky wooden steps.

"Do you think it's ever going to stop raining?" I said loudly, practically shouting.

Mal turned back and gave me a hard look.

Well, what did he expect me to do? All I was trying to do was give Shelby just a few extra minutes to . . . to . . . well, to get herself together.

"Police Department!" Mal announced himself, banging on the door with his fist.

Chapter Nine
Mal

It would have been too easy to kick the door in. I knew Shelby was in there. I could hear her on the other side of the door, scrambling and scurrying around, knocking over furniture in her haste. The oak door's delicately etched glass inset wasn't enough to keep me from seeing what was going on inside. There was enough room through the fleur-de-lis pattern to see the silhouettes of two figures. There *was* somebody else in there with her. Somebody that wasn't me.

"Open up, Shelby! We're getting wet out here!" Jess complained, peeking around my shoulder. She swiped at her hair, dripping water into her eyes, and hugging her arms tightly to her chest.

I stepped aside and pulled Jess closer to the door, to give her more protection from the overhang. It was the best move I could have made, putting Jess between me and the door. It stopped me from pushing against the door as soon as Shelby opened it. She poked her head out, concealing most of her body behind the door.

She had the nerve to try to look and sound natural.

A huge, pink Turkish towel was wrapped around her head and she'd come to the door wearing a robe, as if she'd just gotten out of the shower. Maybe she had. I'd give her that much credit.

"Jessica," she said breathlessly. Then looked beyond her at me. "Malcolm."

Her perfectly capped, laser-whitened smile was weak. She couldn't hold it for very long. Couldn't hold the smile. Couldn't hold my gaze either.

"You gonna keep us standing out here in the rain, Shelby?" I asked, grabbing Jess by the shoulders and steering her ahead of me. Shelby had no choice but to back up.

"Uh ... no ... of course not. Come on in." She made a grand sweeping gesture.

Jess wiped her feet on the plastic grass and daisy welcome mat, and stepped across the threshold.

"We didn't mean to come calling unannounced, Shelby," she apologized. "I'm really, *really* sorry."

Jess made a small sound, hissing through her teeth, as if she'd just been burned.

"It's all right," Shelby said breathlessly, fidgeting with the belt of her crimson satin robe. Red was Shelby's favorite color. I'd remembered that when I'd picked out that very same robe as a gift for her last Valentine's Day.

"No, it isn't," I said, straining to sound civil. "It's so rude."

"What are you doing here, Mal?" Shelby asked pointedly.

I didn't answer right way, but walked leisurely around the room, my hands clasped loosely behind my back. Sometimes being a cop trained to take in details worked against me. I didn't have to go far to collect the evidence I needed. A dozen pink roses in a vase on the coffee bar. Two dinner plates in the sink. Two wine glasses on the table by the couch. A room filled with recently burned candles. And the coup de grâce—one pair of red satin panties hastily shoved underneath her black leather couch. It was the same crimson satin panties that completed the set that I'd given her. The lack of one piece of evidence, one that I was secretly hoping I would find, disturbed me even more than the sight of her crumpled underwear. No condom wrappers.

I was filled with a morbid curiosity. Had she even bothered with protecting herself, and me, while she was playing musical beds? Who was he? Did I know him? Where had she stashed him? There weren't too many places he could hide in a place this size. One way in and one way out the garage apartment, unless he was fool enough to take a leap out of a second floor window. How long had this been going on? Why didn't I know? Maybe on some level I did. The real question was, why didn't I *want* to know?

My head was spinning with the possibilities. The answers as to why Shelby had suddenly become so low maintenance, as far as I was concerned, were staring me straight in the face. A bright crimson beacon shouting at me.

"I said what are you doing here?" Shelby said, sounding more offended the longer I ignored her. I took a step toward the bedroom and thought she would nearly stumble in her haste to block my path. That was a first for me. Usually she was racing me to the door.

Jess spoke up for me. "We were worried about you, Shel. Mal is encouraging everyone in the area to evacuate for their own safety."

"And naturally he came to get you first," Shelby replied, glaring at Jess.

"She was first on my route," I explained.

"Of course," Shelby said snidely. "Seems to me, Malcolm, that Jessica is always first on your route. Always."

"Now wait a minute, Shel," Jess started. "The only reason that we're here was because Mal wanted to be sure you were safe."

"Well, you don't have to worry about that, Chief Loring," Shelby retorted. "I'm being well taken care of. Better than I have been in a very, very long time."

"Is that right?" I challenged.

"Shelby!" Jess gasped, sounding shocked.

"Oh, don't sound all surprised and innocent, Jessica," Shelby said nastily.

For a brief moment, I wondered if Jess had known all along about Shelby's extracurricular activities. Wasn't she the one who tried to give Shelby a warning call just minutes before we showed up?

I wouldn't put it past Jess. She and Shelby were friends. It would be like Jess to stick her neck out for a friend. I don't know which made me madder, the fact that Shelby could cheat on me or the fact that Jess wouldn't tell me about it if she knew. A tiny voice on the inside of me admitted that it was the latter that disturbed me more. I didn't want to think that Jess would ever want to deceive me.

Jess and me . . . well . . . We had a connection that went beyond friendship. If she was lying to me, or keeping something from me, I'd know it. Wouldn't I? Somehow, I'd sense it. She couldn't look me straight in the eyes and lie to me.

Standing here now, facing Shelby, I wasn't so sure. If Shelby could do it, maybe Jess could, too. Maybe all women could. Maybe, all of those comedians were right. Maybe men were just plain clueless when it came to knowing what went on in a woman's head. Or in a woman's heart.

"I don't know what you're talking about, Shelby," Jess said, honestly dismayed. She crossed her hands over her heart. The look on her face, with her eyes as wide open as her mouth, convinced me that she had no idea that Shelby had moved on. I think she was just as hurt because Shelby hadn't shared that secret with her.

"Oh, like you and Malcolm have never—" Shelby began, pointing an accusing finger at Jess.

"Never." Jess didn't let her complete the sentence. Her tone was harsh as she got back in Shelby's face, wagging her own accusing finger. "And you know it. Don't try to put on me something that was all your own doing. I would never do anything like that to you. Not like you . . . You selfish heifer, going after Mal when you knew that I—"

Jess stopped herself, biting her lip, and then clamping her hand over her mouth. Her head swiveled back and forth, looking from me to Shelby back to me again.

That she what? I turned to Jess, hunching my shoulders, waiting for her to finish the sentence. What was she going to say? At that moment, I really needed to know.

She exhaled a long breath and pointed at the door.

"That you what, Jess?" I prompted.

"Nothing," she said, becoming tight-lipped. "You two obviously have some things to work out. You don't need me here clouding issues. If you want me, I'll be waiting outside in the Jeep."

"You don't have to go, Jess. We're all one big happy family here. In fact, why not make it a party? Where is he, Shelby? Get him out here," I ordered Shelby, pointing to a spot on the carpet.

"Excuse me?" Shelby said, sounding indignant.

"I said get him out here," I repeated with more of an edge.

"Why?" Shelby went from indignant to suspicious. I don't think she trusted what I had on my mind to do. I didn't blame her. I didn't trust myself either.

"I need to have a word with him," I explained calmly.

Give this man a medal. I had gotten a choke hold on my patience and wasn't letting go. I couldn't afford to.

"You don't need to say a thing to him, Malcolm," Shelby snapped. "In fact, there's nothing you need to say to me either. So, why don't you please leave?"

My tenuous hold on my patience slipped a notch. "I'm here in my official capacity for Codell County P.D., Shelby. Now, you either tell your friend to get his ass out here so I can say this once . . . and only once . . . or I'll go in there and get him. You don't want that now, do you?"

"You're abusing your authority, Malcolm," Shelby said. "I didn't have to let you in here."

"Half of your closet is full of my things," I said in a tone so icy that even Jess flinched. "If I go in there and get them, I may not be too careful about what I toss out."

"You'd better do as he says, Shel," Jess directed.

Tightening her robe belt around her, Shelby completed the short walk across the room to the door leading to her bedroom. She looked back over her shoulder before stepping inside, closing the door behind her.

Jess expelled another breath. "You have to believe me, Mal, I swear I didn't know."

"I know," I assured her.

She walked over to stand next to me and asked in a low voice, "So, what are you going to do?"

"What do you mean?"

"About you and Shelby."

I snorted in derision. What else could I do?

"Nothing," was my careful response.

"Nothing?"

"That's right."

"You're not going to take this lying down," she said, then bit her lip again. "Oh, wrong choice of words. "Sorry, Mal."

She rested her hand briefly on my arm then took it

away. A noise from the other room made her take a step back.

"What do you expect me to do?" I whispered harshly, glancing back at Shelby's door. "Fighting for a woman who doesn't want you is like . . . resisting arrest," I explained to her. "You can't win. And when you stop fighting against the inevitable, the result is the same. You haven't changed anything. All you've done is pissed everybody off."

"So," she said slowly. "If you're not going to try to work things out, what do you need to see him for?"

I couldn't tell her that I just wanted to see him. I couldn't tell her about the destructive curiosity that just had to know what type of man Shelby had chosen over me.

"I told you. I just need to have a word with him."

"Mal, are you sure you know what you're doing?" Jess asked.

"I thought you were on your way outside?" I said impatiently.

"Maybe we should both step outside, Mal," she insisted, reaching for my hand.

"Why? I'm just doing my job, Jess," I said, squeezing it once in appreciation before letting it fall.

"Are you? I wonder." She didn't sound as if she believed me.

"Don't question me, too, Jess, " I warned her. "I know what I'm doing."

"What *are* you doing?"

"Just passing on some evacuation advice."

"This has nothing to do with an evacuation order, Mal, and you know it," Jess retorted.

"You sound like Shelby. You think I'm abusing my authority, too?"

"Maybe. You're only human. Maybe you're just throwing your weight around for the hell of it because you're hurt and you're angry."

"I'm not angry," I denied, in a cold, flat voice.

I admit, when I drove up and saw the bike parked there, I'd felt the blood boiling in my brain. I'd actually considered leaving my service weapon in the Jeep to remove all temptation.

As I sat there in the Jeep, collecting myself, all rational thought flying out the window, I had visions of me going up there and blowing both their brains out. I'm a man, like any other, who'd just found out that my lady has been creepin'.

Was I supposed to sit back and take that? As I'd walked around her place, mentally filing away all of the facts that supported evidence of her infidelity, I grew closer and closer to going off.

It wasn't until Shelby had accused Jess of cheating first that I snapped back to myself. Seeing Jess's expression, listening to her defend her behavior and mine, I realized that the only person I should be angry at was myself. Maybe I'd gotten too complacent in our relationship, taking Shelby for granted. Maybe, if I'd been taking better care of business, she wouldn't have taken her business elsewhere.

Be that as it may, she should have told me that she wasn't satisfied with how things were going between us. I would have listened. I might not have been able to do much about it. I am who I am. I can't change that. But I would have listened. If she was unhappy, I wouldn't have expected her to hang in there with us. What's that old saying? If you love something, let it go? Right? Was that what I was supposed to do now? Let her go?

It was true. I wasn't angry. Not anymore. I can't pinpoint the exact moment when it drained out of me. I just know that when Jess had torn into Shelby, obviously upset because Shelby had gotten to me first, my attitude did a rapid 180.

"Never" Jess had said. Nothing had ever happened between Jess and me. That wasn't exactly the truth. There was that time I'd shown up drunk at her house. Only Jess's resolve had kept us from going further than we should have. She'd been a lot stronger than I was.

Since that day she turned me down, I'd replayed the events of that night over and over in my mind. Each time, the events escalated further. Each time the events of what "might have happened" grew more intense, until I woke up one morning, aching for her and cursing the fact that she could be so resolute. Had I ever cheated on Shelby? No. Only in my mind. But it was enough. Now, as I stood here faced with the possibility that I'd chosen the wrong woman, it made me wish that Jess had finished her sentence. I really, really needed to know what she was going to say. Shelby had gone after me when she knew what? What did she know?

A moment later, Shelby's new friend emerged from the bedroom. I had to blink, both mentally and physically, to make sure I wasn't staring into the face of my doppelgänger. He came out of the bedroom wearing a pair of dark blue Dickies work pants and boots. He must have been dressing in a hurry, sliding his long arms into his shirt as he came out.

Not a bad looking man. That would have been a real blow to my ego if Shelby was "slumming" with her new man. He was tall, six-foot-three or -four. Dark skinned. He wore his hair longer than mine, though not by much. A small symbol, indicating a college fraternity, was branded over his heart.

"What's your name?" I directed at him, ignoring Shelby's heated glare from across the room.

"You don't have to answer that," she advised.

"Mister, do you know who I am?"

I stepped up to him, inches away from his face. He didn't flinch, didn't back away. But he answered my question.

"You're that cop," he said, his eyes shifting to the badge pinned to my chest and gun still securely fastened in its holster.

"That's right. So I'm only gonna ask you once more. Your name?"

"Evans," he responded reluctantly. "Riley Evans."

"Well, Riley Evans," I said amiably, backing away, "I'm only here for one reason . . . to give you fair warning."

"She doesn't want you anymore," Riley spoke up, trying to anticipate where I was going with this conversation.

"Did she tell you to say that?" I wanted to laugh. Was he going to challenge me for Shelby? If only he knew how unnecessary that was.

"Riley doesn't need me telling him what to do," Shelby said, moving beside him and linking her arm through his. "He has his own mind."

"Good for him," I mocked her.

"Mal," Jess called out a quiet warning, opening the front door. "The evacuation. Remember? This is about police business. Nothing else."

"Of course!" I said, as if the thought that it could be otherwise never entered my mind. "That's why I'm here. To inform you of the voluntary evacuation. We've got shelters open at the high school and the Baptist church. Is that GoldWing out there yours, Evans?" I asked about his motorcycle.

"It's mine," he admitted.

"My advice to you is to stay off the roads if that's your only means of transportation. I don't imagine you'll get far in this weather."

"I didn't expect him to try," Shelby said suggestively. She put her hand on Riley's bare chest, smoothing her fingers over his pectorals and dipping down toward his navel. I turned my back, starting toward the door before she went any further. "We'll be *riding* out the storm right here."

I didn't have to ask what she meant by that parting shot.

"Be careful, Shelby," Jess said. "All kinds of nasty things can happen when you're riding without rain gear."

Jess looked back at me and winked. Had she noticed the lack of condom use as well?

"Let's go, Jess," I said, putting my hand in the small of her back and ushering her outside.

She gripped the handrail, walking carefully down the stairs with considerably less noise than she had when we'd first gone up.

"I'm sorry, Mal," Jess said, her tone subdued, even pained.

"What are you apologizing for?" I snapped.

It came out harsher than I meant it to, making Jess flinch again. That was twice in one day that she'd shied away from me. Not a look I ever wanted to see on her again.

"I . . . I know that must have been very painful for you. If you want to talk about it," she offered.

"I don't," I said flatly.

End of story. Case closed. File this one away under just one of those crazy things that didn't work out. I wasn't the first man who'd ever split with his lady. Law of averages told me that I wouldn't be the last. That thought was of small comfort to me as I passed Riley's bike. I paused for a second, considering what my jail time options would be if I "accidentally" ran over it as I was backing out or if a few rounds from my gun somehow wound up in the tires or gas tank.

"Mal," Jess said, putting a restraining hand lightly on

my forearm. It was as if she could read my thoughts. I guess it was written all over my face. "Come on. Let's get out of here."

She squeezed my arm, silently insistent.

"Get in the Jeep," I told her.

"Not without you."

"I'll be there in a minute," I promised.

"No. Not in a minute. Now," she urged, tugging on my arm. "Right now."

"All right, I'm coming," I relented, backing toward my Jeep. I held the door open for Jess and helped her climb inside.

"You sure you don't want to talk about it, Mal?" she asked, putting her hand against the door to stop me from closing it.

"I'm sure."

"You're positive?"

"Absolutely. How many times are you gonna ask me?"

"Until I get an honest answer."

"This is as good as it gets," I retorted, moving around the front of the Jeep to enter on my side.

"Not good enough, law man," Jess shouted stubbornly.

As I settled in, I tried to strike a bargain with her. "I'll tell you, if you're so ready to talk. You talk to me, then. Tell me what you were going to say up there."

"Up where?" Jess shifted uncomfortably, her expression telling me that she knew exactly what I was talking about.

"You called your best friend a heifer," I reminded her. What could Shelby have done that warranted that?

"Oh that!" Jess laughed uneasily. "Among us girls, that's a term of endearment."

"Heifer?"

"Yeah. Followed closely by 'cow,' and when we're really feeling affectionate 'bitch'?"

"Now who's not being honest?"

"Never mind about that, Mal. We weren't talking about me. We were talking about you."

"No, we weren't, because I wasn't talking."

"Exactly!" she said triumphantly. "You may as well talk to me, Mal, because I'm not gonna stop talking until you start."

Chapter Ten

Jess

"Stop!" I shouted, involuntarily grabbing Mal's arm.

A woman stood on the side of the road waving her arms to flag us down. My shout wasn't necessary. He'd already spotted the van a quarter of a mile up the road. Several emergency flares placed behind and alongside the road sputtered and struggled to stay lit under the rain's constant drenching.

Mal slowed down and turned on his emergency lights. As he pulled behind the minivan, listing to the left on a flat rear tire, he reported back to the station, giving his location and informing them that he was stopping to help a stranded motorist. He relayed the type of vehicle and the license plate number. Mississippi tags, but from several counties north of us.

His red and blue flashing emergency lights and the minivan's flashing amber caution lights barely cut through the gloom of the morning, a gloom that had little to do with the heavy storm system dropping more and more rain on us. The gloom came from Mal himself as he drove, wrapped more in the darkness of his own thoughts than his rain gear. True to his word, or rather his nonwords, he didn't talk any more than he had to—only breaking his silence to respond to radio traffic.

"I wonder what they're doing out here?" I said aloud.

"My guess would be a flat tire," Mal said, in total smart-ass mode. He'd done that because I wouldn't stop pestering him about Shelby. I guess he thought if he gave me enough evasive answers, I would leave him alone. Fat chance of that. I wasn't going to leave him alone. Not ever.

Behind the open tailgate of the minivan, a pile of suitcases, boxes, and bags were scattered on the ground. A spare tire was leaning against the rear bumper.

"I can see that," I shot back. "I meant, what makes a woman risk driving all this way in this kind of weather?"

It had been my experience in dealing with the parents of my students that there was always a reason for an adult's erratic behavior. When a parent acted out of the range of normal behavior, it took a while, but the cause usually presented itself. That wasn't to say that Codell County didn't have its share of, let's say, *eccentric* personalities. Once the run-of-the-mill flakes were identified and I learned how to effectively deal with them, when any of my students' parents acted abnormally and that behavior affected their mental or physical health, I did everything in my power to root out the cause—whether it was drugs, or mental illness, or some other stressor.

"Good question," Mal said, taking my offhand comments into consideration. "Stay here," Mal said brusquely, gathering his hat, coat, and flashlight.

"I can help," I offered.

"You couldn't change a flat tire to save your life, Jess," he said, a not-so-vague reference to the time in high school that he had to change it for me.

"Maybe not," I said easily, not taking the bait. "But I can hold a flashlight for you."

Whether he really wanted to talk was beside the point. Something told me that what he really wanted was to fight. He needed an excuse to work out his anger. Any excuse. I couldn't give it to him. I wouldn't. In fact, I'd taken away the one chance he had to vent his anger. I had to. I wasn't about let Mal vandalize a $40,000 bike just to get his revenge on Shelby.

"Suit yourself. Stay out of the way."

I followed behind him. "Yes, sir," I said, executing a snappy salute. The look he gave me in return instantly drove all of the nonsense out of me.

"Drop it or keep your behind in the Jeep," he growled.

Mal was totally into the job now. Supercop mode.

"Yes, sir, Chief Loring," I replied, respecting his job and the responsibility that came with it. It was the same tone I would have used if stopped by another cop in any other town. There was a time and a place for everything. And this was not the time for me to be acting like this with Mal. He wasn't Mal. Not at this moment. He was the chief of police of the Codell County police department. And he'd just made a traffic stop. Statistically, traffic stops were one of the most potentially threatening aspects of any cop's duties, even in a town as small as ours.

We trudged through the water, approaching the woman.

"Oh, thank goodness you stopped," she called out, clutching her water-soaked sweater to her chest. Her knee-length cotton dress was plastered to her legs. As she jogged to meet us, her once-white tennis shoes were dark gray and seemed, by the way she lifted her legs as she walked, too heavy for her feet.

"I don't know what happened. One minute we were driving along, and the next I'm swerving all over the road." She moved her slender hand back and forth, imitating a fishtailing motion.

"Are you all right?" Mal asked, shining the flashlight into the minivan. He walked behind the van, illuminating the flat tire and another quick look at the license plate.

"Yes, we're fine," she said. "The kids are shaken up. But we're all okay."

On the far side of the van, several feet away from the road, I counted four kids. The oldest seemed to be about nine years old. I recognized that look. A third grader. The youngest was still in a baby seat, screaming its lungs out, announcing to the world what it thought of being outside in this weather. They were all huddled miserably under a big black golf umbrella. It was leaky in several places. Some of the spokes were bent or showed where the umbrella cloth had stripped from the spoke. It was practically useless for keeping them dry.

"Oh, those poor babies," I commiserated, then addressed the mom. "Is it all right if I wait over there with them? My name is Jessica Ramsay. I teach third grade at the elementary school here in Codell County."

"Thanks for stopping, Ms. Ramsay. My name's Brooke."

Just Brooke, I noted. No last name?

"Are those your kids?" I asked conversationally.

She nodded, staring in a mixture of adoration and annoyance at them.

"So well-behaved. You don't see that often in children these days," I continued to make conversation.

"They didn't want to get out of the van," the woman explained hurriedly as to why they were standing by the van rather than waiting inside of it. "I told them they had to. It's so bad out here. I'd seen stories on TV about people who are rear-ended when they pull off the road. If someone didn't see my flashers while I was out here and they were all still inside . . . I did the right thing, didn't I, Officer? I'm not in trouble, am I, for having them out on the road?"

"Yes, ma'am," Mal said automatically, bending down to inspect the flat.

"Chief Loring means you did the right thing by moving them out of the van," I translated for Mal when a look of panic crossed the woman's face. Mal needed a translator since he wasn't in a friendly mood conversationally.

"Have you set the emergency brake?" he asked, reaching for the jack and the spare tire.

"No . . . um . . . I didn't think of that," she said, opening the driver's-side door and leaning inside.

"Get back, Jess," Mal ordered as we heard an eighteen-wheeler roaring toward us on the highway.

I checked over my shoulder at the approaching traffic. There were only a few cars on the road, riding in the big rig's wake. The few cars that were there were moving at a pretty good clip. Too fast for my comfort level. As long as we were standing there, we were one big happy target screaming, "Come splatter us all over the road!"

The eighteen-wheeler moved over into the passing lane as it came up on us, but not before it managed to send up a spray of water and mud. I turned my face away, feeling the cold spray hit my back and legs.

"Good morning," I said as I approached the kids. "My name's Miss Ramsay. What are yours?"

I addressed the oldest one first, acknowledging him as the leader and most responsible. He glanced at his mother before answering. She nodded, giving permission, but I didn't miss how she edged closer to us to listen.

"My name's Carter," the boy said. "And that's Cyrus." He pointed to the next oldest, another boy. "These are my sister Camden, and Ciara is the baby."

"Come on, kids. Why don't we wait over here while your mama and Chief Loring work on getting your tire fixed."

I gestured beyond the paved section of the breakdown

lane. Beyond the road was a stretch of recently mowed grass. Several feet beyond that ran a ditch, already filled to capacity. I heard the water rushing through it as it absorbed the runoff from the road and carried it beyond our sight, past the bend in the road. Past the ditch was a barbed-wire-and-wood-post fence, sectioning off some-one's undeveloped private property. A FOR SALE sign listing the name of the owner was leaning precariously to one side. The lot was left in its natural state, filled with trees and underbrush.

"The tire blew up," Cyrus offered. "Boom! And then we were twisting and turning and going all over the road, and Camden was screaming like a whiny baby."

"Did not!" Camden stomped her foot. "You stop saying that, Cyrus."

"Did, too," he taunted her.

"Did not!"

"Did, too!"

I knew from experience that this conversation would have gone on in just that level of detail and intensity if I didn't do something quick to stop it.

"I know I would have been screaming if I was almost in an accident. It sounds like it was very scary."

"I wasn't scared," Camden insisted.

"Ciara pooped her pants," Cyrus offered.

I knelt down beside the baby and unstrapped her from her seat. By the unique pungent odor and the pale green stains left behind on the seat, I knew that Cyrus was right, at least about this one thing.

"Does Ciara have a change of clothes?" I asked. "A diaper bag?"

"Over there." Camden pointed to the rear of the van where the family bags were stacked. "I'll go get it."

"No, Camden, honey. Don't! Stay away from the road," I called out, reaching out to grab her pink denim jacket as she darted past me. "Your mama wants you to stay over here where it's safe."

I could hear the creak of the van as Mal worked to loosen the tire's lug nuts. Each time he yanked on the jack, the van rocked forward, then back.

"I'll find the bag," I told her. "What color is it?"

"It's green with a big yellow duck on it."

"Green with a big yellow duck," I repeated.

"Uh-huh."

I tried to put Ciara back into her seat. She started to scream again. Her face was red from her cries. She screamed so long and so loud that she never closed her mouth long enough to draw in a deep breath. I thought she might hyperventilate, so I held the baby out to one of the kids, thinking that they could hold her until I got back.

"*Eeee-uuuuu!*" Cyrus said. "I'm not holding her. She stinks."

"Carter?" I asked the oldest.

"I'm holding the umbrella," Carter said, clutching the handle tightly.

"Don't look at me," Camden said, backing as far away from me as possible without stepping out from under the shelter of the umbrella. I looked for Brooke, but she and Mal were engaged in conversation. She stood with the hubcap cover in her hands as Mal loosened each lug nut and dropped it with a small *clank* into the cap.

I didn't want to, but I set Ciara down into the chair for just a second, long enough to take off my jacket and wrap her in it before picking her up again.

"Wait here," I advised the children as I tossed a part of my jacket over Ciara's head to cover her. Ciara whimpered for a moment, then snuggled against the warmth of my shoulder. Checking to make sure that she was well covered, I hurried back to the van.

"Don't mean to interrupt," I said breathlessly. I'd tried

to dodge as many raindrops as I could. Walking up the slope was difficult on the shorn, wet grass.

Mal looked up at me, his eyes widened at the sight of me holding Ciara. He didn't say anything as he turned his attention back to the tire. He lowered his head, seemingly focused on what he was doing. Not fast enough. Not before I saw a small smile tug at the corners of his mouth.

I glared at him, daring him to make a wisecrack about me and my so-called maternal instinct. I didn't see what was so damned funny. He acted like he'd never seen a woman with a baby before—albeit, a stinky, drippy, whimpering baby. What else could I do? I couldn't leave her there. She was cold and wet and miserable.

"Brooke, where's your diaper bag? Baby Ciara here could use a change," I said, patting the child on the back to soothe her.

"Oh . . . um . . . It's over here somewhere," she said as she started to rummage through the boxes.

"Be careful, ma'am! Get back," Mal called out sharply when Brooke leaned on the van for support, making it rock precariously on the jack stand.

"That's all right, I'll find it," I assured her, clamping my hand on her shoulder and pulling her away from the van. "You . . . You go on helping Chief Loring. I'll take care of changing Ciara."

Shoving aside a couple of bags, I found what I was looking for.

"Green bag. Yellow duck," I murmured as I slid the strap of the diaper bag over my shoulder. In a sudden flash of inspiration, I grabbed what looked to be a couple of dark green industrial-strength garbage bags. By the time I'd loaded up, Mal had already taken off the busted tire and was easing on the good one.

"All right, Ciara, honey. Here we go. We're gonna get

that stinky poopy thing off of you," I cooed, rubbing the baby's back in a circular, calming motion.

Out of the corner of my eye, I could see Mal tilting his head to watch me. Only, this time he wasn't laughing. His face was its usual stern mask as he advised, "You may not want to leave those kids too long by themselves, Jess."

"I'm hurrying, I'm hurrying," I replied. I, of all people, should know what could happen by leaving a group of children unattended. I never left my own kids alone for more than a minute. Any longer than that and I didn't know what I'd find by the time I made it back to the classroom.

I checked my jacket once more, cradling Ciara's head to my shoulder as I started down the embankment. I couldn't have been gone more than five minutes. Maybe six. Automatically, I did a quick head count. One in my arms. Two under the umbrella. One. Two . . . only two. Cyrus and Camden. Where was the oldest boy?

"Where's Carter?" I asked, clutching Ciara so tightly to me that she squawked.

Camden pointed, beyond the embankment, past the ditch, and into the fenced woods beyond.

"In there, Miss Ramsay."

"What's he doing in there?" I asked shrilly.

"He said he had to go pee-pee," Camden tattled. "I told him to go right here, but he didn't want anybody watching him."

"Oh, Lord!" I snapped.

Crossing that rain-swollen ditch was bad enough. Carter had gone past the fence and into the woods beyond. Not a good idea in weather like this. It brought out all kinds of animals seeking shelter. It was nothing to drive through these roads and find a deer or two crossing into the night. But sweet, innocent, Bambi-looking woodland creatures weren't the only things sharing these woods. Countryside like this also had its share of predators—stray dogs, wild boar, and coyotes. My biggest fear was snakes. Flood conditions like this were perfect for driving out cottonmouth water moccasins, a nasty, territory-protecting snake with an even nastier venomous bite.

"Mal!" I cried out to him, not bothering to hide the concern in my voice. I didn't want to shield the kids from my fear. I wanted them to know what a dangerously stupid thing their brother had done by going off alone.

Mal popped up from beside the van and was halfway down the embankment before I could scramble up to join him.

"What's wrong?" he asked, gripping my elbows to steady me as my feet slid out from under me, nearly sending me midway down the embankment again.

"In there!" I pointed in the direction Camden had shown me. "The oldest boy wandered off."

Mal swore, making no apologies to me, Brooke, or the kids as he took off after Carter.

"You were supposed to be watching them!" Brooke snapped in recrimination at me. "What kind of teacher are you?"

She followed after Mal, cupping her hands to her mouth and calling for her son. "Carter!"

Ignoring her, I turned to the kids again. "You two listen to me."

I was all teacher then, and they knew it. My tone said "obey me" or get a trip to the principal's office. I needed them right by me, where I could keep my eye on them for every second until Brooke got her family back on the road again.

"Yes, ma'am," Cyrus said.

"I told you not to move, didn't I?" I leaned down into their guilty-looking grimy faces.

"Yes, ma'am," Camden echoed. "But Carter really had to go."

"He couldn't wait five minutes until I got back?"

"He wouldn't go with you watching him. He said he wasn't a baby and didn't need anybody watching him."

"I told him not to go," Cyrus said pompously. "I told him that nobody wanted to look at his peeny-weeny."

"No, you didn't," Camden retorted.

"Did, too."

"Did not!"

"Did, too!"

Oh, for Pete's sake. I sighed, rolling my eyes toward the sky. If it weren't for the smell coming from Ciara, reminding me that someone else needed looking after, I would have put those two in time-out.

"Bring that umbrella over here, son," I told Cyrus. "Hold it over me just like this." With my hand over his, I positioned it just so.

"Miss Ramsay, I gotta go, too," Camden complained. She clutched her legs together, bouncing up and down.

"Don't you two move one inch. Not one inch." I held up my fingers to show them how much I meant it.

"I mean it. I really have to go," she insisted.

"You either have to hold it until your mom gets back, or I'll be changing you next," I said unsympathetically. Kneeling down once more, I spread the plastic bags on the ground.

I peeled off Ciara's clothes and tossed them into the spare garbage bag. She opened her mouth to cry again; but I continued to talk to her, making soothing noises as I swiped at her with over half the box of baby wipes. As soon as she realized that she would be clean and dry, her whimpering subsided, and she was actually cooing and grinning a toothless grin by the time I'd put on the new diaper and a fresh change of clothes.

I tossed my jacket into the garbage bag and did what I could to clean out what had been left behind in the vinyl padding of Ciara's car seat. All the while, I kept glancing up into the woods where Mal and Brooke had gone in to search for Carter. Nervous energy pent up inside of me wanted me to pace up and down the road while I waited for their return. I couldn't go far. Cyrus had the umbrella and his short legs couldn't keep up with me. I couldn't take the baby out from under it. No matter how poorly it shielded us, it was still better than being out in the direct weather.

A moment later, my heart nearly leaped into my throat when I heard the crack of gunfire echoing in the air. *Pop! Pop-pop!* It's was Mal's gun. I knew it was his. I recognize the sound of the gun report. He'd taken me to the firing range a couple of times, helping me to get over my fear of his most lethal tool of his trade.

Camden cried out, and clutched at my leg.

"Mama! Where's my mama?"

"It's all right, Camden," I said, though my mouth was so dry I could barely speak above a whisper. "They're going to be fine."

"What's that shooting?" Cyrus asked.

I shook my head, knowing that I couldn't give a convincing answer. It was better to stick to what I knew I could say. "Don't worry." I patted Camden's shivering shoulders. "Don't worry, baby. It's going to be all right. I promise."

"You promise?" She looked up with worried gray eyes.

"My most solemn promise."

A moment later, Brooke emerged from the forest. She climbed over the fence at the spot where Mal had draped his slicker to protect them from the barbs. Mal and Carter appeared a moment later. He grasped the boy by his waist and hauled him over the fence into his mother's waiting arms. Mal hopped over next. His long legs clearing the fence effortlessly. He retrieved his slicker and tossed it around her shoulders.

"I told you they would be fine!" Cyrus cried out, jumping up and down, and sending the umbrella flailing all over the place. I clasped Ciara to me, shielding her small body from Cyrus's enthusiastic leaping.

Mal grasped Brooke's elbow as they crossed the ditch, making sure that she didn't slip into the water as they waded through nearly thigh-high water. After they reached the other side, I waved my arm, making sure that they saw that we were all right and were waiting patiently for them.

Mal sent Brooke and Carter on up the road ahead of him, staying behind for a few minutes before joining us.

"Mama!" Camden and Cyrus left me and latched onto Brooke as if pulled by a powerful magnet. Very powerful. Nothing stronger than the bond of love. I passed Ciara back to her mother, then I joined Mal, holding out my hand to him and pulling him the rest of the way up the embankment.

"What happened out there?" I whispered harshly.

"Not now, Jess."

He joined Brooke and her children standing next to the van, where Carter was explaining with animated voice and wild hand gestures the events of the past few minutes.

When Mal's shadow fell over him, he looked up and gulped.

"Young man," Mal said, his voice terrible. Even made me want to perk up my ears and listen.

"Yes, sir." I saw Carter's adolescent Adam's apple bob in sheer nervousness.

"Do you know what almost happened to you out there?"

"Yes, sir," he repeated.

"You were told not to move."

"I know . . . but . . ."

"I don't want to hear any excuses from you. You didn't listen and almost got yourself and your mother in serious trouble. Is that what you wanted?"

"No, sir." When he dipped his head, his lower lip starting to tremble, I thought I saw a shift in Mal's expression. I knew him so well. I don't think Brooke or any of her kids would have noticed it.

"No, I didn't think so. It wasn't deliberate, so I'm not going to take you in . . . even though I should have."

"You mean arrest me?" Carter asked, with a noticeable squeak of fear in his voice. "For what? What did I do?"

"Malicious mischief, for starters," Mal ticked off on one finger. "Indecent exposure. Trespassing on private property. Have I mentioned enough?"

Brooke put her arms protectively around her son. "He's just a child, Chief Loring."

"Who needs to learn the value of respecting authority," Mal directed at her. "What do you think would have happened to him if I hadn't managed to scare off those coyotes?"

She shrugged helplessly. "Thank you . . . Thank you again."

"My advice to you, ma'am, is to get back in your van and get off the road as soon as you can. You think it's bad out here now? The weather's only gonna get worse."

"Worse?" Brooke said, glancing involuntarily at the sky.

"If you don't mind me asking, where are you headed?" I spoke up.

"To Biloxi. Still quite a ways to go."

Mal checked the replacement tire once more and popped the hubcap back on. "First chance you get, get yourself a new spare. This is only a donut. A baby spare. It's not meant to be a long-term replacement."

"I understand," Brooke said, nodding vigorously.

"I certainly hope so," Mal encouraged. "Don't go over forty miles per hour until you can get somewhere and swap this out. And keep your emergency flashers on."

While she loaded the kids into the van, I helped Mal put her suitcases and boxes into the rear of the van. He slammed the hatch down, then gathered the remaining flares from the road to extinguish them.

"Remember. Get somewhere, out of this weather. Hunker down until it's passed."

I leaned forward, peering into the van. With a cranking motion of my hand, I gestured for the kids to let down the window. Despite the heart attack that Carter had given me by running off like that, somehow I was going to miss them. The lack of warmth from Ciara nestled against me gave me a pang, an odd sense of melancholy and loss.

"You kids be good," I advised. "Mind your mother, now."

"We will, Miss Ramsay," Camden promised.

"Promise?"

"My most solemn promise," she echoed me. I blew them a kiss, then reached in and placed my hand against Ciara's cheek.

"Good-bye, sweetheart," I murmured, and then backed away.

"Come on, Jess," Mal put his arm around my shoulders, steering me toward the Jeep. "Get inside."

I gave him no argument. I was soaked through to the skin, and oddly drained. I worked with children all day long. But never before had I had this sense of weariness or loss at seeing them go. I watched them drive off, their hazard lights still flashing as they pulled on to the road. Mal coasted behind them for a quarter of mile, making sure that they were all right, before they took the exchange leading them further south. Cyrus's face was pressed to the window as he waved good-bye.

Lifting my hand, I waved until I couldn't see their flashing lights anymore.

As we came up on Bramfort levee and the sandbagging crew site, Mal slowed to a near crawl, working his way through the dump trunks idling by the side of the road and the volunteers milling around the headquarters.

When he cut off the engine, Mal said unnecessarily, "We're here."

"Uh-huh."

"Not too late. I can still take you to the shelter."

"I need to be here, Mal," I said stubbornly. "I need to keep busy. I don't want to think about what could be happening to my house."

"Are you gonna be all right, Jess?"

"Sure. Why do you ask?"

He shrugged. "I don't know. You look . . . sad."

I had just as much to lose as all of those other folks out there. I was worried about my house and told him so.

"I can understand that," he said. "But it's more than that. What is it, Jess?"

"I don't know," I said, lowering my head. "I just can't stop thinking about Brooke and those kids. Do you think they're gonna make it to where they're going, Mal?" My voice quivered.

"I hope so. I've got some friends in the Biloxi police department. I can put out the word to keep an eye out for them."

"Would you?"

"Of course. Why do you sound so surprised?" he smiled at me.

"I know they were a lot of trouble. Especially that Carter."

"He was just being a boy," Mal said, making an excuse for him.

"That didn't stop me from wanting to wring his neck after you brought him back," I said grumpily.

Mal burst into laughter, throwing back his head and slapping his hand on the steering wheel. "If it weren't for you holding that baby, I think you woulda choked him."

My face fell again at the thought of Ciara. "I can't believe it," I said incredulously. "I miss her. I actually miss that squirming, squalling bundle of poop!"

Mal reached out and tucked a strand of hair behind my ear. His knuckles grazed my cheek as he said, "You know, Jess, you handled that bunch pretty well. I'm proud of you."

I smiled. "You think so?"

"Yeah."

"Brooke said I was a lousy teacher."

"No, she didn't."

"She came about as close to saying it."

Mal cleared his throat, shifted uncomfortably in his seat as he said, "Don't listen to her. She was upset and worried about her kids. You're a wonderful teacher. Someday you'll make an even more wonderful mother."

I blinked at him, surprised to hear those words come out of his mouth.

He reached back behind the seat and handed me a windbreaker. Not as big as the slicker he wore now, but it had POLICE stamped with bright yellow letters and reflective tape across the back. I slid it on before I got out of the Jeep. It completely dwarfed me. The sleeves fell well past my hands. I pushed them up and pulled the hood up over my head.

Mal couldn't help himself. He started laughing at me again, a soft intimate chuckle as if the joke was only between us. I don't blame him. I looked like a little girl, dressing up in her daddy's clothes. I didn't have a choice. I had to wear it since Brooke had driven off with my jacket.

"Okay, you've got fifteen more seconds to laugh at me. And then I'm gonna knock you out," I threatened mockingly, balling up my fists and holding them up in front of me. It would have made for a more menacing pose if the sleeves didn't flop over my fists like seal flippers. He reached over and pushed them back on my arms, almost to my elbows, taking as tender care of me as I had of Ciara.

"I'm not laughing at you, Jess. I'm laughing with you."

"Do you hear me laughing?" I said, raising my eyebrows at him.

He tapped his fist against his heart. "On the inside," he said, whispering to me. "I know you're laughing on the inside. Where it counts. It's where we all have to laugh sometimes."

It was good to hear that Mal could laugh. After what he'd just been through with Shelby, I didn't know if he'd had any more laughter left in him. Should I consider it a compliment that I can bring the laughter out in him? Especially if he's laughing at me?

"I'm gonna check in with Myles," Mal said. "See if I can figure out who's running this show."

"When you find out, let me know."

"Try to stay out of the way, Jess," Mal said, adjusting the hood around my face so that it didn't slip forward and cover my eyes.

"I won't be in anyone's way," I said, tilting my head back to look at him. "I just want to help."

"Help me help you try to keep out of trouble."

"Like I told Mama, I'll do the best that I can," I said, smiling sweetly.

Sighing, Mal opened the driver's-side door. "I can't ask much more than that."

Chapter Eleven
Mal

I walked around the campsite, getting the lay of the area. There were several tents set up around the camp, some of them functional, utilitarian, dark green military-style tents, probably taken from the army surplus store, since I'd yet to see any actual military personnel here yet . . . and some of them were regular weekend-vacationer-type tents in bright colors with multiple rooms and zippered fronts.

Each tent had a folding table placed in front of it. On top of the tables were pre-wrapped sandwiches, cups of coffee or bottled water, and a first aid kit. The tarps, which were thrown over the tables to keep the food dry, collected and spilled more water than they prevented. With each gust of wind, any tarp that wasn't tied down to the table legs lifted like the sails of a clipper ship and went spiraling away.

As I walked up the line, greeting my friends and neighbors, it gave me a sense of community pride. There had to be at least a hundred people out here already. Most I knew by name. Some I only knew by sight. Old and young, some well off, some living paycheck to paycheck, all creeds and colors. Black. White. Red. Looked like a vintage Coca-Cola commercial with everyone working together shoulder to shoulder.

They had the same look of desperation and determination. It was the same look on Bull Pearson's face when he was building his retaining wall. That same look was in Jess's light brown eyes when she begged me to bring her out here instead of waiting with helpless frustration at the shelter. Then, I'd been irritated that I'd let her emotional outbursts cloud my judgment. Now, seeing those same feelings magnified a hundred times over, I couldn't be angry at her anymore. I felt an overwhelming sense of awe.

It never failed to amaze me how people could come together. Folks who might not even speak to each other if they saw each other on the street were working together now. Codell County was a small community, with small town closeness and big city prejudices. All of those were forgotten in this moment. They were working harder than some of them probably ever had in their lives. Yet, here they all were.

I shook off my idealistic dreaming. There was a reason why we were all out here. Fear. Nothing but fear. It was my job to do what I could to ease their fears, to get them what they needed, and to keep the peace in the event that they couldn't have it.

I asked a couple of folks about Officer Myles, and they pointed me over in his direction. He was walking the north end of the makeshift command center for this volunteer brigade with Jordan Reeves, a civil engineer on loan to the community college here in Codell County from the University of Southern Mississippi.

"I see you made it," Myles called out to me, waving me over. He didn't say much more than that. I couldn't help but notice how he looked around me, following Jess's progress as she made her way to what turned out to be the heart of the command center. When I glanced back, I saw her huddling with a group of five or six others, cradling a mug of something steaming hot to her lips. Probably coffee. Jess wasn't quite human until she had a couple of mugs of coffee, heavily dosed with cream and sugar, in her.

"Any problems, Chief?" Myles asked.

"Not a one," I said, casually shifting to block his view. There couldn't be two of us with our minds on Jess.

"Glad to see you could make it, Chief Loring," Reeves said, holding his hand out to me. It took me a moment to decide that he wasn't being sarcastic. He wasn't cracking on me because I was late showing up to the camp. He really *was* glad to see me. I was one of the few town officials who knew all aspects of the emergency evacuation plan.

The professor was looking tight around the corners of his mouth. And something told me that the moisture gathering on his forehead wasn't all rain water. The man was sweating. When he grabbed my hand, he pumped it up and down several times with nervous energy. He probably would have kept pumping, too, if I hadn't pulled my hand back.

"You folks have been busy," I observed, looking all around us.

Empty dump trucks were pulling out, spewing dark smoke in the air from exhaust pipes as they rumbled on, passing others with full loads. Some trucks were filled with sand, others with more people.

"We've already been on the phone with reps from the EPA, the Mississippi Department of Transportation, and the Corps of Engineers," Reeves said. "The Coast Guard is on standby."

"Nobody seems to think all of this sandbagging is necessary," Myles said, shrugging his shoulders. "A waste of time."

"Apparently not an opinion shared by most of the folks who live around here," I returned. "Otherwise, we wouldn't be here, isn't that right, Professor Reeves?"

"Chief, I don't want to cause any unnecessary concern. The levees are supposed to hold any overflow from the river," Reeves promised. "So far, they're doing their job."

"The river hasn't crested yet," I reminded him. "Last I checked, we were in for several more hours of this stuff." I pointed at the sky, indicating the clouds still dumping plenty of rain down on us.

"This tropical storm has parked right over us and doesn't seem to be in a hurry to be going anywhere. What happens if it keeps on, bringing not only more rain but strong winds or tornadoes with it? What happens to the levees then if they're torn to shreds?"

"I hope for all of us that it's something we'll never see. Excuse me, Chief. I think I'm needed," Reeves said, nodding at one of the volunteers waving at him trying to get his attention from underneath one of the tents.

"Sure, go ahead." I waved him on.

Myles waited longer than I thought he would before he asked me. "Why'd you bring her here, Chief?"

"She asked me to," I said simply. I was waiting for him to ask me if I always did what she asked me to. I was just waiting. But he didn't. Because he didn't, I didn't have a good enough reason to pop him in his mouth. As jumpy as I was feeling, all I needed was the flimsiest of excuses.

"She shouldn't be here," Myles insisted.

"You don't think I know that? But she's here now. Can't nothing be done about it."

Myles shoved his hands deep into his pockets and

stared down at his feet. "Well, Chief, I was thinking that
. . . maybe I could head back . . . now that you're here,
that is. I could take her back with me. Get her to the
high school."

"You're welcome to try, Myles," I said, sweeping my
hand toward the tent. "Be my guest."

"Are you sure that you don't need me here?"

I shrugged. "I can't say. I just got here. So far, things
look like they're clicking without too much interference
from us."

"Then, I'll just go and see if Jess needs a lift back."

"You do that. In fact, if anything does happen and we
have to bug out of here fast, I want you to make sure that
you take Jess with you."

"You do?"

"Yeah . . . In fact, Myles, I'm making you personally responsible for her. You got that? If there is a break in one
of the levees, I want you to get into your truck and haul
ass out of here. Can you do that?"

"You can count on me, Chief."

"Good man. Go and find her. Stick close by her. I'm
gonna walk the line, see what we've got going on here."

"Yes, sir."

You should have seen the love light in his puppy-dog
eyes. I didn't say that out loud. I didn't want to crush his
tender feelings. Myles was still young. Too young for Jess.
But that didn't stop him from having an old-as-time-itself
yearning for the woman. Poor Myles. I almost felt sorry
for him. Jess looked at him like she did the kids in her
classroom. He didn't stand a chance with her.

"What do you think, Chief?" asked Monique Anders,
who worked the counter at the coffee shop, as she
walked up to me and handed me a Styrofoam cup of
lukewarm coffee and a soggy cream cheese Danish from
a two-handled tray she carried.

I shrugged my shoulders.

"I don't know. I don't know what to think, Monique," I said honestly.

Monique lowered her voice, leaned in close to me and whispered. "Some of us are hoping that if the levees fail, they do so right now."

"That's a helluva thing to hope for," I said, wiping the crumbs from my hands on my pants leg.

"Don't get me wrong, Chief. It's not that I want it to happen. It's just better if it happens sooner rather than later. It's the waiting and not knowing that I can't stand."

From the comments I heard up and down the line, the dread and anticipation had everyone wound up tight.

"If you have to hope for something, hope that the thing we all paid our hard-earned tax money to protect us will hold up."

"That goes without saying . . . but not without praying," she said, smiling.

"Another cup of coffee, Chief Loring?"

"Nah. I think I'm good to go. Thanks, Monique."

I tossed the rest out and crushed the cup in my hand. She took the cup from me and stuffed it into a black plastic trash bag that she had clipped to a belt around her waist.

The sight of the news station's remote truck pulling up near the command center was enough to make me want to get out of there. I'd had enough of those reporters for one day. I should have turned right around and left without checking in at the command center; but I couldn't do that. Not just yet. Not without giving Jess one more chance to leave with me.

Chapter Twelve

Jess

That news reporter stuck a camera right in my face. And me looking like death warmed over. The bright spotlight they'd shown in my face hurt my eyes. And the reporter standing next to me, in full television makeup, was cute, petite, and perky. I hated her. Hated the fact that she could look good in what seemed to me like a monsoon, and I was standing there with Mal's big ugly jacket hanging on me like a parachute.

But I smiled for the camera anyway, and put on my best third grade teacher persona. Maybe some of my kids were watching. I had to be strong, confident, and optimistic for their sake. I could imagine what must be going through their minds. Listening to their parents' worried talk; maybe some of them were already at the shelter, and hearing the rumors of river flooding . . . It didn't take much for active third grade minds to figure out they were all in a lot of trouble.

"I'm just out here doing my part," I said, looking directly at the camera operator, trying not to blink or squint or look like some ignoramus they'd dragged in front of the camera for a taste of local-yokel flavor. I enunciated clearly, distinctly and used complete, grammatically correct sentences. Not that I spoke that way all of the time. When I get worked up, I can sound just as country. But, I was there to represent small-town Mississippi. I couldn't stand it when news crews grabbed the scroungiest, skankiest, most *ignant*-sounding soul to interview. That's right. *Ignant*. A made-up word but it applied—meaning even worse than being ignorant.

"I want to save our town just like everyone else."

The reporter made it sound as if I was holding back the river with my bare hands. I was only dishing up coffee and donuts and offering up whatever encouraging words I could muster as the drenched, exhausted, muddy volunteers came back to the table for nourishment or a Port-a-potty break. It was a small thing that I was doing. But I was here. It was why I asked Mal to bring me. To help out in any way that I could.

I saw him standing on the edge of the small group that had gathered around the camera crew. Mal hated cameras. He hated the spotlight. He was doing what he always did to keep the attention off of himself. Wrapped up in his long dark coat, with the rain dripping off of him, he could have been just another shadow.

It was only when the lightning flashed that I could see him clearly. He was waiting on the fringes of the crowd, evaluating the situation, and waiting for his time to act. Waiting. Waiting. I knew that he would be watching everything and doing nothing until just the right moment.

I'm standing here, talking to the reporter, trying to appear brave, but all the while I'm so scared. I'm scared out of my mind. And the only thing keeping from turning me into a blubbering idiot is Mal's comforting presence watching over me. As long as he's there, I know that I'm going to be all right. I know that he'll keep me safe.

The news reporter moved over to talk to Reeves. She'd just begun the interview when it came—the sound everyone was expecting and everyone was dreading. The warning siren.

It started as a low wail, barely noticeable over the rumble of dump trucks and the shouts of people giving directions about what to place and where, and of course, the ever-present rain. Yet, one by one, we all stopped what we were doing, frozen in mid-action, wondering if we were really hearing what we were hearing.

Where was that sound coming from? What was going on? Did anybody know?

The questions came from all around me. It wasn't until a truck came rumbling through and a voice over a loudspeaker warned us of a break in the Fulsome Road levee that we really knew the reason for the siren. The sound overtook us.

And so did the panic!

I don't know who knocked over the table, spilling coffee and scattering paper cups to the ground. I couldn't even see how many people literally ran into the tent walls, pulling it down as bodies scattered in all directions like a colony of ants when someone jams a stick into the mound.

I remember shouts and screaming, the frantic starting of engines. Sounded like the gunning of engines at the Indy 500. I don't even remember who grabbed my hand and pulled me out from under the tent where I'd been standing and waiting with one of the volunteers. I do remember being shoved, buffeted, and pummeled on all sides, but eventually making it to the area roped off for the parked vehicles.

Someone was holding on to my hand, squeezing it

so tight that I thought the bones would crack. When I finally looked up, it was Mal who was pulling me.

"Mal!" I clung to him for a moment. Only a moment. It was all the time that he would allow for us. It wasn't enough. At the same time, it was too much. I could feel his heart beating, even through his coat. It was beating fast. Fast enough to burst. I could feel him squeeze me for just a second and whisper a few words in my ear. Words that would only come out in the worst of times. Words I'm certain that he would have never allowed himself to say otherwise.

"I love you, Jess Ramsay."

Too much and not enough. I'd waited for so long to hear those words. Over a year. The last time didn't count. The last time he was falling down drunk. Maybe this time didn't count, either. Fear did strange things to a person. Wasn't that what Bull Pearson had said? Maybe, if we survived this, he'd wish he'd never said those words to me.

Mal yanked open the truck door, lifted me inside, and slammed the door. "Get her out of here!"

I knew by the sound of his voice and the look on his face that he'd never take those three little words back. Mal loved me. Loved me above everyone else. Above his own life. You can't ever take a love like that back.

I hadn't even put on my seat belt when the tires started to spin, churning up chunks of mud, grass, and gravel.

"Mal!" I called out to him, putting my hand to the window. But he was already gone. He took off running, shouting orders, and doing what he could to keep the panicked flight from the campsite from turning deadly. So many people. So many vehicles all trying to get back to the road. There had been an evacuation plan for getting out of here. I'd been briefed by one of the organizers when I showed up at the site. At the time, the plan had seemed well-thought out. It looked so good on paper. Now, with the real threat facing us, there was only one element to the plan that mattered. Get the hell out of there.

No one knew how long it would take for hundreds of thousands of gallons of water to come rushing down from the break in the Fulsome Road levee. Now that the Fulsome Road levee was breached, it was only a matter of time before Bramfort was breached, too. Could be hours. Could be minutes. No one was going to wait around long enough to clock the flow.

"Buckle up, Jess."

I turned to see who Mal had entrusted my life to. It was Myles Overton driving the truck. Myles? Was he old enough to drive?

"Don't worry," he said, trying to sound confident. Hard to do since his voice was still cracking.

"I'm not worried," I said. A bold-faced lie if ever I told one.

Myles turned the wheel sharply, barely avoiding a Mini Cooper that had gotten bogged down in the mud as it tried to go off-road to get away from the levee. Myles's Z24 Chevy truck had heavy-duty tires specially made for this kind of driving. He skirted around the miniature car without blinking.

"Maybe we should go back and try to pull them out?" I suggested, looking back.

"Nuh-uh. Mal said don't let anything stop me from getting you out of here, Jess," Myles said, gripping the steering wheel tightly and hunching over as if expecting me to try to take the wheel from him.

"Go back, Myles," I said, grabbing his arm. "We can't leave them there!" I shouted at him. "You're a public servant, damn it! Go back there and serve."

He looked at me like I was crazy, and stepped on the gas pedal, surging ahead.

"We can't go back. There's not enough time."

I couldn't believe that he'd done that. Just couldn't believe it. He left them there.

"Don't worry, Jess. Everything's gonna be all right. Somebody else will come along for them. We'll make it out. We'll make it . . ."

Chapter Thirteen
The River

Living things grow. Change. Adapt. If I am the bringer of life, can any less be expected of me? For too long it has pleased me to remain as I am. For too long I have rested within these earthen walls. I have more than rested. I have become placid. Stagnant. It is not within me to remain as I was.

If anyone had bothered to ask, I would have answered. My only constant is change.

Chapter Fourteen

Mal

She didn't make it. I looked for her, asked everyone I knew who knew her, and called out her name up and down the halls of the high school, the designated meeting place for the evacuees. No one had seen her. No one. Out of the 150 that had checked in at the levee fortification camp, sixty-eight made it back to the high school. Another twenty or so called in to the police station, stranded in trees or on roof tops, waiting to be picked up by copter or boat.

Jess wasn't one of them. She didn't make it out. She didn't make it! Reports kept coming in about the rising water levels. *She didn't make it.* Over seventy percent of the houses in Codell County had water to their rooftops. *She didn't make it.* The hospital reported several cases of water moccasin snake bites. Before this was all over, there would be other water-related injuries. Even deaths. Not all would be drownings. *She didn't make it.*

Three hours since the first levee break was reported. Since that time, several more breaks were called in by witnesses, search-and-rescue volunteers, and the core of engineers as the protective walls around my town continued to crumble. Three hours since all hell broke loose, turning my town into a lake.

On the second floor of the school, someone went into labor. Delivered a healthy baby boy, with her husband falling in a dead faint and me and the school nurse on the phone with the hospital, coaching us until they could get here and take her and the baby back for observation.

Down in the cafeteria, a fight broke out over something trivial. Something about somebody stealing someone's pillow. Tempers were running short, as were supplies. An administrative nightmare trying to keep track of everyone flowing in and seeing to their needs. We had an emergency-response plan and were trying to stick to it. But all I could think was that Jess didn't make it.

Jess didn't make it, and it was all my fault. If I'd just done what I was supposed to, if I'd done what her mother asked me to do, she'd be here. I'd be holding her now, loving her, and consoling others who'd lost their own instead of wallowing in my own agony.

When Myles came through that door, I knew before he ever said a word to me. I'd been calling him for hours on his radio trying to get a fix on where he was. We were able to track the location of the vehicle by the onboard computer. But Myles never answered. Never once. Each time I got no response from him, I kept fighting that sick, sinking feeling in the pit of my stomach. No news was good news. Isn't that what everyone says?

Then he walked through that door, and I knew. It was all over his face. Fear and shame. He opened his mouth, closed it again. Opened it. And closed it again. He looked like a guppy that had leaped out of its fish tank and was now gulping for air.

"Myles, where have you been?" I asked.

He turned back toward the door, pointing listlessly as

if that was an adequate explanation of his radio silence for the last few hours.

"Jess?" I stepped up to him. Every question I could ask compressed in that one word.

Myles started to breathe so hard I thought that he would hyperventilate.

"I'm sorry, Mal. I'm so sorry. I tried. She wouldn't listen to me. She wouldn't get back in the truck . . . I tried . . ."

"What . . . What are you trying to tell me?"

"She got out to go after this car . . . It was stuck . . . I told her that someone was coming. I told her that someone would come after them. But she wouldn't listen to me. You know Jess. Nobody tells her what to do. Nobody. She wouldn't listen to me. Why did you send her with me, Mal? Why did you do it?!"

Myles started shouting at me like it was my fault that I trusted him. Like I was to blame for trusting him with the only thing that ever mattered to me. The closer we drew to each other, the more animated he became. His hands waved around in the air as he jabbered, as if he could conjure her from the air in front of him.

"She wouldn't listen to me. What was I supposed to do? I could hear it coming. Hear it rushing down on us. What else could I do?"

For a minute, I couldn't breathe. I couldn't think. She didn't make it. She didn't make it, and it was all my fault. I gave her to Myles and he . . . he . . .

"You left her there?"

Someone said what I was thinking out loud. Was it me? I don't know. My voice didn't sound like my own. Cold and hard. Stripped of anything that made me human.

"What else could I do?" Myles wailed. "She wouldn't get in the truck!"

"You left her!"

Somebody hit Myles. Hit him hard. Hard enough to bust his mouth and nose open. Was it me? I don't know. I didn't feel any pain in my hand when it slammed into his face. All of the pain was coiled in the middle of my chest, flared out, and made me want to stretch my hands out and wrap them around Myles's throat. I saw red. Red blood. Felt the red. Red-hot hatred burning through me.

Somebody pulled me away from him before I could go through with it. I don't know who. By now, our yelling had started to draw a crowd.

"You left her!"

She didn't make it. Myles left her there. He'd run to save himself. And it was all my fault for trusting him with the only thing that ever really mattered to me.

There was shouting. Lots of shouting. And cursing. Raw, cruel, obscene words hurled at Myles. The words bounced off the walls, seemed to come from all directions. Yet it was only me. All from me.

Myles sat up from the floor, blubbering, wiping at his mouth and nose, looking just like the young kid he was. I sank to my knees, staring at him, and thinking that I should say something consoling. But all I could think was the way Myles's voice sounded when he told me that Jess didn't make it.

"What happened?" I asked, forcing myself to stop thinking like the man and start thinking like the job. It was all I had left now—the job. Do my job now. Why not? I didn't do it then. Not for Jess, anyway. I did it for everyone else. Making sure that every vehicle got away from the command center. Every single one. I stayed so others could go. Maybe, if I'd been thinking like the man then, instead of the job, Jess would be here with me now.

"I did what you told me," Myles said. "You told me to get her out of there. Don't let nothin' stop me. You told me that, Chief. You did. That's what you told me to do so that's what I did."

"I know I did, Myles. I did that." I'd told him to go. It was all my fault. Seemed to be my day for shifting the blame for my mistakes back onto myself.

"After you put her in the truck, I drove like a bat outta hell. Just like you told me. But then we passed this car. It was stuck in the mud. So, she told me to go back. But I wouldn't do it. No, sir. I couldn't. You told me not to stop."

I narrowed my eyes at him. Somebody needed help and he didn't go back. He didn't do his job. Yet, I couldn't fault him. Plenty of blame to go around.

"I . . . I wouldn't go back, so she got out. Said that if I wasn't going to do anything about it, she would."

When he stopped talking and put his hand inside of his jaw to poke at the teeth I'd knocked loose, I yelled at him.

"Keep talking!"

Myles jumped. "She got out of the truck, told me to wait for her. She was gonna go and get them, help them to climb onto the back so we could all get out . . . but . . . but . . . but I could hear it coming. The water. Like nothing I ever heard before. So loud. It was right on top of us. There was no time. No time. She wouldn't get back in the truck, Mal. I swear I did everything I could."

"So, you left her. You left her!"

"I'm so sorry. I swear to God, if I could have done it differently, I would have."

When I die, someone should have those words engraved on my tombstone. I would have done it all differently. All of it. From the first moment I saw her in grade school, to the moment her mama sent me after her when she snuck out to go to that concert, to the time I showed up drunk at her house, to the hour I wasted moving her furniture.

What was I talking about—*when* I died? I was already

dead. A walking, talking husk. All that made me human, all that made me feel was gone. Washed away.

"Where?" I finally managed to ask.

"Where?" A blank look came over Myles's face.

"Where did you . . . did you . . . did you . . ." I couldn't bring myself to say how he'd left her behind. "Where was the car stopped?"

"The road was packed, bumper to bumper. You saw how crazy it was trying to get away from there. So, I turned off the main road, to loop around. Four miles off the main highway, near that old cottonseed processing plant."

I thought about the area. The cottonseed processing plant should have been torn down years ago. It was a nuisance. Just a place for high school kids to vandalize and vagrants to claim as home. It was a fire hazard with its abandoned pallets of rotted, unprocessed cotton, busted out windows, and machinery scavenged for parts and left to ruin.

"When I heard the water hit the back wall of the plant, I knew it was coming. If that building hadn't been there, giving me time to get out . . ."

He didn't finish. He didn't have to. I knew what he was going to say. And I knew what I was going to do. I stood up and started for the door.

"Mal?"

Jarvis Darby, who ran the combination post office and souvenir shop, grabbed my arm. "Where ya goin', Chief?"

I jerked my arm away without answering him.

"You're not going out there, are ya?" Jarvis asked.

"What do you think?" I snarled at him, and Jarvis backed off. Not a small feat since Jarvis was six-foot-four and tipped the scale at 300 pounds. No one made fun of the big man who sold cheap magnolia-shaped refrigerator magnets. But at the moment, he saw the futility of trying to use his bulk to stop me. Nothing short of a freight train was going to stop me. I wasn't going to leave Jess out there. I'd left her once. I wasn't going to leave her again.

"Don't go out there, Mal. There's nothing out there now," Myles said. "When that water hit the building, I heard it. I saw the wall collapse. It's probably a pile of rubble by now."

"Maybe not," Jarvis said thoughtfully. Bless him for his glimmer of hope!

"That plant has been standing since World War II. It survived the hippies making it a commune in the sixties, refitting for polyester production in the seventies, and being a so-called secret rave location through the eighties. You think a few drops of water are gonna take it down?"

Myles lifted his face to me. "Do you think there's a chance? Do you think Jess could have made it? She could have made it into the building, huh?"

I didn't answer him. How could I? He wanted me to make him feel better about leaving Jess behind. I couldn't do it. More to the truth, I *wouldn't* do it.

Chapter Fifteen

Jess

Mal will always come for me. Whenever I'm in trouble, whenever I need him, he'll come. I know he will. It has always been that way. And it will always be—even when I thought I didn't want him to, he was there. I just have to keep believing that. I have to hang onto that belief no matter what. Hang on, Jess Ramsay. Hang on.

My fingers were cramping. And so, so cold. I could barely feel them. But I have to hang on. I have to. Because if I don't, if I let go now, I'm gonna lose it all. I lose my faith, my love, and my life.

"I can't hang on anymore. I can't!"

"Yes, you can. You have to. Come on . . . You can do it. Just a bit more."

I wrapped my arms around the kid that I'd pulled from that Mini Cooper that had gotten bogged down in the mud and tried to draw him closer to me. He was so young. His chin was dotted with peach fuzz. I could feel his heart beating through his thin jacket and even thinner chest. We hunkered on top of stack of crates left in the middle of the main floor of the cottonseed plant.

I don't know what was in those crates, but I know they stank. Smelled like rotting meat. Every time the wind blew through the busted windows, the smell almost made me gag. But we had to stay here. We didn't have much of a choice. It was the only thing tall enough, and sturdy enough, to keep us out of most of the water. Most. Not all. The crate was just large enough for me and the kid to sit on and keep our heads above water.

I felt just like that chick from that James Cameron blockbuster movie *Titanic* after the big ship had gone down. Only, I wasn't going to let this kid bob in the water while I stayed safe. We were both gonna get out of this. All I had to do was hang on until Mal came after me. He was coming. I knew that he would. If he wouldn't come on his own, Mama would surely send him after me. It had been a long time, and she hadn't heard from me. She was probably burning up his cell phone trying to get to him. I'd left my phone in Mal's Jeep.

"Come on, law man," I said, my teeth chattering. "Get off your ass and get out here."

"You mean the Chief? Chief Loring." The kid sounded surprised that I would talk about Mal that way.

"Yeah," I said. "*Chief* Loring."

"You think he's coming for us?"

I nodded my head a couple of times and said, "Uh-huh."

Talking was an effort, and it took all the energy I could muster not to throw up every time the wind changed directions or every time I saw another drowned rat floating by us.

"How do you know? How can you be sure?"

I would laugh if my face didn't hurt so much from trying to keep my teeth from clicking together.

"We've got a connection, Mal and me," I told him. "He'll be here."

"I hope you're right."

"Hope hasn't got a thing to do with it. It's the law of averages."

"Huh?"

"Never mind. You wouldn't understand. I'm not even sure if I understand."

Mal had come after me before. It stood to reason that he would do it again. It didn't matter that reason had nothing to do with why he would come. In fact, reason should have stopped him from coming a long time ago. What we had between us wasn't rational. Wasn't rational at all. What was rational about a man and a woman who could remain friends, almost become lovers, and still remain friends even with the threat of competition for our affection?

"What if he doesn't come? Do you think we should try to get out on our own? Swim out, maybe?"

The thought had crossed my mind. With the water flowing as fast it was, it had to end up somewhere, didn't it? Maybe, somewhere, it tapered off. Maybe the current wouldn't be so strong, somewhere along the way, and the level would drop low enough for us to climb out and walk the rest of the way into town.

Then again, maybe this wasn't all we could expect from the river. Maybe more was coming. It was still raining. It would be just our luck to be almost in the free and clear and another flash flood come along and sweep us away.

On second thought, sitting up here on these crates was sounding better and better to me all the time. There was still half a wall of the plant standing between us and the main flow of water. As long as that wall stood, I was gonna stay right where I was.

"He'll be here," I said stoutly. "I know he will."

"I hope he gets here soon. I'm freakin' freezing. I can't feel my legs."

He was shivering all over. And so was I. Felt like my body could be one big goose pimple. I was squeezing tight, trying hard not to shiver. On top of that, I *really, really* had to go to the bathroom. If it had been just me out here, I would have let the sphincter go.

"Try not to think about it," I encouraged, as much to keep the kid from thinking about being cold as I was trying hard not to think about going to the bathroom. I was also trying to keep my arms wrapped around him. It wasn't an easy task, trying to hold onto him and our perch at the same time.

The pull of the water against us was constant. Yet, at the same time, it kept changing. Sometimes the water flowed generally away from us. Then it shifted in another direction, pushing the stack of crates slowly against the back wall. If the crates hadn't been bound together, shrink-wrapped on wooden pallets by yards of plastic, I think our tiny island would have busted up a long time ago. I counted it as a miracle that the stack held as long as it did.

I guess it was my day for miracles. It was a miracle that me and the kid made it here alive. It was a miracle that the plant walls held, even with who knew how much water crashing down on it.

Closing my eyes, I was suddenly warmed all over with the thought of Mal and the way he'd held me right before he'd put me in Myles's truck. Now *that* was a miracle! The man who wouldn't draw attention to himself if his life depended on it was holding me close in front of everybody. He'd held onto me and told me that he loved me.

Mal loved me!

"He's not coming," the kid said, his voice so soft that I almost didn't hear him over the noise of rushing water and debris crashing and banging into what was left of the plant walls.

"Don't say that!" I snapped. I didn't want to hear that. I had to keep believing that everything was going to be fine. I couldn't keep us and our hopes afloat.

"But it's been hours! If somebody was coming, wouldn't they be here by now?"

"It just seems like forever," I said. "It's probably only been an hour. Maybe two. Give them time."

I was lying through my teeth. By my rough calculation, it had to be three, or closer to four hours that we'd been out here. I could tell by the way my stomach was rumbling what time it was. It was about noon when we'd arrived at the levee site. I'd only eaten a couple of donuts and downed a couple cups coffee. I figured we were out there for maybe and hour and a half before the evacuation order came. It had to be almost five o'clock now.

It was a necessary lie. I did it to keep the kid's spirits up. I couldn't have him giving up on me. I was a teacher. My job was to keep alive the hopes and dreams of over thirty kids in my third grade class. What kind of a sorry teacher would I be if I couldn't even keep one from giving up?

"What's your name?" I asked the kid.

"Aaron," he said. "Aaron Martin."

"Pleasure to meet you, Aaron Martin. My name's Jess."

"Glad you came back for me, Jess." He reached out, covered my hand in his and tried to squeeze.

His back to my chest, my chin resting on his shoulder, I kissed him on the cheek.

"It was my pleasure, Aaron."

"I . . . I didn't want to die. Not out there by myself. When my car got stuck, I got so scared."

"I know . . . I know," I soothed. "We were all scared."

"Why'd that guy do it? Why did he take off like that?"

"Probably scared," I said, trying to think about how I

nearly fainted when I saw Myles's tail lights spinning off, leaving me behind. Nearly made me lose my religion, calling him every name under the sun I could think of. And I could think of a few juicy ones. Most of those names I'd reserved for Mal for when he really got on my nerves.

"He coulda waited for us. He shoulda!"

"Coulda. Woulda. Shoulda," I said. "Can't think about that now, Aaron. What's done is done. Let's just focus on sitting tight and staying afloat until we're rescued, all right?"

"If I ever meet up with him, I'm gonna cave his skull in. And then I'm gonna leave him to die, just like he left us."

"Don't think like that, Aaron. If this place turns into our graves, we can't get to heaven with murder in our hearts."

Besides, if I knew Mal, and I thought I did, Mal would have already taken care of the beat down for us. There wouldn't be anything left of Myles for Aaron to whup up on. Poor Myles. I could only imagine. When he showed up in front of Mal without me, he never stood a chance.

"You believe in heaven, Jess?" Aaron asked me.

"Yes," I answered quickly, without thinking. I had already seen it. I'd already been there. When Mal held me in his arms, whispered those sweet, sweet words to me, I knew heaven existed. I'd been shown a glimmer of how it could be. "There's a heaven."

"My folks said they believed in heaven. They went to church. But I don't think they really believed."

"Why not?"

"You don't know God until you stare him in the face. You can't really believe He exists until you can see Him, touch Him, feel that He's real. I think all of that going to church and reading the Bible is pretending. You're just trying to make others think that you believe."

I had no response to that. I didn't know anything about Aaron and how he was raised. I know how *I* was raised. I was raised up in the church. And even though I'd strayed, I'd always held onto my faith. I knew it was always there, like a lifeline, waiting to draw me back if I went out too far.

"What do you believe, Aaron?"

"Up until the minute you pulled me away from the car and got in here, I didn't believe. I had no reason to."

"What about now?" I asked softly.

Aaron sighed. He stared out across the water that had to be at least twelve feet high now.

"When I saw that water crashing down on us, I thought I was gonna die."

He laughed, a harsh grating sound that echoed across the water. "You know, Jess, my grandmama used to say that nothing turns a sinner into a saint quicker than coming close to dying. All that water, coming down like that, not thinking, or feeling, or caring . . . it felt . . . it felt . . . I don't know . . . like something evil was coming after me."

"The water isn't evil, Aaron. It just is. It's out there doing what it's supposed to do when the rain comes down hard and the levees can't hold the water back. No good or evil in that. It's just nature."

"I know that," he said. "I'm just telling you what I felt. I remember thinking that if Satan existed, he was there, in the water, waiting to take my life. And then, there you were, pulling me out of it, keeping me safe. And here we are now, still alive. It didn't get us . . . I'm alive, and there is only one reason for that. Something my grandmama calls the grace of God. I'm alive because of the grace of God. And for every drop of water that flows by and I'm still alive, I know it's only because of you and the grace of God."

As if there wasn't enough water all around us, I found

my eyes starting to tear up. He was so young and sweet and scared. I sniffled and tried to wipe my nose on my shoulder sleeve without letting go of Aaron.

"If I get outta this alive, Jess, you know what I'm gonna do?"

"Don't make any promises that you can't keep, Aaron," I teased him.

"I mean this one. If I get out of this alive, I'm gonna go straight to my grandmama and thank her for praying for me all those years. You think I can do that without breaking a promise, Jess?"

"You do that, Aaron," I said. I leaned my chin on his shoulder again, as much for comfort as for warmth.

I was tired. So tired. It would have been so easy for me to close my eyes and grab a few Z's. I would only sleep for a moment. My eyelids fluttered a couple of times, then snapped open again. My heart pounded so fast in my chest that it drove all thoughts of sleep from my head.

What was I doing? Had I completely lost my mind? I couldn't sleep. Not now! If I went to sleep, it would be all over.

Mal had better get here soon. I'd been keeping a careful eye on the water level for the past hour. I didn't mention it to Aaron. He had enough on his young mind to think about. It seemed to me that the water was slowly starting to rise. It had risen several times before, but always fell back to a level that I was comfortable with. Not this time. This time the water was steadily rising, and it wasn't going down soon after. Either it was getting higher, or we were sinking.

Without drawing attention to what I was doing, I looked around me, trying to see if I could spot any higher ground. Plenty of trash floating by us, but nothing that looked as if we had to leave our haven. Turning my head around almost as far as I could, I tried to gauge the height of the highest remaining wall of the plant. It was maybe three or four feet taller than our stack of crates. But was it as stable? Could it withstand Aaron and my combined weight if we had to climb on it?

As the water rose another half a foot, I crossed my fingers. It would have to hold. It would have to.

Chapter Sixteen

Mal

Jarvis could only scrape up two or three gallons of gas for the outboard motors for the boats I'd commandeered. It would have to do. I couldn't wait any longer for someone to find a station that wasn't completely under water.

"All right, listen up, people!" I shouted to be heard over the rumble of idling motors. There seemed to be a lot of noise for only three boats. Jarvis Darby was in one of the boats. And the twins, Melvin and Kelvin Price, were in another. I was in the last one. I probably should have taken Myles with me on this search party.

To be honest with myself, I didn't think I could put my feelings aside long enough to let him ride with me. What if I went out to that plant and Jess wasn't there? Could I stop myself from tossing Myles over the side, and kicking him in the head until no more bubbles rose to the surface? I doubted it. Evil, vindictive thoughts, I know. If anyone knew what I was really thinking, they'd probably seriously reconsider hiring me as police chief.

When I took this job, I never claimed to be anybody's

angel. In fact, I think it was the fact that I could be tough, unyielding, that made me one of the more attractive candidates for the job. I knew what had to be done, and I did it. I didn't whine about it or seek the advice of a committee. I did what I had to do.

So, when Myles offered to go out with us, I did what I could to keep from laughing in his face. Too late for heroics now. He should have thought of that when he was gunning his engines, trying to save his own neck.

Instead, I squeezed him on his shoulder and suggested that he go to the hospital to see about that busted nose. Myles was eager enough to do it. I think sending him off let him off the proverbial hook.

He seemed to take my concern as genuine. And, at that moment, it was. As long as I had hope that Jess was all right, I could pass on to him the milk of human kindness. Just let me go out there and not find her. It wouldn't be milk flowing through my veins, but ice water. As God is my witness, I wouldn't think twice about trying to kill that boy again.

Naw . . . It was better for everybody if Myles stayed behind.

"We're heading out to the cottonseed plant. There may be two or more folks who got trapped by the rising water after they left the levee," I called out to them.

Nobody had to ask who we were looking for. By now, my outburst had circulated its way through the shelter. Everybody knew that I was going after Jess Ramsay.

"Jarvis, you ride upstream from the plant. Maybe they made it back to the main road and caught a ride with someone else. Melvin, Kelvin, you two go downstream a ways and search the area between the plant's main drive and the highway. Set your radios to channel four and shout out if you find anything. *Anything.* Any questions?"

Melvin, or maybe it was Kelvin, I never could keep

them straight, lifted his hand. "It'll be getting close to night soon, Mal. How long do we search?"

It was a reasonable question. They all knew how I felt about Jess, even though it took me long enough to finally admit it.

"As long as it takes, fool," Jarvis answered for me.

"Search until it's obvious that it's no longer a search and rescue," I said, thankful that my voice didn't crack when I said it. "Search until I say we've gone into recovery mode."

"Yes, sir," one of the twins said, giving his brother a knowing look. If it was left up to me, we'd be out searching for months before I gave in and changed our search tactics from searching for survivors to dredging the water for victims.

"All righty then. Let's do this," I said, reaching back for the tiller and easing the boat away from them.

The boat's top speed was about forty-five miles per hour. It took every ounce of self-control that I had not to open her up all the way. As desperate as I was to find Jess, I still had to use some common sense. Gas was at a premium. I wasn't going to waste a precious drop of it on an engine that was badly in need of a tune-up. I kept the boat at about half speed, exercising caution and patience. There was a good chance that there were still others stranded out here. I had to be on the lookout for any sign of them.

As we got closer to the plant, I motioned to Jarvis and the twins, indicating at which point I wanted them to fan out. They split off from me, leaving a wide, V-shaped wake in the water.

As Jarvis peeled away, I could see him turn on his spotlight. The area that I wanted him to cover, the main road and surrounding area leading to the plant, was lined with pine trees. The water was so high that little of the trunks could be seen, only the dark green of the tree tops dotted with pine cones. Jarvis swept his light back and forth, up and down. Over the sound of his engine, I could hear him calling out to Jess.

I cut my engine down to a quarter speed, inching through the water at a near crawl. If she answered, I needed to hear her. My ears strained as hard as I could. Yet, all I could hear was the lapping of water and the slowly fading putter of the boats.

"Jess!" I cupped my hands to my mouth and called out. Nothing. Only the sound of my own voice bouncing back at me. "Jess Ramsay!"

Myles had said that there would be nothing left of the plant. He was damned near right. I was coming up on where the plant should have stood. Not much was left. There was more than enough rubble floating in the water to let me know that this is where the plant should have been. And a god-awful stench. What *was* that?

I put my wrist up to my nose, trying to block out the smell—a smell so vile that it turned my stomach. I don't remember anything smelling like this the last time I was called out here. If there was, I would have torn down this place myself with my bare hands.

The remaining wall was about the length of a football field. I cruised the back side of it, controlling the tiller with one hand and shining my search light along the wall with the other.

"Jess!" I called out to her every few feet. "Come on, girl," I said more to myself. "If you're out here, give me some sort of a sign. Give me something. Don't make all of this be for nothin'. Don't make me have to go back and stomp a mud hole in Myles's head."

My radio squawked for my attention. It was the twins reporting in. They'd already gone ten miles up the road without a sign.

I gave them new directions. "Go up another five miles or so and then turn around and head back. Join Jarvis in the trees on the north side of the plant."

"Copy that, Chief."

I had to smile. That must have been Kelvin. He'd applied for a job at the police department. At the time, there wasn't enough money in the budget. I had to make a choice between Kelvin or Myles. At the time, Myles seemed like the better candidate. Right now, I was trying hard not to second-guess my judgment. If I'd had Kelvin as one of my officers, would we be out here now like this?

As I came up on the corner of the wall, I swung a tight arc and started back the opposite side, slow and easy. Not as easy going along this side as it was the back side. There was more debris floating in the water. Crates and bales and bags and a dull, oily slick that made me hope that a stray spark from the outboard wouldn't set the water ablaze.

My flashlight swept over anything bigger than a bread box floating in the water for any sign of Jess. Anything would have been welcome. Anything to let me know that she'd been here.

"Come on, Jess," I whispered, almost in a prayer. "I know you're here, baby. Come on . . . come on . . . Where *are* you?"

Chapter Seventeen

Jess

I was starting to hallucinate, only I didn't know it at the time. You know, the mind is a funny thing. It can make you believe all sorts of crazy things. When your mind joins forces with the strength of the heart, almost anything can happen. With a willing body, you can believe anything.

Hours ago, I believed with everything I had in me that Mal was coming for me. All I had to do was sit tight and have faith, and everything would turn out all right. No one could tell me otherwise. I certainly wouldn't listen to Aaron say anything to the contrary. Every time he tried, I put my hand over his mouth and shushed him. My overconfidence was blinding. I knew what I knew.

Lack of food, lack of sleep, and being pummeled for hours by the constant stream of water, I didn't know where I was. I wasn't even sure who I was anymore. I wouldn't be surprised if there wasn't something in that stinky, nasty water that made me loony. By then, the water had reached us chest high. When it crested, it washed over us, covered our heads.

I strained to keep my mouth and nose out of it. It was so hard. We were strapped to the crates, our legs and feet jammed into the plastic wrap to keep from being carried off by the swift current. Tying ourselves was Aaron's idea. Like a fanatic, I'd convinced him that Mal was coming for us and that this stack of boxes, which had been our salvation, wouldn't turn out to be instruments of our deaths.

In the hours we waited, I lost all track of time. Minutes stretched to hours which seemed to drag on for ages. In a crazy half-dream state, I started to believe that so much time had passed, the water had changed me. I was a mermaid now.

My legs dangled weightlessly in the water. My arms fanned outward, back and forth, back and forth, sending me drifting toward the bottom of an undersea garden, where thirty of my magical mermaid children waited for me with eager, expectant faces.

They had been waiting for me, calling to me. *Jess! Jess!* I should have been there a long time ago. What had kept me from going to them? I didn't have an answer for them. And because I had no answer, there was nothing to keep me from using the last of my strength to get to them.

"I'm coming," I called out, barely recognizing my own voice. It was dry and scratchy. All this water, and I hadn't dared to drink any of it. The feel of it, the smell of it turned my stomach, making me afraid of the things floating in it.

But I wasn't afraid anymore. My bleary eyes stared downward. The water was so cool and clear. Below, my children waved to me. Called to me. I could hear them calling my name, getting louder and louder. Their voices were so loud, they sounded like thunder rumbling.

"I'm coming," I repeated. And without another moment's hesitation, I tore the plastic strips binding me to the crate and let myself slip into the water. It cradled me in a watery cocoon. It felt so good to let go. So good. It had been so long since I'd felt this sense of peace. For so long I'd been cold and tired and scared. Not anymore. It was all over now. All over. And to get that peace, all I had to do was let go.

"Jess! Hang on, baby! Hang on!"

No!

I didn't want to hang on. Not anymore. It hurt too much to hang on. Why should I hang on when it felt so good to let go? Hanging on meant more pain and despair and fear. Why should I?

I kicked my mermaid legs, fighting against whatever it was keeping me here against my will. As I broke the surface, water splashed in my face, and I caught a mouthful of that vile liquid. It burned going down. Gasping, choking, I tried to turn my head away, only to have it pressed hard against something warm—warm and strong. Long arms wrapped around me, hauling me from the water and onto something that thrummed and rocked and swayed. A boat. What was a boat doing down here in my undersea garden?

"Jess! Open your eyes, baby. Come on, wake up!"

Rough hands against my face, tapping me just short of a slap.

I tried to open my eyes, but there was a blinding white light that hurt. I threw my hands up, covering my eyes with my forearm. "No!"

Moaning, I tried to turn over and crawl to the edge of the boat. I knew there was pain up here. Let me go! Let me go back!

"Jarvis, turn that light out! Jess, where are you going? Wait!"

The same hands that had pulled me from the water and hauled me into the boat kept me from going back into the water. They drew me back, pressed my cheek tight against someone's chest. Not just someone. Mal! Oh, my God!

"M-Mal?"

I couldn't believe it. He was here? Was he really here? Or was this just another hallucination? When I felt his lips press against my forehead, his large hands stroking my hair, I knew that this was no illusion. He was here. He'd come after me.

As if there wasn't enough water already around us, I started to cry—big, fat, crybaby tears rolled down my cheeks. I was blubbering loudly, shamelessly, clinging to him as we sat on the bottom of the boat. Mal wrapped a blanket around me. It was rough and moth-eaten and smelled like gasoline. I didn't complain. I was so happy to be alive . . . so thankful that he'd found me. Only, it wasn't just me, was it?

"Mal, w-w-where's Aaron?" My teeth chattered so badly, I almost bit my tongue. I hung on to him. My fingers clenched and dug into his arms.

"Don't worry, he's here. The twins have got 'im. You just sit back and rest now, Jess. The boy's all right."

"He's all right?" I repeated.

"Yeah." Mal cradled me to his chest, rested his chin on top of my head. "He's gonna be just fine . . . thanks to you."

As I leaned against Mal, I pounded his arm weakly with my fist. "No thanks to you! Where have you been? What took you so long, Mal Loring!"

Mal's soft laughter caressed my ears, comforting me as much as the blanket he held wrapped around me. "You know, you're one helluva woman, Jess Ramsay."

All around me, there were more voices. More laughter. They were all laughing at me, including Mal and Jarvis Darby and the twins, Melvin and Kelvin. At the moment, I didn't care. I was so grateful to be alive.

"And d-don't y-y-you forget it!" I was blubbering again, snuggling closer to him, closer than I'd even held Aaron when I thought we were staring death right in the face.

"Come on, Jess," Mal said, starting the motor. "I'm taking you home."

"What home?" I said bitterly. My voice cracked. "You don't think my house is still standing. Not after all of this, do you?"

After all of this time, I hadn't thought about it. I couldn't bring myself to think about my pride and joy completely submerged.

"Mine is," Mal said. He'd said it so quietly that I almost didn't hear him over the roar of all three boats and the whoops and hollers from Jarvis and the twins.

"You're coming home with me, Jess Ramsay . . . where you belong."

Mal didn't talk much after that. I know him. I know what it took for him to say that to me. It was up to me to do the talking, to say the things that needed to be said. And there was so much of it . . . so much I wanted to say to him. But before I said a word, there had to be an understanding between us.

Chapter Eighteen

Mal

A touch of hypothermia was all; but that could be easily treated. Keep her quiet. Make sure she took the antibiotics that the doctor had given her for all of the water that she'd swallowed. And most of all, keep her warm. No problem following those doctor's orders. I had just the right cure for her.

To make room for more critical patients, he'd released Jess into my care. I should have taken her to her mother's. Ms. Ramsay had been calling me every ten minutes since I'd let her know that I'd found her daughter.

Thank heaven for the hospital. I had to turn off my cell phone once inside. Otherwise, I would still be on the phone with Jess's mother. She wasn't an easy woman to placate.

I could have taken Jess to the high school with the rest of everyone else who'd been driven out by the high water. That's where Aaron had gone after he'd been released from the hospital. The twins told me that he'd been asking about Jess nonstop.

By now, the story was all over the shelter about how

she'd kept him safe, body to body entwined for safety on top of the boxes. And as truth mingled with gossip, more than once, a few sly comments from some dirty-minded individuals found their way back to me. I didn't need to deal with any of that. Not now. And neither did Jess.

So, I didn't take her to any of those places. When I took her away from the hospital, I took her to the place she should have been all along. I took her into my arms and took her to my home.

It wasn't two stories, like Jess's house, but it sat up high, on sixty acres of property that had been in the family for generations. And it wasn't in any damned flood-control zone, either. It has been here forever and always will be.

When I pulled up into the drive, Jess had been sleeping. Her head was resting against my shoulder. She looked so peaceful, I almost didn't want to wake her. It would have suited me just fine to sit out here with her, just watching her, holding her, and thanking God that I'd found her.

The sudden stillness must have wakened her. She sat up, her eyes wild and confused, crying out. Not just crying out. Calling out my name. "Mal!"

"It's all right, Jess. I'm here." I soothed her, squeezing her shoulder.

"Where are we?" she asked, looking around. It was pitch black outside. Even though it had stopped raining, the clouds had not broken. No moon. No stars. Just inky blackness.

"We're home, baby," I said.

She grabbed the door handle to the Jeep, pushed on it to let herself out.

"Wait for me, Jess."

She stood outside, leaning against the Jeep and staring up at the sky.

"You know, I think it's clearing up," she said.

"That's just wishful thinking," I said, feeling terrible for being the one to dash her hopes. "The front has stalled over us."

"That means at least several more days of this. Oh, Mal!" She moaned. "I don't know how much more I can take of this."

"It'll be all right, Jess," I assured her.

"You know, law man, I don't think I thanked you for coming after me."

"Nope," I agreed. "In fact, if my memory serves me, you threatened to have me replaced when the next mayor is elected."

"Oh," she said, lowering her head against my chest. "Well, you know I didn't mean it, don't you, Mal?"

This was a side of Jess I didn't see very often. She was soft, vulnerable. Even vaguely flirtatious. Come to think of it, I don't think I'd ever seen this side of her. Not directed at me, anyway.

"Maybe you had the right idea," I said. "Maybe it's time to go into retirement."

I thought about what I'd done to Myles. A wave of shame as deep as the one that had washed over Jess before she fell off those crates came over me. I'm not sure that I deserved to be the town's representative of law and order. The fact that I could do that to one of my own was eating me up inside. While I had been looking for Jess, I'd managed to push it to the back of my mind. Now that it was still and quiet and my mind was at ease, the memory of what I'd done kept pushing itself to the front. Poor Myles. He'd only done what I'd asked him to do. It was my fault for putting so much on him.

"And do what?" she scoffed. "You're not fit for anything but being a cop."

"I don't know." I shrugged. "Maybe I could teach."

"There isn't room in the school district for both of our crazy souls."

"I have to do something, Jess. I can't go back knowing what I did to Myles."

"Don't be too hard on yourself, Mal," Jess said, trying to assuage my guilt.

"Maybe I won't give it up completely," I conceded. "But, when things settle down, I'm going to give a nice, long vacation serious consideration."

"Something else you need to be giving serious consideration to," Jess said. She didn't have to say much more than that. I knew what she was thinking. I guess that ESP worked both ways. But no surprise to us. We had a connection, Jess and me.

"I know," I said, staring down at my feet, shifting uncomfortably. I was hoping that this conversation would wait . . . wait until after Jess had rested, after she was feeling stronger. Or maybe it was me that needed the strength. For too long we'd been fighting the feelings. Now that the fight was over, I didn't know if I had the strength to move forward.

"Tell me something, Mal."

"What do you want to know?" I had to talk to her now. No ducking. No hiding. My love for her was out in the open. Time to air it all.

"Did you . . . do you . . . I mean, with Shelby . . . Did you ever tell her that you . . . um . . . that you loved her?"

"No." I answered quickly, with a definitiveness in my voice that she could not mistake.

"Why not?" She turned her face up to me. And for a moment, I thought I saw disbelief reflected in her eyes. Not that she thought that I was lying. I would never lie to Jess. Not intentionally. The disbelief that was there was more like incredulity. She couldn't believe it.

"I mean, you two were together, weren't you? She was

your woman. I know she's been here . . . slept here . . . She told me so."

"She told you that she did?"

"I've known almost from the very moment when you two started sleeping together . . . when we were seniors in high school," she confessed. "Seems as though even back then Shelby had a bad habit of leaving her panties to mark her territory."

"What?" I shook my head, not comprehending. I knew from recent experience that Shelby was careless about her underwear. But Jess's reference to high school made absolutely no sense to me.

"Mal," Jess said in that tone she used when she wanted to show disapproval to her students, "I found her panties under your bed. Don't you remember that day when you were studying for exams and I'd come over to help you do some chores?"

"Of course I do. One minute we were fine, hanging out, the next thing I know, you're tearing out of there."

"You didn't expect me to make up your bed knowing that you and Shelby had been rolling in it, did you?"

"Jess, I never slept with Shelby when she was in high school. What kind of man do you think I am?!" For a moment, I was hurt. How could she think that of me? I supposed the tables were turned. How could I have thought that she would have hidden Shelby's infidelity from me?

Jess shrugged, lowering her gaze. "A human one. She was going after you pretty hard, Mal."

"But she was in high school!" I snapped. "I wouldn't have slept with her. That's statutory rape."

"But I found her panties under your bed!"

"I don't care what you found. I'd never . . . never . . . Jess, oh, God!" I moaned. "Is that why you bugged out of there so fast? Is that why I didn't hear from you for weeks . . . and why you kept trying to set up me and Shelby?"

"Yes," Jess admitted, breathing hard. "Yes, it was."

"Jess, why didn't you tell me? Why couldn't you have just talked to me? All this time . . . we could've . . ." I couldn't even bring myself to think about the time we'd lost over what could have easily been explained . . . maybe not so easily. There was only one way Shelby's panties could have gotten under my bed. She must have put them there on purpose to drive a wedge between me and Jess. Shelby and I didn't get intimate until her junior year in college.

I placed my hand on the back of her head, tilting it back. I wanted to see her eyes, and I wanted her to see mine.

"Jess, I never wanted any other woman but you. But you . . . You weren't having it. Weren't having me. You kept pushing me on Shelby. I thought that's what you wanted. I swear . . . as I live and breathe, I never told Shelby that I loved her. Did she ever tell you that I did?"

"No." Her mouth quirked, the beginnings of a smile. "That was one detail she left out. So, why didn't you tell her? There were bets around town about when you two would be walking down the aisle."

"Did you bet?"

"I didn't have any money," she quipped. "Otherwise I would have."

"That's cold."

"Don't change the subject," she insisted. "Why didn't you ever tell her that you loved her? I have to know, Mal."

I shrugged. The answer was simple. "Because I didn't."

"And you would never lie?"

"Not about that, Jess. I love you. You know that I do."

As the stars and sky and sea is my witness, I did. I hugged her closer, squeezing her tightly and rocking back and forth.

"So . . ." I began.

"So what?"

"So, since it's time to play true confessions, your turn to tell me something."

"If you're talking about that 'heifer' comment . . . No, it's not a word of endearment."

"That's not what I'm talking about."

"Oh. You want to hear that I love you, too, I supposed?" she asked, laughing.

My answer was overly confident. "I already know that you do."

"Oh really?" Jess raised her eyebrows, challenging me. "What makes you think that I do?"

"You trying to tell me that you don't?"

"You're so smart, law man. You figure it out."

"All I want to know is this . . . When you were out there, did you let that boy feel you up?"

"What?"

I didn't think I could surprise Jess anymore. Or put her at a loss for words. This time, I did.

"That boy? You mean Aaron?" she asked.

"Yeah." It didn't escape my notice that Aaron's name was on her lips when I pulled her out of the water.

"Mal, he's just a boy." Jess was laughing even harder at me. It wasn't funny, damn it. I'd heard more than my share of rumors since we'd rescued them.

"He's old enough," I said stubbornly. "And you were out there for a long time. Things happen."

Shelby had shaken my confidence. I needed to know that the woman I'd given my heart to belonged to me and only me.

"Not those kinds of things," Jess insisted. She placed her hands on either side of my face, stood on tiptoe, and pulled my face down to hers. And then she kissed me. The sweetest, softest kiss I'd ever known.

"I love you, Malcolm Loring," she whispered. "I always have."

"You're the only woman there will *ever* be for me, Jess."

Hearing the words was enough for her. Satisfied with my answers, all the ice within her seemed to melt away. Leaning against me, I felt her start to tremble. She couldn't have been cold. I was holding her too tight for that. And I don't think she was scared. Not anymore. I wasn't going to let anything hurt her again. Not ever. Jess was trembling because she was crying again.

"Sh . . . baby . . . Don't cry, Jess. Don't cry." No more reasons for tears.

I kissed her on both eyelids, her cheeks, and tasted the salty trail of tears that led to her lips. Salt gave way to sweetness when she opened her lips to me. Doubt gave way to desire as she opened her heart to me. Pain gave way to pleasure as she opened her soul to me.

Jess's blanket fell to the ground, and so did we, in a tangle of arms and legs, hands and hearts. We were laughing and crying at the same time, gasping for air and grasping for skin. Damned clothes. Too many clothes. And buttons and zippers and ties. They were nothing but nuisances now, keeping out the weather and keeping us from each other.

We wasted no time. Too much of it had already been lost. No, not lost. We'd foolishly given it away. All of that sparring and snapping and circling each other like mad dogs. What did we think we were doing? I don't know. But I do now. I wasn't going to waste another breath pretending like I didn't want this woman by my side.

It had taken almost losing her to make me come to my senses. I wouldn't make that mistake again. Tonight, I was gonna use every one of my senses to complete my connection to Jess. Mentally. Emotionally. Psychically. Physically. All of it. I wanted all of her.

In hindsight, it wasn't the best of all possible locations to make love to her for the first time. This wasn't how I'd imagined it would be. If I'd been more patient, I could have gotten her to the house, to my room. I should have at least tried to make it to the front porch. But Jess didn't complain. So I wasn't going to either. At least I had the good sense, the presence of mind, to pull the condom out of my wallet.

There was nobody around for miles. Nobody to complain about the noise. Jess and I filled the night air with the sound of our lovemaking—our voices rising and falling on the wind, as wild and swift as the waters that overtook our town.

At one point, I thought maybe I could have been drowning—completely overtaken by my emotions. It was too much. I couldn't think, couldn't speak. I could barely move. When I thought I couldn't hold on another moment, when I thought I'd lose myself forever, staring down into Jess's sparkling eyes as I moved in and out of her, she always brought me back. She was my lifeline.

Sometime around three in the morning, I picked Jess up and carried her into the house. When I crossed the threshold with Jess in my arms, I felt a shiver run down my spine. It was an omen. Because the next time I carried Jess like this, I swore to myself that it would be as my wife. I just knew it. I think she felt it, too. Because she kinda murmured something and wrapped her arms around my neck.

I brought her to my room and laid her down on my bed. I had to brush aside a few pairs of pants, some newspaper, and yesterday's breakfast dishes. I didn't claim to be the neatest man on the planet. But I sure was the luckiest. Jess Ramsay was mine. Finally mine. If I wanted to be honest about it, I'd have to say that was the way it always should have been. If I have anything to say about it, it's the way it always would be. Just my woman and me.

Chapter Nineteen

The River

It is not in my nature to be selfish. I am a giver and a nurturer of life. If during the course of my travels, I claim a life, I will always restore—one for one.

If anyone had bothered to ask, I would have answered. From my liquid loins, life springs eternal. From silt to sea, my path is not one of straight, predictable flows, but infinitely cyclical.

Chapter Twenty

Jess

I don't know what time it was that I rolled over. I didn't want to know. What did I need to look at the clock for? I wasn't in any hurry to go anywhere. For now, I was right where I wanted to be—safe, secure, and one hundred percent satisfied.

Stretching like a cat, arching my back, and practically purring, I rolled over on my side and pulled the blanket almost up to my nose. Whatever time it was, it was still dark. I was glad about that. I didn't want Mal to see that silly schoolgirl grin on my face. He already knew what he could do for me, how he could get to me. My clawing his back and screaming his name like a banshee should have been proof enough of that. I'd stroked everything else that night, I didn't have to stroke his ego, too.

Mal scooted behind me, pressing his chest against my back and draping his arm across my stomach. When I sighed in utter contentment, he raised up on his elbow and kissed my cheek.

"You awake, Jess?" he whispered.

"Barely."

"Try to get some rest," he said, kissing me again, and stroking my hair.

My grin changed to an all-out laugh. "Now, just how in the world am I gonna do that, Malcolm Loring?"

Already, I could feel Mal stirring behind me—a not-so-subtle pressure against my back. Throbbing. Lengthening. He was ready for more.

I couldn't help but laugh at him. He'd been the one crying uncle, begging me to stop touching him so that he could get some sleep before heading back in. Now, here he was, speaking volumes to me without saying a word.

"Pay no attention to the man behind the curtain." He gave a deep-throated chuckle. I liked the sound of Mal's voice when he laughed. It was such a rare occasion when he did so.

"Oh, I don't know," I replied, turning my face back toward him. "He's pretty insistent."

"A cold shower will take the fire right out of me."

"Does that really work?" I sounded surprised, hopeful. Drenching myself in ice-cold water had never worked for me. All it did was make me wet and cold. It didn't take my mind off of Mal. If anything, it made matters worse. I kept thinking that if only he were there, holding me, shielding me from the icy spray . . . There were times I thought I'd go out of my mind, climb the walls with wanting his touch. I tried everything to get Mal off my mind. Cold showers. Exercise until I dropped from exhaustion. Prayer. Meditation. If they'd had a medication for what was wrong with me, I would have gladly had the doctor write out a prescription. He was in my blood. Under my skin. And now, completely in my heart.

"No." Mal grunted, responding to my question. "But I'd better try something before I go back in to work."

He rolled away from me, and I groaned in disappointment.

"Do you have to go in?" I complained, even though I already knew the answer to that. Mal was many things to me. Friend, now lover. Protector. But even with all of that, he was also the chief of police. And others, beside myself, needed him as much or more than I did now.

"I know they've been calling me, but I've turned off the ringer. When they really need to get a hold of me, they'll page me."

"Don't answer it," I said, only half seriously. "Tell them you're taking care of business in a different kind of way."

"I won't be gone long, Jess," he promised. "Believe me." He paused, as if another thought occurred to him.

"What?" I asked, prompting him to tell me what was on his mind.

"You'll be all right," he assured me. "The river will never reach you here."

"I'm not afraid," I said stoutly. That wasn't the complete truth. I had to stretch the truth somewhat to make him feel okay about leaving me alone.

He smiled at me. It was the kinda smile that read through my stretch of the truth. He was grateful for my effort but he wasn't buying it.

"I'll call you as soon as I make it to the station."

I nodded, then made a show of punching my pillow into a more comfy position, and rearranging the blanket around me.

Now, it was Mal's turn to moan a complaint. I guess the thought of me, lying in his bed, not a stitch on, was enough to give him reason to consider his options and his dedication to his job.

"Go on," I said, waving my hands in a shooing motion. "Go do what you have to do. I'll be just fine right here."

"You got that right," he retorted. He leaned back on one elbow. "Anybody tell you lately how incredibly sexy you are, Jess Ramsay?"

"Lately?" I echoed, raising my eyes, staring at the ceiling, and tapping my chin with my index finger. "Let me think. There was this time that . . . No, that doesn't really count. He didn't mention *incredibly*. It was just your plain-old, garden-variety sexy."

It surprised me how quickly Mal fell into the role of jealous lover. His dark eyes narrowed and his chin jutted forward. "Who the hell was *he* telling you that you're fine? You'd better be yanking my chain, woman."

"Play your cards right and I'll be yanking more than that when you get back, Mal Loring." I used my ultrasexy seductress voice.

I know. I know. It was a cheesy pickup line. And given some more time, I probably could have come up with something more creative. But I don't think Mal minded. Or even noticed. The way I lowered my voice, giving him my most direct stare and a half smile, got the effect I wanted. I didn't often get the opportunity to play the role of the temptress. The way I was feeling right now, I wasn't playing. Not anymore. I couldn't get enough of him. His look. His touch. His taste. I had a captive audience and didn't mind taking complete advantage of that fact.

Mal reached and pulled the blanket aside, baring me to my waist. All of a sudden, I felt shy again. I reached for the blanket again, laughing self-consciously, but Mal stopped me.

"Don't," he said, his voice raspy.

"You want to me to catch my death of cold?" I tried to make a joke of it.

"I just want to look at you."

"Why?" I wasn't fishing for compliments. I was having one of those not-so-rare moments when I doubted the power of my own attractiveness, and his sanity.

"What do you mean 'why'? The reason should be pretty obvious. At least," he said, allowing his eyes to slide over me, "the reasons are obvious to me. I'm seeing two big reasons right in front of me."

I know . . . I know . . . a cheesy pickup line. But it got the effect he was looking for. He didn't need to come up with anything better. He had me hooked. I couldn't help myself. I'd never seen Mal quite this way. Not directed at me, anyway. The time he showed up at my house drunk didn't count. Not by a long shot. He hadn't been in control of himself then. Not like now. He was in full control.

"Let me look at you, Jess," he ordered, sounding very much like the control freak he was.

Neither one of us had turned on the light. There was a small reading lamp on the nightstand beside the bed, but Mal didn't reach for it. Instead, he reached out with one hand, and grabbed another condom. The other hand was extended palm outward, and covered my left breast. His hand was large and rough, calloused by hard work. Yet his hand was also tender. Oh-so-tender in the way he touched me.

I looked down at him, saw that his eyelids had drooped closed. The half-moons of his thick eyelashes were stripes of inky darkness against his face. Mal caught his lower lip between his teeth, a low moan rumbled in his throat as he slowly closed his fingers over my skin. He squeezed and released, using his thumb to rub across my nipples.

Inching forward on the bed, Mal cupped my breast and drew himself close to me. He rested his cheek on my chest for a brief moment, listening to the erratic pounding of my heart, before turning his head aside and flicking his tongue over the most sensitive parts of my breast. He caught the nipple between his teeth, giving it a gentle tug.

I couldn't help it. I gasped out loud, making his eyes

fly open. He lifted his face to me, his expression strained.

"I'm sorry. Did I hurt you, Jess?" His voice was heavy with concern.

"N-no!" I stammered. It felt too good to hurt. Placing my hand on the back of his head, I guided him to the right side.

"Equal treatment under the law, I always say," I panted.

In the darkness, I saw the flash of Mal's grin before he switched to the other breast. Swirling his tongue around the puckered skin, he worked his mouth skillfully, deliciously raising the nipple on that side to its full peak.

By now, I was literally squirming. Arching my back, clawing at his skin, I'd lost all of my bashfulness.

"Give me that!" I commanded, holding my hand out for the foil packet. It didn't take long at all for me to unroll the pale red latex. "You're getting adventuresome, law man," I remarked. "This box is cherry flavored."

Then, I reached for him, grasped him midway between the base and tip and eased him between my thighs, yawning open and lifting to invite him in.

There was no room for hesitancy in his bed. There was barely enough room for Mal and me. The way we twisted and writhed, strained against each other, we rolled back and forth, covering almost every inch of his king-sized bed. We were entwined with each other, tangled in the blankets. His sheets somehow wound up around my hips, blocking his access.

With a frustrated tug, Mal pulled the sheet aside, tossing it to the floor. At the same time, he managed to grasp my hips and slide into me, swift and slick, with a guttural cry that was part victory, part ferocity, and part curiosity.

There was still so much we needed to learn about each other. Even as long as we'd known each other, there was still so much we could learn from each other.

Maybe, when our pulses subsided and our senses cooled, we'd try to reason it all out. Not now. Now was not the time for reason. This was the mindless moment where reason has no place. There's nothing rational about passion. Passion is all-consuming, instinctual, and primal. If you have to try to explain it, you don't have it. Mal and me, we had it. Again and again and again—until I was the one gasping for air, begging for mercy and respite.

At first, I wasn't sure that he'd heard me laughingly cry "uncle." The creak of the bed springs, the rhythmic pounding of the headboard against the wall, even the rumbling roll of thunder in the overcast sky drowned out my halfhearted attempt to reign in our passion. If he had heard me, I'm not sure he wanted to. Something in the way he clutched me brought to mind a kind of desperation. No, not quite desperation. More like fear. For a moment, I thought I saw fear reflected in his eyes. What was he afraid of?

I was so touched by the sentiment. Mal wasn't the type of man who scared easily. Silly man! Didn't he know that I was here to stay?

Mal and me had always been together, whether we knew it or not, whether we wanted to admit it or not. I was his woman. He was my man. Nothing would ever change that. I suppose this was all still new to us. It would take him a while to finally accept that. So, I gave him his moment of uncertainty, even as I gave my heart to him.

When his passion finally overtook him, I could feel him shaking, struggling for control. He wasn't ready to let go. Not yet. I could hear it in the way he groaned, a long, unwilling lament. The fact that he didn't want to let me go fueled me. It felt so good to be needed. He wanted me. Mal wanted me!

"Jess!"

He breathed my name upon my skin, raising chill bumps with the sheer emotion of it.

"I'm here," I soothed, stroking his head and smoothing my hands over his perspiration-soaked skin.

"Maybe I don't need to go into work after all." He tossed the suggestion into the air. He sat up on one elbow, staring down at me again.

"You know better than that," I returned. "You have to go in."

"I don't want to leave you," Mal confessed.

"I'll be all right."

"This has nothing to do with you. I'm just being selfish."

"Or greedy," I suggested with a sly smile.

"That, too." Mal grinned back.

"So, law man, what are you going to do with me?" I couldn't stay here and I couldn't hang out at the police station. Maybe I could go to the high school and help out there.

"Marry me," Mal said, without missing a beat.

I blinked. "Wh-what did you s-s-say?" The words stumbled off my lips. He didn't miss a beat, but I certainly did. My heart was thumping all over the place, flopping around in my chest like frogs in a gunnysack.

"You think I'm gonna go back to your mama, tell her that I've had you here, all night, without putting a ring on your finger?" He was teasing me. He had to be!

"So, you're only proposing to me because you're scared of my mama? Mal, you ought to be ashamed of yourself!" I reached out and thumped him in the middle of his forehead. I should have knocked him out for giving me a scare like that. I could do it, too. I'd taken a self-defense class or two from him. It would serve him right if I knocked him unconscious for teasing me like that.

Mal was smiling at me; but he wasn't kidding. I could

tell by the look in his eyes, and by the way his voice got all soft and low.

"Next time I see your mama, Jessica Maydean Ramsay, I want to be sure that I can look her straight in the eye when I do it."

"You're serious, aren't you?" I had to ask.

"You thought I was playing?" He sounded like I'd hurt his feelings. If he was kidding around, he'd put on one hell of a poker face. I didn't know whether to play along, pretend like I believed him, or call him on it.

"No. I thought you'd lost your mind," I confessed.

"Yeah, a lot of good lovin' will do that to a man," he quipped. "Really, Jess. It's been on my mind for a long time."

"Even when you and Shelby were—"

"I don't want to talk about her right now," Mal said sharply.

"I know. I'm sorry, Mal. I don't know why I brought her up."

Mal sat up, rolled away from me. For a moment, I thought I'd really pissed him off this time. He didn't say another word. Just climbed out of bed and headed across the room. When he stopped at his chest of drawers, my anxiety turned to curiosity. With his back to me, I couldn't see what he was doing. But I heard the scrape of a drawer as he pulled it open. He rummaged around for a moment. I could hear objects being shoved aside.

"What are you doing?" I asked.

"I want to show you something," he said, his voice quiet.

"What is it?"

"Give me a minute. I know it's here somewhere . . . I gotta . . . Here it is . . ." He was speaking more to himself than me. When he turned around, he held a small bag in his hand. I reached over and turned on the night-stand lamp.

"What have you got there, law man?" I tried to keep my tone light. But curiosity was eating me up inside.

"Here," he said, unceremoniously tossing the bag onto the bed next to me. It landed with a small thump onto the blanket. Whatever it was, it had a weight and substance to it.

Pulling the covers up around me, I sat up and reached for the bag. And I tried not to grimace. It was small, white, and plastic, and covered with finger prints, as if it had been handled several times. Several hundred times.

The logo on the bag was worn and faded. Still, I recognized it. It was from Bauman's, a jewelry store downtown that had closed years go. *Years.* I peeled open the drawstring bag and peered inside. Inside the bag was another box. Not just a box, but a jewelry case, red velvet trimmed in gold ribbon.

I held the bag open, hardly daring to reach my hand inside. If this was a joke, it was a cruel one. A mighty cruel one. I wasn't laughing. And neither was Mal. He wasn't even smiling. Just standing there beside the bed. Naked and magnificent. Silent and expectant.

"You gonna wait 'til Christmas or are you gonna open it?" he finally said.

I reached inside the bag and took out the box. Still, I didn't open it.

"Mal, how long have you been holding on to this?" I asked, my voice soft and trembly.

"February 14, 1982," he said promptly.

I did some quick mental calculations. He would have been thirteen years old then. And I would have been nine, almost ten. What kind of a gift could a thirteen year old afford from Bauman's? I tried to think back to what he was doing back then. He hadn't always been a police officer. Not at thirteen years old. Mowing grass if I'm not mistaken. And a paper route. He had a dark green ten-speed with a black and white seat and playing cards stuck in the spokes that made a racket whenever he rode by.

Slowly I cracked open the box. A small gold heart locket reflected the light from the nightstand back at me. The locket was engraved in a fine, filigree script. *Mal loves Jess.*

"Oh, Mal . . ."

I could barely breathe for the painful lump resting in my throat. He must have saved all of his paper route and grass mowing money to be able to afford this. It was 14-karat solid gold. Not gold plated. Not gold trim. Real gold. It was too much. It was just too much. It was . . . just the locket.

"What happened to the chain?" I piped up.

Mal gave me a half smile.

"Don't you remember your fourteenth birthday?" he prompted.

"You didn't want to give me the locket then?"

"You were all gaga for that trunk-necked, football playin', unibrowed senior at Codell County High School. What was I gonna give you a heart locket for?"

"Oh, him!" I waved the thought aside. "All the girls were crazy for him. That didn't mean anything." I smiled sweetly at Mal. "He didn't mean a thing to me."

"So, when you took him to your junior prom, that didn't mean anything either?"

"I asked you!" I reminded him. "But you had to work. Remember?"

"I guess there's enough blame to go around for why we aren't together, huh, Jess?" He sat down on the bed facing me.

"It's not too late for us, Mal."

"I know, Jess Ramsay," he said, cupping my chin in the palm of his hand. "That's why I'm giving this to you now. You've always been in my heart. Since you didn't believe me telling you, I thought maybe you'd believe me showing you."

"I believe you, Mal," I whispered. I swallowed hard, forcing down the lump. Fluttering my eyelashes, I wasn't trying to flirt, but hoped that by blinking fast, I could hold back the tears. It didn't help. If anything, it made the tears flow even faster.

"I swear," he murmured, brushing aside my tears with the balls of his thumbs. "You are the cryin'est woman I ever met."

He leaned close, would have kissed me again, but his pager went off, rattling and shifting around the nightstand.

Sighing, Mal reached over and checked the number, though he really didn't have to. We both knew who it was.

"You coming into town with me?" he asked, distractedly.

I nodded, not trusting my voice.

All of a sudden, Mal was all business, as if someone had suddenly thrown a switch. All of the toying and tenderness drained from his face. He was the chief of police again. The outside world intruded on our haven.

I suppose I shouldn't complain. The man I love had just confessed that he'd always loved me. What more could a woman ask for?

Chapter Twenty-One
Mal

I'm not sure what possessed me to ask Jess to marry me. It just popped out, before I could take the words back. I guess it was something subconscious inside of me, just dying to get out. Now that it was out there, I couldn't take it back, even if I wanted to. Which I didn't. I don't have a problem with the thought of sharing my life with Jess. It's all I've dreamed of for as long as I can remember.

I just didn't like speaking without thinking. That part really bothered me. I'm not an impulsive man. In my job, I couldn't afford to be. When I say something, I mean it, word for word. It's not like me to just pop off without thinking. Though, you probably couldn't tell that by my actions lately. Just ask Myles.

Not when it came to Jess. With that woman, all bets were off when it came to saying what I would or wouldn't do. Today there was something in Jess's eyes, staring at me like that, so sweet and sexy and kinda helpless—what else could I do but ask her to marry me? I would do anything to keep her safe. Move mountains, if I had to. Even if that mountain was my own stubborn pride.

Maybe I had been too quick to ask her to marry me like that. Jess was as practical as the next woman. But I'm sure she has also had her fantasies. Neither one of us could have ever imagined that her "moment" would come like this. Over the years, I'd dreamed up a thousand ways I could propose to her . . . and do it up right and proper. Flowers. A fancy dinner somewhere, hiding a ring in a glass of champagne. Or maybe a picnic. Maybe an announcement over the PA at a basketball game.

I never expected I'd be standing naked as the day I was born, holding onto a trinket I'd bought when I was too young to know what real love was, asking her to share my name. Still, I'd said it.

It wasn't until we'd dressed and were headed back into town before I realized that despite all of her crying and kissing, she hadn't given me an answer.

I pulled up in front of the high school, idling the engine.

"You gonna be all right?" I asked her again.

She nodded tightly, pressing her lips together so hard they'd almost disappeared. We'd only gone through a couple of roads, almost impassable because of high water. Each time she heard the water splash up around the tires, she'd gripped my arm, or her arm rest, and bit her lip to keep from crying out. Something told me that I shouldn't have brought her back here. Not yet. It was too soon. On the other hand, I couldn't leave her out there by herself.

"I'll be fine," she tried to assure me. "You go on, law man. You've got work to do."

The words coming out of Jess's mouth said "go," yet the look on her face said "stay." She was a bundle of contradictions. I knew why she was trying to make me feel better. But I wish she'd be more honest with me. More honest with herself. She was scared. More than scared. Jess was terrified.

But Jess had always been an independent woman. She didn't like to admit weakness. I wasn't expecting her to go all damsel-in-distress on me. I just wanted her to know that I was here for her now. Fully. Completely. It was okay for her to let her guard down in front of me. I was strong enough for the both of us.

Instead, she opened the door to the Jeep, ready to run into the high school. The sky was still dark, but I knew by the thickening of the clouds that the rain wasn't through with us yet. And with the river out of the levees, there was no way of knowing how high it would get before it crested.

"Call me if you need anything," I yelled out after her. She turned around for a split second, blew me a kiss, and then ducked into the school.

Shifting my Jeep into gear, I followed the horseshoe-shaped drive out to the main road. I turned on the radio, pressing buttons until I found a news station. More information about the election. Some fluff entertainment news and sports statistics. I listened with only half an ear until the weather report came in. Then my ears perked up. Mentally, I was comparing what the broadcast news was saying about our weather condition to reports from the local weather bureau. So far, both were right on the money. Rain and more rain.

The police station was only six miles from the high school. But with several city streets blocked off due to high water, it took longer than I expected to get there. Even then, I had to park the Jeep several blocks over and call in for a boat to come and get me.

Roderick Dawson responded to my call. He idled up to me, moving slowly and trying not to create a great wake. It really didn't matter. I was already standing waist deep in water, raising a bit on tiptoes from the neon orange life vest that I'd strapped on.

"Here, Chief, let me give you a hand," he offered, extending his hand to me and helping me climb over the edge. The boat tilted far to my side as I scrambled up. Roderick leaned back, shifting his weight and righting us.

"I didn't expect to hear from you, Chief," he said, before restarting the motor. When he adjusted his bright yellow rain slicker, I saw that he'd come out to get me armed. His service revolver was strapped down in his shoulder holster.

I have no illusions about our secluded corner of the world. As safe as we want it to be, hard as we try to make it so, it isn't always the case. For every good Samaritan we get who is willing to lend a helping hand in time of need, there are those who are just as quick to take advantage of our troubles.

"You didn't think I'd come into work? Why not?"

Roderick shrugged. "You know, with everything that's happened . . . I thought you might want to take it easy for a while."

I guess he'd heard along with everyone else about what happened out there with me and Jess.

"How is Ms. Ramsay?" he asked, when I didn't comment.

"She'll be all right. She's already back at the high school. You know Jess Ramsay. She's not one to let anything keep her down for too long."

"But after what she's just been through, maybe she should rest. Maybe you should both rest," Roderick said emphatically.

"We can rest when our businesses and homes are no longer waterfront property," I retorted.

"Still," Roderick hesitated.

My eyes darted to his hand on the outboard motor

controls. I couldn't help but notice that we were still traveling at a snail's pace. Not even ten miles per hour. Was it caution making him travel so slowly or was it something else? A voice in the back of my head was telling me that he was stalling. But why? On some level, I already knew. On another level, I didn't want to know.

"I could take you back to the school," Roderick offered.

"No thanks," I said.

"It wouldn't be no trouble at all, Chief. I could—"

"What's going on, Roderick?"

Enough jacking around with instinct and suspicions. I wanted to know what he was trying so hard to keep from me. I hadn't worked with the man for seven years not to know when something was up with him. It was one of the reasons he'd dropped out of our once-a-month, Saturday night poker games. I could clean him out every time, just by reading his pitiful poker face.

"Chief," he began, then closed his mouth.

"What is it, Roderick? Go on. Spit it out."

"I'd rather not say, sir."

Finally, he pulled up along the side of the police station, which was actually a multiple-function building containing the police headquarters, county courthouse annex, and rental office spaces, most of which were occupied by bail bondsmen and lawyers.

"We've moved the command center up to the third floor," he said. "We've got sandbags around the front of the building, so you can get in, but there's still at least a foot of water inside on the first floor."

Two out of our fleet of six patrol cars were still parked in the front of the building. I could see where the water had gotten inside.

"Where are the other cars?" I asked him, pulling open the door and sloshing through the water toward the stairs.

"Brooks and Grady were in their cars when the levees

failed," he said. "I think they're okay. And Rusty's was being serviced. I don't know if the shop is under water or not. Myles has the other one. He's at home . . . uh . . . resting."

I didn't have to look at Roderick's face to tell that he wasn't too pleased with me at that moment. I didn't blame him. I wasn't too proud of myself, either. Eventually, I'd have to account for my actions.

"Elevator's out," Roderick pointed out.

I glanced at him. "Oh, yeah?" My tone dripped with sarcasm.

A handwritten sign with the words "Voyage to the Bottom of the Sea" was pasted with gray duct tape against the elevator call button. Another sign, more serious in tone, was in penned in a bright red marker, "OUT OF SERVICE. DO NOT USE."

"How's he doing?" I asked, and felt another pang of conscience hit me. I hadn't called to check on Myles since I took Jess home with me. Come to think of it, I hadn't called anyone.

I expected some serious repercussions. Myles would be perfectly in his rights to bring charges of assault against me or sue me. None of those things ran through my mind when I was throttling him, or when I was resting in Jess's arms last night. Now, with a cooler head prevailing, I was starting to think about those things as I climbed through the darkened stairwell. The emergency lights, powered by a generator, cast a dim orange glow.

"We moved your office to one of the courtrooms," Roderick said. "No phones. We're communicating through two-way and cell phones. I've been acting as watch commander since yesterday."

"You're the one who needs to rest," I said. "As soon as I check the schedule, I'll rotate you off and someone else on."

"Don't worry about the schedule, Chief," Roderick said. "You've got other stuff you need to handle first."

Again, the cryptic remarks. I glanced back over my shoulder but didn't ask Roderick what he meant by that. I guess I'd find out soon enough.

As soon as I pushed open the door to the courtroom I had a gut feeling that I'd be getting quite an education. I looked around the room. Four out of five of the most influential people in Codell County were all inside waiting for me. If anyone had decided to take over the town by wiping out all the decision makers, they'd made it easy for them by congregating together like this.

The buzz of conversation stopped as soon as I entered the courtroom. My gaze swept across the room, noting those who met my gaze straight on and those who avoided me.

Russell Colby, the current mayor, sat closest to the door and looked for all the world as if he'd rather be the furthest away.

He took out a wad of tissue from his pocket, breaking eye contact with me by making a show of clearing his sinuses into the crumpled white Kleenex.

"Chief Loring," Sandra Reed, the superintendent of schools, greeted me with a cool nod as she stood on the far side of the room stirring tea in a Styrofoam cup. The Lipton tea bag tag dangled from the edge of the cup, wrapped around the orange stick stirrer.

I was kinda surprised to see Sandra here, dressed as she was, too, in blue jeans and a large gray sweatshirt with the Mississippi State Bulldogs logo emblazoned across her chest. Her shoulder-length, dyed jet black hair, usually done up in an elegant French roll, was pulled away from her face with a simple rubber band. I know it must have killed Sandra to be seen out in public like this. Sandra's idea of casual was wearing a single strand of natural pearls rather than the cultured double strand, to emulate her mentor, former first lady Barbara Bush.

I wasn't surprised with the sour expression she gave me. Sandra didn't like me. Not since I locked up her son on a drunk-and-disorderly charge. I'd tried not to. Did everything I could to get the boy to go home without incident.

But he was hell-bent on showing his "homies" that he could be down, instead of going on home to his mama like he should have. He tried to take a swing at me, and not with his hands, either. I wasn't going to let some snot-nosed, nineteen-year-old gangsta wannabe try to pee on me. No sir. Not in this lifetime. If he'd kept his pants zipped, he wouldn't have a record to this day that kept him out of the private university his mother lobbied so hard to get him into.

Beside Sandra in the courtroom, dressed in blue work Dickies, matching pants and shirt, was Rashad Tyrell, recently elected to the town council. Rashad met my gaze head on. I wasn't encouraged by that. I knew that Rashad used the old stare-at-'em-at-the-bridge-of-the-nose to make it look as though he was looking you straight in the eyes. It was an old public servant's trick, one that had often served me well.

"Well, well, well," I said, surprising myself with how pleasant I sounded. "The gang's all here. Good morning, folks."

I stepped into the courtroom, moving toward what I presumed was my desk. Someone had the presence of mind to bring up some of my personal effects—a picture of me and my dad holding up an 800-pound bluefish marlin that we'd caught off the coast of Florida on a fishing trip, a rookie baseball card signed by Hank Aaron, a picture of me, Jess, and Shelby taken at a Frankie Beverly and Maze concert, and oh yeah, my nameplate. I suppose that made this desk mine. Anyway, I acted like it was mine.

Making a pointed effort, I ignored the looks from what remained of my staff, those that were able to somehow paddle their way into town, as I stood at the desk and started to rifle through the stack of manila folders sitting in my "in box."

"What a night, eh, folks?" I said, forcing myself to sound conversational. "What's everybody standing around here for? We've got work to do. *Don't we?*" It was a question within a question within a question, layered with all kinds of unspoken innuendo.

"How's it going, Mal?" Brenton Michaels, the town administrator, greeted me with what I was thankful for— a true sense of warmth. Brenton and me go way back. He'd put my name out there, in front of Russell, after he'd been elected and was looking for a new top cop to solidfy his position. Somewhere in our family tree, I think me and Brenton are related. Though, you'd never know it to look at us. Brent's flaming red hair and face full of freckles didn't necessarily scream soul brother.

"Can't complain," I replied.

"And how's Jess?"

His concern was genuine, so I answered him with all sincerity. I think he could hear the relief in my voice.

"She's gonna be all right. In fact, she's down at the school now, doing what she can to be of service."

"Chief Loring," Sandra spoke up, clearing her throat delicately. "If you have a moment . . ."

"Something tells me that I'm gonna have all day," I snapped, but I was still smiling. Enough to make my face hurt. What else could I do? I'd been in the wrong when I'd gone after Myles like that. Dead wrong. It was a miracle that the good leaders of Codell County didn't all storm my doorstep the day it happened. I don't know what they would have done if they'd interrupted Jess and my reunion.

"You may want to rethink that tone, Chief," Sandra suggested, setting her tea aside on the table with a barely audible thump. It was as impressive as a sound could be from a Styrofoam cup. Her motion, followed by the downward pull of her lip, was deliberate, meant to call up images of errant school kids and school marms with rulers wrapping on knuckles. She didn't scare me. Not one bit. Now, Jess's mom, Ms. Ramsay, there was a woman who knew how to put the fear of God into you with just a look.

"My tone?" I repeated, raising my eyebrows and taking a step toward her. Job on the line or not, she wasn't going to come up in my office and tell me how I should behave. Well, technically, this was the courtroom, not my office. But it had been commandeered and possession was nine-tenths of the law.

"Now, Mal," Russell rumbled. He was a thick, heavyset man, who in his day might have cut a fine figure. "Take it easy."

"What has my tone got to do with why you've ambushed me here today?"

"Nobody's ambushing you, Chief," Rashad replied, giving me that middle-of-the-nose gaze again.

"It's not your tone, it's your attitude, Chief Loring," Sandra snapped. "And you're one to talk about ambushes. What gives you the right, the unmitigated gall to attack Officer Overton?"

I had no answer to that, no acceptable answer anyway. But I didn't give her the satisfaction of knowing that she'd scored a point over me.

"Mal didn't mean it, Sandra. He was just under a lot of stress," Russell stepped in. I almost laughed. I'd seen better performances of good cop/bad cop on reruns of *Law & Order*. The original version, not those *CSI* or *SVU* spin-offs.

"We're all under a lot of stress, Russ," she retorted.

"That doesn't mean we can go around taking out our aggression on the first convenient person. Contrary to your belief, Chief, your officers don't have to take abuse from you."

Again, I kept silent. In fact, my jaw hurt, I was clenching my teeth so tightly together. Up until the time I snapped with Myles, when did I ever give them the impression that I could abuse my staff?

"Tell us that you're sorry, Mal. A nice apology and some restitution to that young boy and it'll all be over with, won't it?" Russ kept talking quickly. And he was sweating. I knew that look. He was lying.

Who did he think he was fooling? I hadn't allowed myself to think about what was going to happen to me. I was too preoccupied with Jess. Now that she wasn't here, and I was thinking more clearly, the weight of my actions was resting heavy on my heart. I could have killed that boy. Killed him with my bare hands. No apology could fix that. It would do Myles an injustice to make-believe that it would. He wasn't a fool. If I went to him, with half-assed, insincere words, meant more to save my hide than to soothe his feelings, he'd see right through it.

No, I would have to apologize to Myles in my own way. But I wouldn't go with an agenda. I wouldn't do it to try to salvage my job. I would do it because it was the right thing to do.

I held up my hand. "Don't try to shine me on, Russell. Just say what you came here to say. Am I fired or what?"

Putting the question out there like that bluntly shocked them into silence. I don't see why. I always was a put-it-out-there kinda guy. I didn't give any bull and I didn't expect any either, not from my so-called colleagues, coworkers, and friends.

"Nobody said anything about firing you, Mal," Brenton said.

"Not yet," Sandra qualified.

"We just think you might need to take a break, is all," Russell added. "Give yourself some time off."

"Rest?" I echoed. "In the middle of one of the worst floods to hit our town since 1927?" I shook my head. "Humor me, folks, just how much time are we talking? Hours? Days?"

When no one was forthcoming with a response, I added. "Weeks?"

"Just a couple, Mal. Three, four at the most. Just long enough for the press to get bored with your story and let it go," Brenton offered. "It's already been picked up by AP. You're statewide news, right alongside the pictures of street signs nearly covered up with river water."

"We don't need the kind of publicity your tantrum brought to us," Sandra continued. "We're fighting poor public perception as it is. Everyone already thinks we're the poorest, most backward state in the union. And you want to go off and pull a stunt like this! It's deplorable. Our chief of police acting like a lovesick moron!"

"A month off of work?" I said, starting to pace. I'd been thinking that I needed a vacation. But this was different. This was no frolic on the beach. I couldn't see myself sipping on chilled fruit and umbrella-filled drinks and working on my tan. This was my job they were talking about. My reputation.

"Is that with or without pay?"

"Given the state of emergency that we're in, Chief, do you honestly think we could afford to keep giving you a salary?" It was Sandra's turn to sound incredulous.

"So, what am I supposed to do?"

"Hope that Officer Myles doesn't sue you and the city for damages."

"And if he does?" I prompted.

"Then, I hope you're a praying man, Chief. Because

we'll be taking that badge, your job, and your soul before we're finished with you."

"Go to hell, Sandra."

Again, I congratulated myself. I'd said it with the utmost pleasantness. It's easy to be pleasant when you mean every word.

I reached into my jacket pocket, pulled out my badge and ID and tossed them on the table beside her tea cup.

"If it's poor perception you're worried about, folks, let me save you the trouble."

"Mal, what are you doing?" Brenton asked me. "Don't do anything stupid, now."

"Too late for that," Sandra retorted. The look on her face was triumphant, as if she'd always wanted my badge but just didn't have enough political pull to get it. Stupid me. I played right into her hands.

Maybe they'd done me a favor. If I was that far gone that I was beating up on my own people, then maybe it was time for me to go.

"I'm not going to fight you about this," I told them. "There's already been enough of that, wouldn't you say?"

My service weapon joined my badge on the table.

Then, without another word, I turned around and headed for the door. I didn't look back, not even when Roderick called out, "Need a ride to your car, Chief?"

Naw, I guess I didn't. As mad as I was, I figured I'd better wade through a couple of miles of waist-high water before I went back to Jess. As hot as I was, maybe I could evaporate some of this water around us.

By the time I made it to the school, there were people all around. Everywhere I turned, everywhere I stepped, there was either a body or evidence of one. The good news, they were all alive. Survivors of the flood were all pouring into the high school. Even people from the

other shelters, those that had been overrun, were somehow making it in.

The cafetorium—the combination cafeteria and au-
ditorium—each of the classrooms, and the gym were just
about filled to capacity. I knew most of these people. Not
all of them were from Codell County. The rising river
had folks from the neighboring counties converging on
the high school, seeking refuge.

"Chief Loring," someone waved me over. It was Stan
Jordan, the school's basketball coach and sometimes
driver's education teacher.

"Got a minute, Chief?"

I bit my tongue to keep from making a wisecracking
remark. Speaking of saving jobs. The last time I answered that question, I'd put my job at risk.

"Sure, Jordan. What do you need?"

"Another set of hands. We got a wave of families in
about an hour ago that could sure use something to eat."

He pushed a loaded cart toward me.

"Take these to the math and sciences wing on the first
floor. And when you're done, check with a Mrs. Mitchell
of the Red Cross. She's handling distribution of the
extra clothes and blankets."

"Sure. Why not." How could I refuse? It wasn't as if I had
anything else to do. I didn't have a job to go to anymore.

As I ferried relief supplies back and forth, from blankets, to dry clothes, to sandwiches, I wondered how
many people we could continue to cram in before we
were overrun.

"Chief," one of the high school students called me
from down the hall. "Mr. Gerardo is asking if we have
any more blankets. Three more families just came in."

I shrugged helplessly. I'd raided the Red Cross's stash
of blankets that they'd brought with them. I'd taken as

many as I could, knowing that others would soon follow me with their own requests for extras.

"I don't know, Lisa. I'll check with Mrs. Mitchell," I promised. "Right after I deliver these meal boxes."

"Yes, sir. I'll tell him."

Continuing down the hall, I pushed the rolling cart. It was just meager food in the boxes. Ham sandwiches, potato chips or animal crackers, and dried fruit. Couple that with bottled water or boxed fruit drinks, it was hardly enough to satisfy hunger.

Under the circumstances, it was the best that we could do. So far, few complaints. But the gratitude wouldn't last if the refugees got wind that the reserves were rapidly depleting. And still they came. By the boatloads, rescue teams ferried survivors in, dropped them off, and turned right around to find more.

In chatting up some of the folks I knew, I'd learned that some local grocery stores had promised more food would be forthcoming. Every grocery store, convenience store, mom-and-pop shop that could do so without endangering themselves would stay open twenty-four hours a day. Those that could were giving supplies away. Others were taking IOUs, trusting in good faith that they would later be compensated.

There was still so much that was needed—formula for babies, diapers, medicine to treat injuries, antibiotics, antiseptics, bandages and splints, painkillers.

The list of needs was ever growing. And with each family I handed a meal to, I could feel myself getting more and more anxious. We'd all heard the weather reports. More rain was coming, with few signs that it was letting up. Now was a helluva time to be taking a "vacation."

I'd been asked to step aside from my position, but that didn't mean I couldn't still be of service. I'd already put my name on the list of volunteers for night patrol. From

the reports that came back to the station, it was the most
hazardous duty so far. With only searchlights to guide
the patrollers, there were far too many incidents of res-
cuers themselves falling into the rising waters.

I wasn't scheduled to patrol until late, but that didn't
stop me from hanging around, doing what I could. What
was that old cliché? You could take the badge from the
man, but you couldn't take the man from the badge. I
was cop, first and foremost. I wasn't in charge, but that
didn't mean I couldn't take charge.

To hell with Sandra and Russ and Brenton. To hell
with all of them. Chief of Police was just a title. If I
couldn't be one here in Codell County, I'd go somewhere else and apply for a job. I was good at what I did.
Somebody, somewhere, would believe that, see that in
me, and give me the job.

For now, my résumé would have to wait. I had to keep
my head in the here and now. Today, the river was raging all around us. And as mad and as badass as I thought
I was, for now, the river was top cop.

Chapter Twenty-Two

The River

Through the ages, I have had many names. None have done me justice. What is the purpose of a name? That which attempts to classify. Is that the purpose of the name, no matter how inadequate?

If anyone had bothered to ask, I would have answered. There is no name that can define the indefinable. I am forever changing, not only myself, but the land that borders me. As I reach out and alter the face of the world, I am also changing those that would seek to name me, and by naming me claiming to control me.

Could it be that I am the one who classifies? It is I, as I flow through the ages, that bends and shapes the lives of man. I am the ultimate controller, the final claimer. My touch is indescribable. Inescapable. I am the identifier. For no man can remain the same after knowing me.

Chapter Twenty-Three

Jess

Mal didn't tell me what happened when he went to the station that morning. He didn't have to. The fact that he'd shown up an hour later at the high school and spent the rest of the afternoon there told me everything I wanted to know. Had he been fired? That remained to be seen. For now, he wasn't acting as chief of police. He couldn't have been. Instead of sitting at his desk, passing out orders to his officers, he was busy making runs back and forth between the classrooms.

Being ready, willing, and able to protect and serve wasn't something Mal did between the hours of eight and five. Whether he wore the badge or not, Mal wasn't going to stop doing what he was born to do.

By late that afternoon, the rumors were running rampant through the halls of the high school. As rumors usually go, some were just downright stupid. I wouldn't believe them if someone had paid me.

I'd heard everything from Mal walked out on them to Mal was physically thrown out of the building. Kicked out of his own office, down the stairs, and into the street like yesterday's garbage.

No one who knew Mal would ever believe that non-sense. Still, there the rumors were, hovering over the shelter, reminding him at every turn that in that moment when he'd lost control, he'd lost some of Codell County's respect.

It didn't take long for Mal to gain it back, though. He wasn't going to let a few whispers, a few stares, even a few challenges of his authority stop him from doing what he was supposed to do. He and his staff were trained to act in disasters. What kind of man would he be if he turned his back on his town because a few shortsighted individuals, more concerned with public opinion than with what was best for this town, had turned their back on him?

Where he had to, he took orders from those who directed him to do what they wanted him to do and where they wanted him to be. And, in the absence of clear-cut leadership, Mal was the one giving the orders. I couldn't have been more proud of him in those moments. Because I knew how hard it must have been for him.

"Here, law man," I said, handing him a Styrofoam box and a cup of coffee. "Take a break."

He'd just spent the past hour with Mr. Gerardo and the Red Cross volunteers going over the numbers of how many people were actually crammed in the school. They'd spent the better part of the day assigning families to any remaining empty rooms.

Mal blew on the still-hot coffee, cooling it before taking a sip.

"Black, no cream, no sugar?" he asked.

I rolled my eyes at him. Even if we had those luxuries in our emergency rations, I would never doctor his coffee that way. Like so many other things in his life, Mal liked his coffee uncomplicated.

"How's it going?" I asked, tilting my head toward a quiet corner of the room.

Mal shrugged, following after me. I wasn't necessarily talking about the relocation effort. What I really wanted to know was how he was holding up.

"Wanna talk about it?" I asked softly.

"Nope," he said immediately, staring straight ahead. I guess he saw through my poor attempt at digging for information. We sat down, our backs against the wall. Folding our legs cross-legged, we rested our dinner plates in our laps.

While Mal munched, I studied his profile, noting the tightness in his jaw, the narrowed eyes. As he ate, he crunched down on his food. I had to wonder if he was grinding more molars than food. Mal was still upset about this morning's turn of events and wasn't doing a very good job of hiding it from me.

"Fair enough." I kept my tone even, forced lightness to keep from making the situation worse. "What do you want to talk about then?" I let him pick the subject.

"If you don't mind, Jess, I don't feel much like talking about anything at all."

"You shouldn't keep all of that stress bottled up, Mal. Sometimes it helps to get things off your chest," I suggested.

"Yeah?" He swung his gaze around, one eyebrow lifted in utter sarcasm.

"Yeah," I encouraged.

"The last time I let it all off my chest, *Dr.* Jess Ramsay, since you're so good at playin' pop psychologist, I near 'bout beat a man to death. Is that enough stress relief for you? Tell me I ain't a prime candidate for anger management."

He covered his face with his hands, laughing without real warmth. "Now I'm sitting here, trying to figure out how in the hell I'm gonna get through the rest of this day without poppin' somebody in the mouth for reminding me all about it. I can't take a step without hearin' about me and Myles and the good folks of Codell County who think I'm better off sittin' on the sidelines taking a much needed *vacation.*"

Mal held up his hands, crooked his index and middle fingers to put imaginary quotation marks around the word vacation. Then he sighed, took the last of his coffee in one gulp and crumpled the cup convulsively into his fist. "Folks have been wagging their tongues all day about me. You'd think that a man had never lost his job before."

"They let you go?" I thought I'd prepared myself for the worst. But I hadn't. Not really. I never expected that they would let him go. Not when they needed him so much. "Have they lost their ever-lovin' minds?!"

"The whole world's gone crazy, Jess. Including me."

"Don't you dare start feeling sorry for yourself, Malcolm Loring!" I whispered tightly. I reached out and clamped down on his forearm. My fingers dug into his flesh. When Mal winced, protest clearly in his eyes, I continued without letting up the pressure.

"Don't you even dare. You need to keep it together, law man. If not for yourself, for me. Call me selfish, but I need you to be strong for me. This whole town needs you to stay strong. Only they're too stupid to know it."

"I appreciate the sentiment, Jess," he began, and I could hear the conflict in his voice.

His face showed the strain as he admitted more to himself than to me, "But they were right. I'm not any good to them as I was, hauling off and beating the crap out of Myles and then dropping everything to go after you."

"You didn't mean it, Mal. You were under pressure, a lot of pressure, and well . . . for a minute . . . you lost it."

"Don't you see, Jess? Don't you understand? I, of all

people, can't afford to lose it. Not like that. Those who hired me, who I swore to protect, have to have faith, trust, and confidence in the man they've picked to do the job. I violated that trust. And because of that, I don't deserve to wear that badge. I screwed that up. Nobody but me was responsible for that. I made that mistake."

"Saving my life and Aaron's wasn't a mistake. Not in my book."

Mal gave me that half smile of his. The one that always makes my heart give a crazy skip. He reached out, brushed my hair away from my face.

"I didn't mean it like that. I just meant that I should have handled things differently."

"If you had, I might not be here with you today," I said matter-of-factly. "Everything happens for a reason, Mal. Everything."

"If I had a chance to do it all over again, you know I would, don't you?" he confessed.

"Even the part about Myles?"

"He left you," Mal said, his tone suddenly turning hard. "He hurt you. Heaven help anyone who tries to hurt you. No, ma'am," he said, changing his mind about how he'd answered my question. "I wouldn't do a single thing differently."

"There you have it, then," I said, snapping my finger as if I'd solved all of his problems with the magic wave of my hand. "Why are you torturing yourself about something you can't change and probably wouldn't even if you had the chance? It's a perfect example of the "Serenity Prayer.""

I kept a small card of the "Serenity Prayer" in my desk at school. The pale blue glossy card with gold calligraphic script was well worn from all of the times I'd reached into the desk, fingering it, when I was one step away from running screaming out of the classroom.

Twenty-four eight- and nine-year-olds can be quite a

handful. And since I couldn't lay a hand on them these days when they got out of hand without risking a lawsuit, it helped to have the power of the Divine on my side. I wished I had that card with me now, so I could pass it on to Mal.

"Changing the things I can and accepting that there are some things that I can't," Mal paraphrased the prayer. "I don't have to tell you how hard that is for me, Jess."

"That's because you're a control freak." I fluttered my eyelashes at him.

"Takes one to know one." He smiled back, and leaned his face close to mine. "I don't recall you minding my being a control freak when I . . ." He leaned even closer, putting his hand in the small of my back, and whispering the last words to me to make sure that no one could hear his words but me.

They didn't have to hear what he had to say. I imagined that anyone could tell by the look on my face the kinds of things Mal was saying to me. As he massaged my lower back, letting his hand drift lower and working his fingers underneath the waistband of my jeans, I squirmed and bit my lip to keep from moaning out loud.

"All right, law man. That's enough!" I scooted back away from him, trying to put some distance between us. "Don't you have a river to go plug up or something? A stranded motorist to rescue?"

"Three hours," he said. I wasn't sure if he was letting me know when his break was over or asking for that time with me.

"Why don't you make good use of that time and find one of the empty cots and try to get some rest, Mal."

"An empty cot? Have you slept on one of those things? I know folks around here are grateful to be alive. But it's like sleeping on iron rods with a beach towel tossed over them for comfort. How is that supposed to help me relax?"

"You ought to try. You're not going to be much good to anybody if you collapse from exhaustion."

"I gotta keep movin', Jess," he said. "Working keeps me from thinkin'."

"Just what every citizen wants to hear, a law man who turns off his brain while he's on the job."

I'd said that to him as a joke, to put the smile back on his face, but it was the wrong thing to say. Mal *wasn't* on the job. The people who'd given it to him had just taken it away.

Oh, perfect timing, Jess! Way to go! One of these days, my mouth was going to get me into a world of trouble. Looks like this was one of those days.

He stood up abruptly. "Leave the cots for the refugees. I'm on the midnight-to-six boat patrol," he told me. "I've got a room over at the motel. Figured it was best I hang around close to here instead of trying to go home while the river's up. Gonna head over and get some rest. Are you coming or what?"

"If I do," I said, wagging my eyebrows up and down, "you might not get as much rest as you think."

Mal choked back a laugh. "It's a risk I'm willin' to take."

I was glad that I put the smile back at his face. On second thought, why did the thought of my making love to him make him laugh so hard?

Holding his hand out to me, Mal helped me off the floor.

"*Oomph!*" I made a small sound of complaint as I stood up. I consider myself to be in reasonably good physical condition. Yet, the last few days had taken their toll on me. My muscles were sore and cramping. And, if I turned the wrong way, I could hear my knees, elbows, or neck pop.

Mal then draped his arm across my shoulders, leaned close and whispered suggestively, seductively. "Poor baby. How about I give you a massage when we get to the room? How does that sound, Jess?"

That question worked for me on so many different levels. The sound of Mal's voice, low and gravelly, sexy and sincere, sent shivers all through me.

"Ummm," I hummed in my throat, leaning my head against his shoulder. "Sounds just fine to me. Give me a minute to tell Mr. Gerardo that I'm on my way out."

"I'll meet you outside by the Jeep," he said.

I was glad Mr. Gerardo didn't say anything about the goofy grin on my face when I checked in with him. I didn't want to have to explain to him how easily the promise of a man's touch could make me give up my altruistic duties. But a back rub was a back rub. How could I resist a luxury like that?

"You leavin' us, Ms. Ramsay?" he asked.

"Yes, sir. But only for a while," I promised, quickly gathering my bag and jacket from one of the storage cabinets. "I should be back around midnight or so."

"You've pulled quite a long shift today, Ms. Ramsay. You may want to consider taking it easy. Keep off the roads until some of this has passed."

I shook my head vigorously back and forth. A definitive no! Like Mal, I couldn't stay away either. More than one of my students had shown up here at the high school seeking shelter. I'd promised that I'd be back around to see them. I couldn't disappoint them. Seeing a friendly face, even in the midst of all this chaos, helped to give the frightened eight- and nine-year-olds a sense of normalcy.

"I'll be back, Mr. Gerardo."

"Be careful, Ms. Ramsay. It's bad out there. And it's getting worse."

"I'll be all right," I assured him. I was with Mal Loring. He would never let anything hurt me. Never.

Mal was in the driveway, with the Jeep's engine idling, when I dashed out to meet him. I pulled open the door and climbed in. Yet, Mal didn't pull off right away. Instead, he sat listening to the radio. There was an official, someone other than Mal, begging the public to seek shelter. She went on to give a list of road closures. The list seemed to go on and on and on.

"It's bad, isn't it?" I asked, biting my lip.

"Yeah," he said, reaching for the ignition and turning it off. "I've never seen worse. Though, I hear it's close to the flood of 1927."

He didn't even try to sugarcoat the truth. What would have been the point? At least he'd spared me the gruesome details of how many were known dead or still unaccounted for. I know he knew.

"You sure you want to go out with me, Jess? We don't have to, you know. We could stay here, at the high school, where it's safe."

"According to the report, most of the high water is to the north and east of us," I told him.

"But the river line could shift," he warned me. "When it crests, we could be S-O-L."

"You've got access to a boat, don't you? You could call someone from the station if we got stranded."

"Yeah."

"Then we're covered. Let's go. I can't wait to be with you, Mal."

To put it bluntly, I wanted to strip naked and lie in his arms, and have him, if only for a while, make me forget why I was seeking solace and refuge.

I buckled my seat belt, making sure the click was audible.

"Drive," I said, pointing toward the road.

"So bossy," he commented.

Mal turned up the windshield wipers to their highest speed, and the defroster fan to clear the condensation forming on the inside.

The motel was just a ways up the road. The parking lot was crammed full. The vacancy sign, usually glowing a bright red neon, was turned off.

"Looks like the other half of Codell County is here," I murmured, as Mal navigated between the parked cars. "How'd you manage to get a room?"

"I called in a couple of favors," he said.

"What kind of favors?" I pressed. What I really wanted to know was how often Mal was here and under what circumstances. I wasn't stupid. I followed the news. And even when the motel wasn't covered in the local newspaper, the town gossip grapevine was just as efficient and often had the juicier details.

More than once, Mal and his officers had set up stakeouts and stings to stem the flow of drug traffic and prostitution that seemed to find the motel a haven. Situated right along the highway, the motel was at the perfect crossroads, with intersecting highways leading to points north and south of the border, and east and west.

"I could tell you," Mal said, easing the Jeep into a parking spot. He flipped the keys in the ignition, shutting off the engine. "But then I'd have to kill you, Jess."

"Anybody ever tell you that you're full of it, Mal Loring?" I glared at him.

"All of the time," he admitted.

"Seems to me that sooner or later, you'd get tired of hearing it and would try to do something to change that perception," I grumbled, unbuckling my seat belt.

"Weren't you the one reminding me about the 'Serenity Prayer'? Can't help it. It's the way that I am. Besides, I don't want to change." He reached and pinched my cheek. "It's my unique charm that makes you so crazy in love with me."

"Hah! That's where you've got it all wrong, law man. You're the one in love with *me!*" I corrected triumphantly, stepping out of the Jeep and slamming the door behind me.

Mal started for a flight of stairs, fishing the room card key out of his pocket. Our room was on the third floor.

"We've got just under three hours before I'm back on duty. You want to waste it harping over small details?" he asked over his shoulder.

I made a face at his back as I grasped the handrails, climbing up after him. "A little under three hours, huh?" I mocked him.

"Two hours and forty-five minutes," Mal corrected.

He didn't even sound winded as he rounded the corner and started up the last stretch of stairs. He was in perfect, peak physical condition. Then again, I already knew that. The way he'd made love to me at his house, I thought he'd never stop. That silly grin split my lips again. By the time he'd caught his second wind, I was ready to shout "uncle" and kick him out of his own bed.

Then he did that thing, that thing with his lips and tongue . . . There was no way I was going to stop him after that. By the time he'd made his way past my navel, I was completely recharged. Like the Energizer bunny, I wanted him to keep going . . . and going . . . and going . . . Until it was Mal's time to call for a brief respite.

"Two hours and forty-five minutes," I echoed. "That ought to be just enough time to make you remember just who's crazy about who, law man!"

Chapter Twenty-Four
Mal

Jess was right. I was crazy about her. Crazy for her. She'd barely cleared the threshold of the room before I pulled her inside the room, slammed the door shut, and pressed her against it.

Fumbling in the darkness, my hands found their way under her T-shirt, even as my knee nudged her thighs apart. The soft, faded gray cotton of her T-shirt contrasted with the decorative purple lace of her bra. The flimsy lace and elastic may as well not have been there at all. One quick tug was all it took. It came off in my hand like wet tissue paper.

"Well?" she whispered, her voice both taunting and tantalizing at the same time. "Who's the crazy one now?"

"I give," I muttered. "You win."

"I don't believe you." She laughed at me. "I think you're *trying* to lose!"

"With you as my consolation prize," I conceded, "you'd better believe it."

Jess's hands worked the buttons of my shirt, pulling

the shirttails out of my pants and running her palms over my chest.

"Poor baby," she crooned. "You do need consoling, don't you. Let me . . . Let me be the one."

Outside, the whole world seemed as if it could wash away. Rain continued to fall. Even three floors up, I could hear it hitting what should have been the pavement below. Instead, the parking lot was quickly turning into a small lake. It was only ankle deep when we took our room, but there was no telling what we would find once we left it again.

I pushed the thought out of my mind. Inside this room, we were away from the cares of the world. We were warm and safe and dry. Was it selfish of me, for just this short time, to stop thinking about everyone else? Was it selfish of me not to care if the whole damned state floated away? As long as Jess and me were out of harm's way, what did it matter? In less than three hours, I would be all about my duty. But for now, I was all about Jess. I needed her now more than ever.

Being ambushed on my job like that had left me shaken, even unsure of myself. Those were my friends, people that I worked with every day. If anyone understood me, I thought they would. I'd worked with these people, grown up with half of them. Why didn't they support me? I guess it didn't matter now. What was done was done. I could go back, sour my mind and my heart with their betrayal, or I could focus on the here and now.

As I held on to Jess, clinging to her as desperately as I had the day I pulled her from the water, I knew exactly what I was supposed to do, and where I was supposed to be. No doubts. No concerns.

When I slipped my hand down the front of her jeans, Jess moaned and clung to me. She was trembling.

"You cold, Jess?" I asked. The air conditioner was

blowing hard. Refrigerated air wafted from the grates lining the top of the AC unit and stirred the yellow and orange striped curtains.

"No," she admitted. "Just scared."

"You don't have to be afraid, Jess. I'm here."

"I know, Mal. I'm not scared for me."

"What? You worried about me?"

"Yeah."

"Don't be. You know I'll be all right."

"We've never faced anything like this before. I trust you to know your job . . . but this . . ."

"We've been trained for disasters, too, Jess. You don't have to worry."

"I'll try not to," she promised. "You'll have to forgive me if I slip up, every now and then, let my concern . . . my feelings for you show through."

"Of course not." I wrapped my arms around her, then lifted her up.

"Three hours?" she whispered to me.

"Two hours, thirty-eight minutes," I replied, nuzzling her neck.

"Not enough time, law man," she complained. "It's just not enough."

"I know, Jess," I commiserated. "But we'll just have to make do."

When she put her hand against my cheek, caressing me, and giving me that smile, I knew I would have given her eternity, if I could have.

I carried her over to the bed and leaned forward. Jess reached behind her and pulled the covers back as I set her down. Before I slid under the covers next to her, I tossed my wallet on the nightstand, unbuckled my pants, and dropped them to the floor beside the bed. When I settled under the covers next to her, Jess snuggled against me.

For a moment, we lay there, staring into each other's

eyes and holding on to each other. Neither one of us spoke. She didn't say so, but I knew that she was listening—listening to the sound of rain and wondering when it would all stop.

I was doing my own listening. I listened to the sound of her gentle breathing, and the rustle of the bed covers as she shifted to make herself more comfortable. I heard the hum and rattle of the air conditioner cycling on and off, and the muffled chatter of the television in the room next to us.

Over the sound of the rain, I could hear motor boats crisscrossing the town as if it were some sort of lake resort. The chopping sound of helicopter blades cut the air. Whether they were military or news helicopters, I couldn't be certain. Searchlights continuously swept the area.

I faced the window and could see a light rake across the side of the building, focusing its beam through the tiny gap in the heavy, industrial curtain panels.

"Jess," I ventured.

"Yeah?"

"I don't want you to go back out there tonight."

"Why not?" Her carefully arched eyebrows knitted together in confusion.

"I just don't want you to, that's all."

If the military was out there doing flybys over us, that meant that the flooding situation had gotten worse. And not just localized to Codell County.

Saying "because I said so" never sat well with Jess. I had to give her more than that if she was going to do what I'd asked of her.

"I got this room up here, on the third floor, for a reason, baby. Even if the river continues to rise, you'll be as safe here as you'd be at the school. Maybe safer. It'll be easier to shimmy up to the roof, if you have to, for an air rescue."

"But Mr. Gerardo needs my help, Mal. I have to go back," she insisted.

I didn't want to argue with Jess. Not now. But I didn't want her to know just how afraid for her I was. Why worry her unnecessarily?

"They have enough volunteers, Jess! They can do with one less."

"I promised the kids I would come back. A good third of my class managed to make it to the shelter, Mal. They need me there."

"And I need you to stay here!" I said it louder, with more emotion than I'd intended. My fear fed on itself, growing from a tiny knot in the pit of my stomach to a giant, flaming ball threatening to engulf me.

"Oh, for the love of . . ." I took a deep breath, reigning in my impatience and my concern. "Jess, why won't you just listen to me, for once, without arguing with me? I told you I don't want you going back out there, and I mean it."

"Mal!" She sounded shocked and, I was certain, more than a bit irritated. "That's not like you." She paused, reconsidering her words. "Well, maybe not the ordering me around part. That much I can expect from you. But I never thought I'd hear you say that I should bury my head in the sand when someone needs my help. When have you ever condoned anyone shirking their responsibility, law man?"

"I'm not asking you to shirk anything, baby. I'm only asking you to help me keep some peace of mind when I go back out there. I'll be able to focus better knowing that you're safe."

Jess sat up, put the pillow behind her back, and folded her arms across her chest.

"And you don't think I'm gonna be worried sick with you out there, knowing at any minute the river can swallow you up, or you could be buried under a ton of mud? How do I know some jerk, caught by you or one of your officers, looking for a chance to loot, won't pop a cap in you, Mal? It's not fair to ask me to sit back and do nothing while you're putting yourself at risk. You know it's not."

On some level, she was right. Her fears were just as valid as mine. When Jess and I do marry, she's gonna have to deal with a whole new set of fears . . . not just this one disaster. When we get married, she's gonna have to deal with the day-to-day stresses of being a cop's wife. Maybe I didn't work for Codell County PD anymore. But being a cop was all I knew. If I couldn't be one here, I'd look until I found my place elsewhere. Maybe she hadn't considered that yet. Or maybe she had. Maybe this was her way of dealing with the fact that any time, any day, I might walk out of that door and might not ever walk back in. That was my job. My responsibility. Not hers. She didn't have to put herself at risk.

"This town took my badge, took my job, took my self-control and my self-respect," I said, trying hard to un-clench my teeth. "You think I'm gonna let it take you, too? I'll be damned if I sit back and let that happen."

"Nothing's going to happen to me, Mal. I know that you won't let it. I have complete faith in you."

She closed her eyes, leaned forward, and rested her forehead against my chest. Then she turned her head and placed her cheek against my chest. I know that she could feel my heart beating—so wild and fierce and strong for her and yes, filled with fear. This time, I wasn't asking her because it was the right thing to do—like me asking her to leave her house because she needed to evacuate. This time, I was asking because it was the selfish thing to do. It was selfish of me to want to keep her safe.

"Just think about it," I encouraged, squeezing her

shoulder in comfort . . . and to let her know that I didn't want to argue with her anymore about it.

"We've got two hours and ten minutes, law man," she said. "Clock's ticking . . ."

"That wouldn't be your biological clock, would it?" I teased her, tried to lighten the moment that had suddenly become thick and heavy with our unspoken fears.

Any other time, a crack like that would have gotten me a good thump to the jaw with her small, but surprisingly compact and painful fist. Those Billy Blanks Tae-Bo exercise tapes that she sometimes followed—though not meant to teach defensive maneuvers—certainly had given her enough skill to connect with my face a couple of times. I didn't help myself any, either, by insisting that she take the self-defense course that I gave a couple of times a year—a class designed especially for women.

"I never did ask you, Mal," she said, her voice deceptively sweet as she sat up suddenly and straddled me across my hips. Her knees were on either side of my thighs. "How *do* you feel about kids?"

"Depends," I choked out.

The question had come out of left field. I wasn't sure how to answer her. And the weight of Jess sitting on top of me, pulsing ever so slightly against me, was another distraction.

I know Jess loved working with kids. You couldn't be a schoolteacher, stay in the field for as long as she had, and not love kids. One thing was for sure, she certainly didn't do it for the money. Her pittance of a salary barely paid for her to develop a mild sense of "like" for some of those midget monsters. The way she'd taken to Brooke's kids and the way she'd carried that baby as if it were her own, it surprised me to see Jess in a maternal role. That tiny glimpse into one's possible future had me thinking.

"Depends?" she repeated. "On what?"

Jess leaned forward and drew her fingernails lightly across my chest. I could feel gooseflesh raising on my arms and thighs.

"Depends on whose kids they are. Most knuckleheads runnin' around here these days, I wouldn't have on a bet."

"Not our kids," she insisted. "Our kids won't be bad. They'll be perfect angels."

"Ours?" My mind flashed back to Jess with those kids by the roadside. The way that she'd held onto that baby. So easily. Perfectly natural.

"Sure, law man. Yours and mine."

"Just how many kids you figure on having, Jess Ramsay?"

"Umm . . . That all depends on you." She shifted her hips dangerously close. Any closer, and there was the good possibility that within the next nine months, we'd be having this discussion with the addition of one.

I stretched out my arm, reaching for the nightstand. I should have been reaching for the Gideon's Bible stashed in the nightstand drawer. Maybe that would have given me the strength I needed to resist her tempting invitation to get started, right away, on a family. Instead, I reached for my wallet and the condoms that I'd placed there before we left my house.

"We ain't having kids until we've stood before God, the minister at the church, enough groomsmen in tacky tuxes and bridesmaids in pink chiffon, and five hundred of our closest friends and relatives to say our I do's," I promised her.

"You know I don't like pink," she retorted. But that didn't stop her from helping me unfurl the condom. A soft sigh of sheer pleasure escaped Jess's lips as she lifted slightly on her knees and repositioned herself.

I lifted my hips, meeting her with an upward thrust as she settled down to meet me. Neither of us moved. Not intentionally. But I felt Jess settle further into the mattress as she adjusted to me being inside of her. Then, as if encouraged by an unspoken cue, she began to rock her hips back and forth. Before I'd gotten into the flow and timing of her rhythm, she changed up on me and started up again with a slow, grinding, circular motion.

With my hands on her hips, I kept her motions minimal. It was an exercise in restraint. We only had a couple of hours, but I wasn't going to rush because the clock was spinning the time faster than we'd wanted.

Those tiny movements alone sent ripples through me. Ripples quickly became shock waves as the sound of her breathing, harsh and staccato, the sight of her breasts, full and swaying just out of my reach, and the feel of her thighs pressed warm and tight against mine took me to a place in my head that I probably didn't need to be— but would fight like my life depended on it to remain in.

An irrational fear crossed my mind. I imagined spilling into her, the force of my orgasm breaking through the condom and making us parents before I was ready. I know these things were supposed to be quality tested. I don't know what their method was, but I do know me. The way I was feeling now, there was no force on this planet, mechanical or otherwise, that could match the powerful emotion building inside me. Maybe the rational, responsible thing to do would have been to stop, to reign in runaway emotions before they got completely out of hand.

By the sound of Jess's voice I knew that it was way too late for that. As much as she tried to control the feelings rising inside her, she was well beyond the point of trying to exercise any self-control.

For a moment, I played the part of observer, watching the range of emotions cross her face as she went from teasing me to totally enraptured. Jess threw back her head, exposing her throat as she lifted her face to the ceiling. Her mouth was open wide as she gasped for air.

She lifted her hands, clutching her head by grabbing handfuls of her thick hair.

Moaning, writhing, jutting her hips forward in ever-increasing intensity, I don't know if she was aware that I was watching her so closely. I never stopped moving inside of her, driving her closer and closer to the edge. I had to admit, I was more turned on watching her than focusing on my pleasure.

"Nuh-no!" Jess moaned in dismay, as her back arched and tremors wracked her body.

I didn't want her to hold back. I wanted her to be in total release. Too many times as we went through the day, our lives, we had to maintain control. Don't do this. Don't say that. Never cross the boundaries of socially accepted behavior . . . not if you wanted to endure the whispers and the finger-pointing.

Here, in this room, with just the two of us, we could be as passionate and as unbound as we wanted to be.

"Let go, Jess! Don't worry, baby. I've got you. I won't let you fall!"

"Hold me, Mal!" Jess cried out, clutching me with all her strength.

"I've got you," I soothed, stroking her back, easing her, relaxing her as she fell against me. As her tremors subsided, I couldn't help but think that I didn't hear the sounds of the world all around me anymore. Especially the room next door and the television. I didn't blame them. Who wanted to listen to boring television when there was a real live lovefest going on next door?

Chapter Twenty-Five

Jess

I guess there would be many things that I'd learn about Mal as we grew closer together, and, as he so eloquently put it, after we'd stood before God and man to say our vows. One thing I learned really fast, something I never thought would be possible, was that the man was a hard sleeper. Not just hard, but loud.

When his head finally had hit the pillow, he'd opened his mouth and let out a rumble that made me think the walls were crumbling down. There went my ill-conceived notion that cops were supposed to be light sleepers. You know, jump up out of bed instantly alert, ready to serve and protect at a moment's notice.

Poor baby. I reached up, stroked his forehead, wiping away a thin film of perspiration that had collected on his face despite the cranked up air conditioner. He must have been absolutely exhausted. The time had passed when he was supposed to be out there, patrolling the town, looking for stranded citizens. We'd overslept. Even though he was snoring loud enough to keep me from my rest, I wasn't going to wake him. Not even to make him roll over.

Once we finally shared a home, and a bed, I'd buy him a crate full of those Breathe-Right strips—the kind you stick over your nose. They say it's supposed to help. Too bad I didn't have any with me now. Even cramming a pillow over my head didn't seem to help. Let's face it. During his waking hours, the man was swift, silent, deadly. I guess he made up for all that stealth in his sleep.

No matter. I really wasn't sleepy anymore. I'd gotten some rest. Actually, right after Mal had me screeching and reaching for the rafters, I fell into what could only be classified as a light coma. I collapsed on top of him, trembling and sucking in air as deeply as my lungs could hold.

I'd clung to him, feeling ashamed of myself. I'd practically attacked him, using him like a drug to make me forget my fears. As he stroked me, whispering into my hair, I don't think he minded.

Mal snorted through his nose, rolled over and draped his arm over my waist. As he did so, he murmured something in his sleep. I listened closely.

Jess.

I heard my name. He'd called out my name, then smiled the most angelic smile. Even as he was smiling, he was stirring. His dreams, whatever they were, were powerful enough to reach out to the waking world and touch me.

With his arm across my stomach, I was able to feel the deep rumbling within. How long had it been since I'd eaten? That sandwich and coffee with Mal before we left the school had long since been burned away. I grinned in the darkness. Yes, sir. Forget the Atkins or South Beach diets. I'd found a better way to melt off the pounds. It was called the Mal. A steady diet of him would have me slimmed down to nothing in less than no time.

Unless, of course, one of these days we have an accident with the condom. We were trying to be careful. Sometimes, we were just too vigorous. Unless we tone it down, something's bound to happen . . . it'll take about nine months to develop. And that would not be acceptable.

"You'd better hurry up and get me to chapel, law man," I whispered. I wasn't going to curb my enthusiasm for him. And heaven forbid if he should suddenly go all saintly and celibate on me. After finally winning him, I couldn't see letting him go cold turkey.

Cold turkey. My stomach rumbled again at the thought of food. I *was* hungry.

I started to reach for Mal and wake him, then thought better of it. I remembered seeing a convenience store across the highway. Carefully, I eased out of bed, making sure not to disturb Mal. Tiptoeing to the window, I pulled the curtains back a crack and peered across the street. There weren't any cars moving up and down the highway. Roadblocks, newscasts warning motorists and the threat of more rain kept even the most foolhardy off the roads.

I saw a couple dash across the street, even at three in the morning, heading toward the hotel, carrying a plastic bag. The store must still be open. Glancing behind me, I spied Mal's keys and wallet on the nightstand. Mal was still asleep. I'd only planned to be gone a few minutes. No need to wake him up. So, I pulled on my jeans, T-shirt, and my shoes, kissed my man on the cheek, and whispered, "Be right back, law man. Sleep tight."

He barely stirred, mumbled something, then reached up to crumple his pillow under his head.

My hero! Ready to leap up at a moment's notice. Maybe by the time I got back, I'd have something to fortify him before he went back on duty. As I reached for Mal's keys, they barely made a jingle as I stuffed them into my pocket. Then I reached for Mal's wallet.

Faster than a rattlesnake strike, Mal's hand shot out and grabbed my wrist. Not hard. Just enough to make me shout. Then instinct took over and I broke free of his grip in a maneuver that he'd taught me in self-defense class.

Mal sat up grinning at me. I noticed that he started to rub his own wrist. I don't think he expected me to remember so much of what he'd taught me.

"You! How long have you been awake?"

"Long enough," he replied. His eyes swept over me, noting that I was fully dressed. "Where do you think you're goin', Jess?"

I tilted my head toward the door. "Across the street to that convenience store. I don't know about you, Mal, but I'm starving."

"And obviously broke, if you've resorted to pilfering."

"I wasn't pilfering!" I made sure to sound injured and indignant, turning up my nose. "I was borrowing."

"You could have asked."

Sitting on the edge of the bed, I briefly touched his cheek. "I didn't want to wake you up. I thought I'd just pop across the street, grab some energy food, and be right back."

Mal kissed me on my forehead. "You're sweet. But I know you and your idea of energy food. You'll come back with an armload of chocolate-covered donuts, some beef and bean burritos that have seen their better days, and a liter of Coke."

"Sprite," I corrected.

"Yeah. That's what I thought." Mal tossed back the covers, then shooed me away. "I'd better go with you."

"You don't have to! The whole point of me going is for you to get your rest."

"I'll rest easier knowing that you won't be bringing me back a sack of overpriced ptomaine poisoning."

Mal leaned over and scooped up his underwear and

pants from the floor. Umm-umm-umm . . . That man had the cutest, tightest butt. Made me want to reach out, right then and there, and give it a pinch. I shifted my legs, sitting on my hands to stop the impulse. We'd stand a better chance of making it out of the hotel room if I didn't concentrate on the tightness of Mal's rear.

Mal stuck his long arms into the sleeves of his shirt and buttoned up quickly.

"The keys," he said, holding his hand out to me.

"Fine," I grumbled, pulling a long face. But I couldn't be mad at him. I don't know who he was trying to fool with that food-poisoning excuse. Truth was, he'd probably miss me when I was gone. Even though I'd only be gone for a few minutes. I couldn't help grinning. Guess I'd proven my point. He was *sooo* crazy in love with me.

"Get the lead out, Jess," Mal said. He was already at the door, holding it open for me while I sat on the bed.

"Looks like the rain could be slacking off," I commented, turning my face to the sky. It was still pitch black. Toward the eastern sky, I thought I saw a break in the clouds. A few pinpoints of light dotted the sky.

"Maybe," Mal said, though not very convincingly.

"It had better. I'm starting to grow mold with all of this dampness in the air."

I started down the stairs, Mal trailing behind me. When he held the Jeep door open for me, he let out a huge yawn, but tried to cover it by turning his head.

"Are you gonna be all right, law man?" I asked.

"Of course I am. What makes you ask?"

"Maybe it was something in the way you yawned so wide, I heard your jaw pop."

"I'll be fine."

"You don't have to go out, you know." I wanted to bite my tongue even as I made the suggestion.

"Yes, I do," he returned, scowling at me. "You know that I do."

"Yeah, I know," I said. "You're Robocop without an off switch."

"Kinda like your mouth," he retorted.

"You weren't complaining about my mouth when I—"

Mal cranked up the engine, drowning out the rest of my comment. But he flashed me a guilty-as-charged look before putting his hand on the gear shift and slipping the Jeep into reverse. Putting one hand on the headrest behind me, Mal took the opportunity to caress and massage my neck before he looked back over his shoulder, backed the Jeep out of the parking spot, and headed for the motel exit.

Normally, I didn't make it a habit of shopping at convenience stores. Mal called them local stop-n-robs, for all the obvious reasons. If they weren't being held up by some idiot with a gun, the owners were jacking up their prices so high, you had to wonder if there was more "con" in the convenience part than was necessary.

"I wonder if they have any chocolate-covered donuts?" I said aloud, as I climbed out.

"Sometimes, I wonder how you've managed to keep yourself alive this long eating like you do, Jess."

"What?" I sounded surprised. "You think my system can handle an oat bran muffin this early in the morning? Eating that healthy would throw my system into shock."

"What's really going to throw your system into shock is when you start tipping the scales at two hundred pounds."

"More of me to love," I quipped.

"I'm serious, Jess. You need to start eating better."

One thing I didn't need was for Mal to tell me what I needed. I knew I needed to do better. And, as soon as things got back to normal, I would try to eat more balanced meals. Now, I'm not delusional enough to say that I was going to try the *D* word. I'd tried diets before and they never really worked for me. Diet was something you adopted, a change in lifestyle. It wasn't something you "did" for a few months. For me, diet had the same number of letters as fail.

"If it makes you feel any better, Mal, I'll only get the baked, not fried, potato chips."

"Oh yeah. That gives me the warm, fuzzy feeling right here." He thumped his fist against his chest. "Or is it here?" The hand dropped to his stomach.

Smiling sweetly at him, I pushed open the door, noting the electronic chime announcing our entry to the store.

The clerk behind the bulletproof glass encasing the register barely looked up from the nudie magazine he was reading to acknowledge us. He couldn't have been more than eighteen or nineteen years old. I could practically see the acne medication on his red mottled face. His hair, a stringy, greasy color somewhere between moldy wheat and mud, was tied in a ponytail. His bright blue and yellow store uniform shirt was wrinkled and stained, as if he'd slept in it. His name tag, reading "Todd," was pinned on upside down.

"Good morning," I sang out cheerfully.

He looked up, his eyes red and bleary.

"Got any breakfast food?" I asked.

"Aisle four." He gestured with a hand decked out in multiple silver rings. "Pop tarts and beef jerky."

"Umm . . . yummy," Mal muttered under his breath. He turned to the kid behind the counter. "How about cereal, eggs, milk?"

"Cleaned out yesterday," the kid replied, flipping another page of his magazine. "The manager said we should get a shipment in tomorrow, if they can get a truck through." He shrugged. "But I wouldn't hold your breath. We got frappuccino."

"Here. Make yourself useful." I picked up a small basket and slipped the handles over Mal's arm.

"Just how much stuff you plan on getting?" he asked, alarmed.

"When we run out of cash, we pull out your credit card."

"What's this 'we' business?" he complained.

"I'm broke, as you so insensitively reminded me, law man."

The first thing I reached for was a package of chocolate-covered donuts. I followed that with a couple of Dolly Madison fruit pies. *Tsking* in shame, Mal put them back and instead tossed in an apple from a barrel near the register.

"What?" I protested. "This is breakfast food. It's fruit!"

"I like my fiber uncomplicated," he remarked as he moved over to the coffee machine and pulled out a couple of supersize cups.

"Then why bother with coffee?!" I called out to him. "Why not just grind the whole beans between your teeth and wash them down with a swig from the river?"

The look he gave me was none too pleasant. Another thing I would have to note about Mal. He didn't wake up in the best of moods. Then again, on most days, neither did I. But wasn't it going to be fun waking up mean and grouchy together for the rest of our lives?

"Lots of cream and sugar," I reminded him as I moved down the aisle that Todd indicated.

I could hear the coffee machine stir to life as Mal pressed the button. The smell of reasonably fresh-brewed coffee wafted through the store, tickling my nose.

I went up and down the aisle, picking up items I knew that I'd want and calling out to Mal to ask him his preferences. "Hey, Mal, what about this?" I held up a box of crunchy, cinnamon-flavored granola bars.

"Yeah, sure." He didn't sound too enthusiastic, but under the circumstances, it was the best that I could do. When I joined him at the coffee machine, Mal started to rummage through my convenience-store finds.

"Put it back, put it back, put it back," he said to over half of my would-be purchases.

"Nuh-uh. You go and put it back," I shot back. "You've had your shot of coffee. It's my turn."

I put the items into the basket that he'd set on the counter and shoved it back into his arms.

"Let me show you how a real shopper shops," Mal bragged, starting back down the aisle. I blew my lips at him, sounding dangerously close to the horse from that sixties comedy show *Mr. Ed.*

While Mal went browsing, I doused my coffee with another eye-popping dose of cream and sugar. Blowing on the top to cool it, I leaned back against the counter and watched my man go shopping. It was kinda funny, kinda cute watching him picking up items, comparing prices, reviewing ingredients. For as long as I've known Mal, I don't think I've ever seen him in this light.

Shopping together never came to my mind as one of those things that would make me fall deeply in love with him. I mean, roaming around a convenience store at three in the morning wasn't exactly a romantic venue. But it wasn't the location that mattered. It was just being with him. That's when I knew that beyond a shadow of a doubt that this was it . . . This was true love. This was the man for me.

Was I sending out some kind of love vibe? Could he read my thoughts? Could he feel the love pouring out of my heart to him? I don't know. Mal stopped what he was doing and looked up at me. He didn't say anything. He

just looked at me. Then he smiled and turned down the
far end of the aisle, heading toward the refrigerated
cases where the dairy products should have been. There
were a few, pint-sized cartons of milk left. He had to dig
for those, way in the back of the cooler.

"You sure you don't have anything else in the back?"
Mal called out to the clerk.

"Nope," Todd answered.

"Have you even looked?"

"Dude, I told you that we've been cleaned out. What
we got is what we got. You don't believe me, you can
check back there yourself."

This early in the morning, Todd wasn't coming out
from behind the bulletproof cage. He was locked inside.
Nothing short of a fire would bring him out again. I
didn't blame him. It was a rather creepy time of night to
be shopping.

"Don't give him an excuse," I cautioned Todd. "He'll
do it if he thinks you're holding out on him."

Todd simply shrugged his shoulders, then lowered his
head. At three in the morning, I don't think Todd cared
if Mal helped himself to the cash register, let alone a carton of milk.

Mal started for the door that was clearly marked
EMPLOYEES ONLY.

"Mal, what do you think you're doing?" I called out
to him.

"Back in a minute," he said over his shoulder, and continued to the back of the store.

"You can't go back there, Mal . . . Isn't that breaking
and entering or something? If you're gonna go ransack-
ing the man's store, don't you need a search warrant?"

"I don't need a warrant. Probable cause," he retorted.

"Hey, what are you two . . . some kinda cops or something?" Todd wanted to know.

"Why?" I challenged, raising my eyebrows at him. "You got something to hide?"

"What? You mean like a hidden stash of . . . rib-eye steaks? Sure, lady. I'm only working in this dump until my black market supplier can take the load off my hands and make me filthy rich."

"You're funny, Todd," I said, opening up my package of chocolate-covered donuts and popping one into my mouth. "You ought to take that act on the road."

"Anything's better than this place," he grumbled. "You gonna pay for those?" Todd prompted as I went through three of the six donuts in less than a minute."

"Nope. My boyfriend will," I mumbled, licking melted chocolate from my fingertips. Not very ladylike, I know. But I was hungry. And I wasn't going to let a good dose of chocolate go to waste.

"Your boyfriend?" The corners of Todd's mouth quirked up.

"Yeah, my boyfriend." That Todd was starting to irritate me. Why was it so funny to him that I had a boyfriend?

"You ought to take your own act on the road, lady."

"I don't get it."

"You expect your boyfriend, the cop, to pay for donuts. Now that's funny!"

"Mal!" I called out, glaring at Todd. It was time to go. "Come on now. Let's just get what we can and go."

When he didn't answer me, I thought I'd give him a gentle prod. I walked over to the door, pushing on the door to make sure that he heard the chime. "I'm leaving, Mal!"

No answer from him.

"Mal!"

Chapter Twenty-Six

Mal

I'd heard Jess call my name the first time. I didn't mean to ignore her. But I'd seen a pallet of cardboard boxes in the back of the store. If I could trust that what was on the labels was actually in the box, the contents looked more nutritious and fulfilling than the empty calories that Jess was loading up on. It's not that I'm a health nut. I just found that the older I got, the harder it was to keep off the extra pounds. I'd rather do what I can now than spend extra time I didn't have at the gym trying to work it off.

And then the store entry door chimed. Was she leaving?

"I know you are *not* trying to rush me," I muttered, digging into the crate to grab a couple of boxes of whole wheat crackers and a tin of tuna packed in spring water.

Where was she going to go? I had the keys. She wasn't going anywhere. Then, I remembered how Jess had climbed out of the Jeep and threatened to walk all the way to the levee when I said I wouldn't take her. Sometimes, I wondered if Jess enjoyed being stubborn just to see if she can make me cave in. Well, I wasn't giving in. Not this time. She'd thank me for my good dietary sense the next time she complained about gaining five extra pounds from all of that junk food she was eating.

I would have kept on foraging in the back storeroom if it weren't for Jess's tone the last time she called out to me. She wasn't needling anymore. Or impatient. Or even annoyed. The last time she called out to me, her voice was shrill.

Something went cold in me at the sound of her voice. Whirling around, I dropped the crackers and tuna, sprinted out of the storeroom and ran right smack dab into the most stupid rookie mistake a man my age could make. It was a good thing I was as old as I was. Otherwise my mistake could have been fatal.

It didn't take me long to snap to what was going on. Sizing up a situation in a split second was one of my specialties—honed by an instinct for self-preservation. Without thinking, I was diving for the floor, even as I saw Todd behind the counter, quickly shoving in cash as fast as his ringed hands could move at the urging of an armed assailant. Jess was kneeling close to the door with her hands interlaced on top of her head, and another, possibly the lookout, turned to fire in my direction.

Two shots. *Pop! Pop!*

Exploding bags of potato chips and plastic liters of soda rained over my head as I scrambled out of the way. I heard Jess scream again, warning me.

"Mal, watch out!"

Hunkering down behind shelves, I looked up and caught Jess's reflection in the security mirror hanging near the front corner of the store. She was breathing hard, trying to keep calm. Her shoulders lifted up and down with each breath.

"Shut up! I said shut your mouth!" The lookout aimed the gun at her. The look she flashed him, cold and defiant, made me want to call out my own warning. She didn't even flinch.

Please, Jess. I prayed. *For once, keep your mouth shut. Don't tick off the man with the gun.*

My mind was racing with a thousand possibilities of how I could handle this situation. I was kicking myself at that moment because my own gun was probably still sitting on the table back at the station. My gun and my badge. I couldn't even properly identify myself as a police officer to these bozos. Not that I expected simply announcing who and what I was would make them drop their guns and give up. But at least it would take their attention off of Jess. I guess I'll have to teach them a lesson vigilante-style. I can just imagine the hell I'm gonna catch from Sandra Reed if I tried to take them on my own.

"Did you get 'im?" one of them called out.

"I d-dunno." The lookout sounded confused. "I think s-s-so."

"Well, what are you waiting for, stupid? Go and check. And if he ain't, you put one right in his head and make sure."

I heard Jess choke back a cry. Her voice was raw as she said, "I'm betting that you're not as dumb as you look, boy. Do yourself a favor and just take the money and go."

Aw, Jess! What are you doing?

I didn't want her to help me. I wanted her to keep her mouth shut. I could handle this myself. It wasn't ego that had me irritated with Jess. It was concern. What was she doing drawing so much attention to herself?

Keeping my eye on the mirror, I could see the lookout, moving indecisively toward my location. Could he see me? The security-monitor screen mounted overhead so that the cashier could see at all times was divided into four sections. At any given moment, my location could pop up on the screen. For a moment, I lay low, then inched away from where I'd originally dove, trying not to give myself away by crunching on the chips or slipping on the vanilla-flavored Coke bubbling on the floor.

Risking a glance up, I saw the lookout in the next aisle over. In a moment, he'd round the corner and find me. I did what any self-respecting, self-preserving soul would do. For all intents and purposes, I was dead. I didn't move. Didn't blink. Didn't twitch an eyelash. I didn't close my eyes, though. But left them wide open and staring blankly.

"Well?" the one closest to the register called out.

"What?"

"Well, did you get him?"

"Y-y-yeah."

The lookout couldn't have been standing more than six feet away from me. Either he was blind as a bat or he didn't want anything to do with any killing. Whatever the reason, he didn't come closer to investigate. If he'd had any sense, he would have noticed that, for a gunshot victim, there wasn't any blood.

Was it true what they said? That God watched out for fools and children? The lookout had the blessing of divine intervention with him on that day. Because if he'd come any closer to check on me, I had to try to disarm him . . . any way I could. No guarantees that I would take his obvious youth into consideration. If he was old enough to carry a gun, he was old enough to be aware that some way, some how, somebody was gonna have to try to take it away from him.

Another footstep moving closer to me. Heavy breathing. Labored, strained. Then another footstep, sounding unsteady. I tensed, getting ready.

Come on, boy. Don't be stupid.

One more footstep, then the unmistakable sound of retching. The kid dropped to all fours. I heard his palms smack the linoleum floor as he groaned and heaved. No, the boy didn't have a taste for killing. It wasn't in him. The thought of it made him sick. He was a petty thief, not a murderer.

As he stood up, stumbling toward the front of the store, he called out, "C-c-come on, D-Denny! Let's get out-out-out of here."

He was scared to death. Could barely get the words out of his mouth through his stutter.

"Freakin' idiot! I don't believe this," the one still holding Jess at bay at the register shouted. "I told you to keep your fat mouth shut, Darryl!"

Items crashing to the floor. Agitated steps grew louder, then softer. Louder again. Denny was pacing. If I were Denny, it would be a toss-up of who I wanted to shoot more, me or his partner, Darryl. He was probably thinking what I was thinking. Now, along with their images on security tapes, there were names to go on. Denny and Darryl. They were as good as caught.

What a couple of morons. I couldn't wait to submit the tape to that *World's Stupidest Crooks* show.

Several more shots rang out in rapid succession. Not a revolver like the one that had fired at me, but a semiautomatic. Not in my direction. Directly overhead. I heard the sound of exploding electronics . . . the acrid smell of burning circuits. The air filled briefly with wisps of blue-gray smoke. Denny, bless his muddled, trying-to-make-a-plan brain, was taking out the security cameras and monitors. Too bad. I was looking forward to seeing their dumb faces exposed to all of America for their ill-timed, ill-conceived stickup.

With Denny taking out the cameras, that evened the odds. I couldn't use the tape. Then again, they couldn't see me on the monitors, either. There weren't very many mirrors set up through the store, replaced by a security camera system.

"Come on, come on! Fill up that freakin' bag, man! Move it," Denny urged.

Risking being caught, I lifted my head and tried to catch them in the security mirror as Denny waved his piece in front of the bulletproof glass at Todd.

Todd shoved the bag through the money slot. "Here, dude. Just take the money and book outta here, all right?"

"What the hell is this!" Denny suddenly snapped. I heard the plastic sack rustling as if he were going through it. "This all there is?"

"That's all we got, dude. I swear . . . It's been kinda dead around here with the flood washing away everything in sight," Todd pleaded.

"You're gonna be dead . . . real dead . . . if you don't get up some more cash, dude!" Denny snapped.

I debated what, if anything, I could do. My guess is that Todd had already made the money drop for the hour. Anything larger than a twenty dollar bill would have been counted, stuffed into a plastic sleeve, and dropped into a cash collector. He couldn't get at it, even if his life depended on it . . . which, by the frustrated sound of Denny's voice, it did.

"I told you, that's all. Don't believe me, ask the chick . . . or her boyfriend. Yeah, that's it . . . go ask the cop. He'll tell you!"

Hearing Todd's frantic rambling, I changed my mind. Denny and his sidekick Darryl weren't the morons. Todd was. What advantage did he think he'd gained by telling them I was a cop? If I could have done anything, didn't he think I would have done it by now? Or maybe he blurted it out because he was trying to scare them off. I doubted these two would be impressed by the flashing of my badge . . . even if I still had it.

"You mean the one you just shot?" Jess spoke quickly. "Yeah, that's a real smart idea, Denny. Hang around here and ask bonehead questions, waiting for other cops to show up, when you could have just been satisfied with your haul and gotten out of here!"

Jess! Stop drawing attention to yourself, I wanted to yell at her. I didn't like playing possum. Every bone in my body said jump up and take them on, badge or no badge. Weapon or no badge. But this wasn't the movies, and I wasn't Robocop. I didn't have superpowers. I couldn't stop time or turn myself invisible. Hell, I didn't even have a Kevlar vest. All I had was my training and my wits . . . though I'd never know it by the way my mind was racing.

What did I know? There were two of them, and they were both armed. Denny was the so-called brains of the team. He gave the orders. Darryl was the lookout. As soon as they were out the door, if Todd hadn't already tripped the alarm, I'd put in the call to the station, sending somebody right out here. All Jess had to do was be cool and everybody would stay safe.

"Denny, man, he was a c-cop. Man, I sh-shot a freakin' c-c-c-cop!"

Darryl wasn't sounding confused anymore. He was scared. Good. That's the way I wanted him. I wanted him scared and on the run.

"I'm n-not hanging around here. They're g-gonna be all over us."

Okay, Denny's sidekick just rose a notch in my estimation. Maybe he wasn't completely brain dead. And I was beginning to think the stutter was a true speech impediment by the impatient way Darryl responded.

"There's only about a hundred in here, man!" Denny

snapped. "How far you think that's gonna get us?" He turned back to Todd, placing the muzzle of the gun against the bulletproof glass point blank. That is, I reckoned it was bulletproof. Was Todd willing to gamble that it was? I doubted it.

"You're holding out on us," Denny declared. "You got fifteen seconds to give it up. Or I start firing."

"Look at him," Jess said. "You think he's ready to die for this dump? There *is* no more."

She spoke slowly, distinctly. Kinda like the voice she used when she was talking to her classroom.

Jess, I swear, if you get out of this without a getting a bullet, I'm gonna kill you myself for taking chances with a couple of hotheads like those two.

"Maybe I don't stop at just drilling glass?" Denny suggested. His expression in the mirror was distorted as he leered down at Jess. He swung the gun toward her, easing the muzzle down her cheek and pushing it into the soft hollow of her throat.

"C-c-come on, luh-leave her alone, Denny. Let's just guh-guh-go."

Good boy, Darryl. I just might spare you when I get my hands on you. My fingers curled and clenched into tight fists. If he touched her again, I couldn't guarantee that I'd be playin' possum for much longer. Everyone's attention was on Jess and Denny.

"Wha-we have t-to go," Darryl insisted.

"A hundred dollars," Denny said again. "Might be worth it."

"Worth what?" Darryl asked, then called out in exasperation. "I ain't st-staying around here, whu-whu-whu-waiting to be scooped up, while you get your *rrrr*-rocks off."

"Porno boy ain't goin' nowhere," Denny said, indicating Todd. "The cop won't be talking. All you gotta do is watch the door. Five minutes."

He grabbed Jess by the chin, tilting her face up to him.

"Don't you touch me!" she snapped, jerking her head away.

"Five minutes," he said. He cast his eyes back toward the store room. "I hear they say that once you go black, you never go back."

"Touch me and you'll never . . . ever . . . again. I promise you," Jess said through clenched teeth.

One part of me wanted to strangle Jess. She couldn't keep her mouth shut, not even to save her life. The other part of me wanted to salute her. If he took her down, he wouldn't do so without a fight.

Later, when we got out of all of this, I'd have to sit her down and have a nice long talk with her about life-or-death situations and how to make sure she got out of them with her life intact. This was no joke. Denny was a dangerous man.

"No, D-Denny. I'm-muh-muh leaving. Now!" Darryl started toward the door. Denny stuffed the money bag in his shirt, then started after him.

"Yeah, right. I'm coming."

I heard the door chime again and sent up a small prayer of relief. Relief for me and relief for them. Smart boys. That move just saved their lives. They were on their way out the door when I started to rise. I'd barely straightened when the door chimed again.

"No! No! Let me go! Take your hands off of me! Are you crazy!"

I stood up and started for the door. Too late. Much too late. I saw the look of disbelief on Jess's face as Denny grabbed her by her hair and arm and dragged her out the door.

"No! Jess!" I shouted, running now full speed toward her.

"Mal!" she croaked. Denny's arm had shifted, crooked around her throat.

Denny looked up at me, surprised to see me. "So, the dead has arisen!"

He raised his gun hand, pointing at me. But Jess's struggles had him off balance. His shots went wild, taking out the kiosk of prepaid phone cards to the left of me. He didn't bother with trying for another shot, but instead dragged Jess outside.

As I passed the cash register, I shouted at Todd. "Call 9-1-1!"

All I could think about was the look on Jess's face as Denny hauled her out of the door. Her relief at seeing that I was okay was outweighed by her fear and pain as he nearly choked the life from her. As I knew she would, she didn't go with him without a fight. The scuffs of her heels against the tile floor were evidence of that.

Her eyes locked with mine, sending me a message that I had no trouble understanding.

Do your job. No matter what.

Chapter Twenty-Seven

Jess

Mal was a poster child for the police force. If I believed in reincarnation, I'd venture a guess that he'd been a cop in a previous life, too. It was what he did. It was who he was. That's why I knew beyond a shadow of a doubt that he would be all right.

Okay, maybe I had a smidgen of concern when that idiot Darryl recklessly fired at him in the store. Lucky for him he was a lousy shot. From where I was kneeling, I could see how badly his hand shook when he'd taken aim. He'd also jerked the trigger back, instead of a steady squeeze, as Mal had taught me in a gun-safety class. Not that I'd ever wanted to carry one of those things, but Mal had insisted that there was more danger in ignorance. To help me get over my fear of the weapon he carried, he taught me how to fire, clean, and lock it away. That's how I knew how inexperienced Darryl was with his snub-nosed thirty-two.

When he'd gone back there to finish the job, I admit that I was nervous. I didn't believe for one second that Mal could be dead. Not even when the kid came back

and told us that he'd done it. I couldn't believe it. I
wouldn't believe it.

This was Chief Malcolm Loring they were talking
about. I'd known Mal almost all my life. I knew what he
was capable of. And dying like that just wasn't one of
those things. Mal was Mal. No snot-nosed kid with an
itchy trigger finger was gonna take him down. If he
could, I'd have to stop believing that there was justice in
the world. I wasn't ready to do that. Not as long as men
like Mal walked the earth.

As much as I sometimes teased Mal about being a cop
and hated the fact that he'd always let his job come between us, I always expected him to do his job. No matter
what. Right now, his job was to get me the hell of out this
mess that I'd somehow found myself in.

"Move, bitch!" Denny twisted my arm behind me, shoving me outside. He had to make it rough, because I wasn't
making it easy for him to take me along with him. There
were so many statistics out there . . . the kind that read that
once a victim gets in the car, they were as good as dead. I
wasn't ready to be a victim or a statistic. Not when I was so
close to becoming a wife. I wasn't going to let this jerk
cheat me out of seeing the look of joy on my mama's face
when Mal and me finally walked down the aisle.

We passed Mal's Jeep. My mind started racing. Where
was his spare set of keys? Did he keep a spare set? Could
I get inside, start the engine up, and pull away before
Denny could stop me? I had to try.

When I lunged for the door handle, Denny reached
up, grabbed a handful of my hair, and yanked back.
I cried out, tears stinging my eyes. I swear, if he pulled
out a plug of my hair, I was gonna make him pay for that.
I'm not vain about my hair. But I don't want some idiot
tugging on it whenever he has a mind to. Mal is the only

man I'd let grab handfuls of my hair. And I'd better be grabbing a handful of him, in return.

"Don't even think about it!" Denny snapped. He pushed me aside then leaned close to the windshield, reading the Codell County Police Department parking decal on the windshield.

"Stinkin' pig," he muttered and took aim at Mal's Jeep. One shot to the tire. One shot to the radio.

"You didn't have to do that!"

"Yeah, right. Big Piggy doesn't seem like the type to cut us any slack. I don't want him following us."

"Mal will follow us on his hands and knees if he has to. All you did was tick him off, Denny boy." Was I boasting? Did Denny buy it?

Denny pushed, tugged, cursed and pulled while I did everything I could to delay him. Dragged my heels in the mud, clung to him, used every part of my body to stop him from pushing me inside the truck. I just knew that once I was inside, I was as good as dead.

"Hey!" I complained as my head thumped against the roof. "Cut it out."

"Shut up!" Denny raised his hand as if he were going to slap me.

"You shut up, you crazy son of—" I shot back, risking the blow.

I know . . . I know . . . It was a stupid thing to do. I should have gotten in quietly, meekly, and done what they'd asked. But I was gambling that Denny wouldn't shoot me. All I could think was that any moment that I could eat up was time that I'd given Mal. He'd already lost precious seconds when Denny had turned to fire at the store, driving Mal back inside.

"Grab her legs!" Denny panted. He was pushing me from behind while I braced my feet against the frame of the truck. It was no easy trick. The rain was coming down hard, making it hard to see, hard to get a good grip on the truck's frame.

"Whu-what do we nuh-need her f-f-for?" Darryl demanded, reaching for my ankles. I kicked at him, connecting soundly with the heel of my boot. He yelled, grabbing at his face. "My nuh-nuh-nose! Sh-she broke muh-muh-my nose." His voice was muffled as he tried to staunch the flow of blood.

"Let go of me! Take your hands off of me. I'm not going anywhere with you!"

This time, Denny twisted my arm in earnest, making me cry out in pain. I thought I heard something snap, and a spike of fire run down from my shoulder to my wrist. *God, that hurt!*

When he pulled his gun from the waistband of his pants where he'd jammed into his belt, he got my full attention. He pulled it out and pressed the muzzle against my temple. It was still warm from his shooting at Mal.

"You settle yourself down or so help me, I'll rip it off. You got that!"

Nodding mutely, I slid into the truck, sandwiched between the two of them. The truck's bench seat had seen better days. Cracked, dark blue vinyl was taped with silver duct tape. Several springs still poked through cotton stuffing that looked aged and yellow and smelled as if some animal had marked it as its territory with its urine. I gagged, as much from the smell as from the throbbing pain in my arm.

Denny climbed behind the wheel and cranked up the engine. Body rusted through and through or not, the truck's engine sounded strong and tight. What did they have in this thing? A rocket engine?

When they'd pulled me into it, I'd tried to memorize as many details as I could. Early model truck. 1972, maybe. Or '73 body style painted with gray primer.

Louisiana plates. These were out of town boys, come across the state border looking for a quick score. From the looks of the busted steering column and the wires dangling from it, this wasn't necessarily their vehicle. Probably boosted for the sole purpose of making this run into Mississippi.

Boy, were these two in for a surprise. There was nowhere in Louisiana where these two could hide. Mal would track them across the state border, across the planet to get them. And he'd do it even if I wasn't involved. He would do it because they'd come into Codell County to start some mess. What were they thinking?

Being this close and personal to them, small details were becoming apparent to me. These two were young. Really young. The older one, Denny, couldn't have been more than eighteen or nineteen. And the other one, Darryl, bore a striking resemblance to Denny. Similar hair color and facial features. Ash blond hair, high, angular cheekbones, narrow chin. Denny's eyes were brown. Darryl's were blue. Both had hooked noses. Correction, Denny's was hooked. Thanks to me, Darryl's was now broken.

"L-l-l-l-look what she duh-did, Denny," Darryl whined, his breath making a whistling sound as it came through his nose. He held his sleeve up to his nose, grimacing in pain. "She's tr-trouble. Duh-duh-dump her. Luh-luh-let her go!"

The way he looked to Denny for direction, I wondered if there wasn't some hero worship involved.

"Yeah, Denny," I said. "Why don't you be smart and let me go."

"No way, lady. You're my insurance policy. My get-out-of-jail-free card." Denny explained. "Cops won't get too close to us as long as we got her. All we need is some breathing room. Just enough time to lose them on some back road."

Cradling my broken my arm against my waist, I glared at Denny. "That's what you think."

"It's what I know. As soon as we put some distance between us and the cop, if you act right, we'll let you go."

I didn't believe that. They'd let me go all right. Dump my body out without bothering to slow down. Use me as a speed bump, if they had to. I shook my head, forcing out a laugh. "That's the problem, boys. You don't understand what you're up against. Malcolm Loring won't let you get too far. He's coming down on you. There's no where you can run to, no where you can hide that he won't eventually track you down."

"He's just one man," Denny said in derision. "What's he gonna do?"

"You'll find out," I said with the kind of confidence and finality that was starting to work on the younger one.

Darryl's hand gripped the steering wheel so tightly that his knuckles whitened. "W-w-we could luh-luh-let her go," he suggested.

His foot eased off the gas, slowing the truck down. I couldn't tell by how much. The speedometer needle was broken. Even though it seemed as if we were going at least eighty miles per hour by the way trees and street poles flew by at a blur, the orange needle struggled to register above twenty miles per hour. My eyes cut to the fuel tank register. Could I trust the full-tank reading? Had these two stopped to fill up before taking the store? With a full tank of gas and these two hyped up on adrenaline, this could make for a very long ride.

"Come on, Denny. Listen to him," I said, jerking my thumb back toward Darryl. "Let me go."

"Not yet," Denny snapped. "You just keep your eyes on

the road, Darryl. Keep driving. Do what I tell you and everything will be all right."

"She's nuh-not wor-worth it fuh-fuh-for only a hundred d-dollars, bro."

Were they related? Was Darryl Denny's younger brother? If they were related, maybe I could play on Denny's sense of responsibility for his younger sibling. That is, if he had any sense. I had my doubts. What kind of brother could he be, putting a gun in his hand and encouraging him to kill?

"You'd better listen to him, bro," I instigated. "Only a hundred dollars and for what? You're already facing armed robbery, attempted murder, aggravated assault, and kidnapping charges for starters. If anything happens to me, they'll slap a manslaughter charge on you, too. We're talking serious time. Felony charges. Are you ready for that?"

Denny was starting to consider the consequences. Despite his warning for me to keep my mouth shut, my words were getting to him. I knew they were. He chewed on his lip, tapping his heel against the filthy, crushed-beer-can-littered floor mat. His entire leg shook with nervous energy.

"Duh-Denny?" Darryl prompted. "What should wuh-we do?"

"Shut up, Darryl. I'm thinking. You keep driving. And hurry it up! Dude, you drive like a freakin' old man."

Darryl stepped on the gas, surging forward. Over the rough road, every rut, every bump sent me bouncing up and down. The exposed springs gouged into my back, cut into my legs. I moaned, trying to remain seated while minimizing the jarring of my arm.

Denny glanced back over his shoulder. I looked, too. I couldn't see anything, not through the rain. Maybe, in another half hour, the sun would rise. If it didn't cut

through the clouds, at least it wouldn't be as dark. I
knew Mal was back there, though. I could feel him. It
was the only thing that gave me hope.

We rounded a tight corner, tires squealing and slipping across the rain-slick road. I slid across the seat, jam-
ming up against Darryl. For one insane moment, I
contemplated grabbing onto the steering wheel, then,
quickly decided against it. Who did I think I was? One of
Charlie's Angels? If I tried to take the wheel from Denny,
the struggle for control could send us all crashing. The
best thing I could do to keep us all alive was to sit still
and wait for the cavalry to come charging over the hill.
Come on, cavalry. Get your butt out here!

"Head up that way." Denny suddenly pointed, indicating a turnoff from the main road.

"No! Not that way!" I cried out.

The turnoff sign read, FULSOME ROAD. FIVE MILES. There
was no way out that way. Mama had told me that it was
under water. Though I'd wanted to bring the truck to a
stop, I didn't want to do it by taking a plunge into flood
water. Fulsome Road ran parallel to the Fulsome levee.
When the rain had started, it was one of the first roads
to become impassable.

"I thought I told you to shut up!" He raised his hand
again.

I didn't flinch. Didn't bat an eyelash. One of us had to
use our heads.

"You'd better listen to me, Denny. You can't go this
way. It's completely flooded."

His sneer clearly said that he didn't believe me. For
the first time, I was starting to feel panic and fear growing in my stomach. I'd seen the river's fury up close and
personal. I wasn't ready for a repeat performance, especially with this arm. Maybe it was broken. Maybe it was
only sprained. In either case, it was useless to me. I

didn't think I'd be able to use it to swim out of trouble if I couldn't make them listen to me.

"Darryl." I turned my pleas to the younger brother. "Fulsome Road is under water."

"Don't listen to her. She's just trying to give her boyfriend a chance to catch up to us," Denny advised his brother.

"I'm not lying!" I cried out. "Sure, I want Mal to catch up to you. You deserve to be caught. What you don't deserve is to drown . . . to senselessly throw your lives away because you were too stupid to listen to reason. Please, I'm telling the truth. Turn around now before it's too late."

We were still moving forward, following the slow dip in the road off the main highway that would eventually wind up running the length of the levee.

Denny swung his gun around. I wasn't sure if he was pointing it at me or at Darryl.

"Keep going," he ordered his brother. "Don't listen to her. She's lyin'. You can see that, Darryl, can't you? She's just tryin' to muck with your head."

"Turn around!" I countermanded. Another half mile or so up the road would be a small wooden bridge. During a flash flood, a bridge was no place to be.

Denny's eyes narrowed as he drew his lips back into a snarl. "Keep talking. Just give me a reason to dump your black ass out right here."

"Fine," I snapped. "I'd rather take my chances with a bullet than die slowly out there. If you won't listen to me and believe me, believe your own ears. Cut the engine, Darryl. You can hear it. You can hear the water."

As long as I lived, I would never forget the sound of the river coming down on me when I'd stopped to help that kid Aaron. The cold, crushing power of it. Mindless. Unrelenting. Unyielding. I'd never known such terror.

Except the terror I felt when I heard the sound of Myles's truck pulling away from us.

Darryl lifted his foot, allowed the truck to come to a rolling coast.

"What do you think you're doing?" Denny demanded. "There will be cops all over us. Don't stop."

"Sh!" Darryl hissed at him.

"Darryl! We gotta keep moving, bro."

"I suh-said shut up! You h-h-hear that, Denny?"

"I don't hear . . . any . . . thing . . ." Denny's voice trailed off.

Darryl stomped on the floor, pressing the high-beam switch to the left of the brake pedal. The headlights shone through the trees, catching the horrific and strangely mesmerizing scene in midaction as several trees toppled before our eyes. It looked as if black coffee poured over the earth, ripping at trees at their bases, carrying them along. There was no more Denny could say. He made a strange, strangled, gurgling sound.

"Back up!" I shouted, pounding Darryl on his shoulder. This time, I did grab for the steering wheel. I couldn't help it. I had to. He wasn't moving nearly fast enough for me.

"Yeah . . . uh . . . yeah . . ." Darryl acknowledged, jerking on the gearshift. "I'm guh-guh-going."

"Hurry up!" Both Denny and I were shouting at him. Darryl was driving as fast as he could, but in reverse. Not fast enough. The tires couldn't get a purchase on the mud-slick road.

Leave it to these morons to steal a truck with bald tires. I braced myself as best as I could with my good arm as we slid forward, despite the whine of the engine and the effort of the transmission.

"Drive, Darryl!" Denny was shouting. "Get us out of here."

"I'm truh-truh-truh!"

He couldn't even get the word out. There was stark
terror in Darryl's voice as he worked the gas, brake, and
gearshift all at the same time. His voice cracked like a
young boy just reaching puberty. I felt so sorry for him.
He was young. Too young to be put in this situation because of his idiot of a brother.

Darryl spun us in a wide arc, trying to get the nose of
the truck pointed back the way we'd come. He turned
too sharply. The truck tilted to the left. Our combined
weight sent us all sliding to one side of the truck. I
landed on top of Darryl. Denny landed on top of me,
crushing me against him.

"Get off of me! Get off of me!" I batted at Denny with
my good hand. "Get out! We got to get her back on her
wheels!"

Denny stepped on my hip as he tried to right himself.
He reached for the truck's handle, and was about to
push it open, but then swore when the first wave hit us.

I don't know who screamed the loudest, me or the boys.
None of us was wearing a seat belt. So when the water
washed over us, we spun as the truck spun—like wet towels
in a spin cycle at the Laundromat. Over and over and over
and over we tumbled. Water rushed in through the floor,
entry made easier by the holes eaten by rust.

Darryl had gone into full-time panic mode, yelling
and screaming and clawing at anything within reach. Including me.

Instinctively, I held my breath. As I felt the ice-cold
water lick at my feet, rise up to my knees, and encircle
my waist, I drew in as much air as my lungs could hold,
speaking quickly before the water covered my mouth.

"Crank the window down!"

"Are you crazy, lady?" Denny cried out.

"It's our only way out!" I snapped. "If we stay here, we

die. You got that, boy? If we stay here, we'll drown. If we can get out, swim to the surface, we may have a chance."

"Darryl can't swim," Denny sobbed.

"Can you?"

Denny nodded, looking with wild eyes all around him as the water made it to his chest. He was as scared as a trapped animal.

"Then do something good for him for once in your miserable life. *Help him!*"

There wasn't much time left for talking. I grabbed Darryl's hand and made him clench on to the back of Denny's belt. Then, pointing at the window crank, I gestured for Denny to start cranking.

Thank God for the good, old-fashioned amenities of this '72 truck. If it had been a newer model, with all electric windows and doors, we probably would not have been able to get out as quickly as we did.

I say quickly. It seemed like an eternity, climbing out of what was trying to become our watery grave. As soon as the window came down, what little pocket of air we had left was quickly swallowed up as the water rushed in.

Denny hauled himself out of the window, grabbing on to the outside door handle for leverage. I scooted out of the way, treading water, and pushed Darryl ahead of me. With whatever strength I had left in my good arm, I held onto Darryl's belt loop. Once I'd cleared the window, I started kicking, kicking hard to propel us away from the truck. Using the direction of the bubbles escaping from the waterlogged vehicle as my guide, I fought for what I prayed was the surface. I didn't look back. Not once. Why waste the energy?

I had enough of a fight on my hands kicking against the current. It was strong. So strong. Despite our combined efforts, Denny's and mine, I was starting to doubt whether we could fight against it. What could we do?

Two mere mortals against the might of an overswollen river. My only hope was that we'd bob to the surface, like two corks, and somehow make our way to the tree line. My only hope. How quickly my faith had changed. Wasn't it only just a few short minutes ago when Mal had been my only hope?

Do your job, Mal. Do your job!

Chapter Twenty-Eight
The River

I spread my arms wide and cover the earth, sweeping with me in my course all things—both natural and man made. It makes no difference to me. As I am designed by the Creator to flow on, I am resigned to accept that all things may be gathered into the bosom of my embrace. I carry all along with me without consideration, without judgment, without discrimination.

If anyone had bothered to ask, I would have answered. I do not choose what to embrace. I do not choose what and when to release. That choice I leave to my Creator and time—for only they are best suited to determining a natural course of events.

Chapter Twenty-Nine

Mal

"Call 9-1-1!"

I pointed at Todd as I sprinted for the door. I don't think he heard me. He kept pacing back and forth in the small area behind the counter and the bulletproof glass, his hands clamped down on his head, and moaning.

"Oh, man! Oh, man! Oh, man! I am so fired!"

Later for him. I didn't have time for this. My first impulse was to go busting out that door, tearing after Jess. Then, the thought of having a couple of slugs pumped into me as soon as I stepped out in the open stopped me cold. Cooled my hot head right off. Slowed me to the point where I almost skidded into the door, trying to back pedal. Looked like one of the cartoon characters, trying to stop in midcharge, kicking up dust while coming to a screeching halt.

Come on now, son. Use your head. What do you think is gonna happen as soon as you stick your head out that door?

Just to test the theory, I pushed on the door and immediately jumped out of the way. Sure enough. Denny was waiting for me and fired three more rounds at the store. He was firing wild.

"Get down!" I warned Todd, even though at the moment, he was a lot safer than I was. Safer and smarter. He wasn't coming out from behind that booth. Not for anything.

The shot spread was all over the place. The glass to the right of the door cracked, looking like an overgrown spider's web. The second bullet went low, but managed to shatter the glass. I didn't hear where the third bullet struck. Probably skidded off into the tall grass of the vacant lot right next to the store. Or maybe it struck the wall.

Looking around, my mind racing, I figured there had to be another way out of here. A back door. One I could use and come up on Denny unseen.

"Boy, where's the other exit?" I called out to Todd.

Todd still wasn't with me. He was hunkered down behind the counter. But I could still hear him mindlessly muttering and sobbing at the same time.

Useless! He was useless to me now. Frustrated, I risked poking my head up to stare out the window. More shots fired.

"I don't believe this shit!" Now he was firing at my Jeep. *Aw, hell naw! My woman and my truck?! He had to be out of his mind.*

Jeep out of commission. No sign of backup. Time for Plan B.

"Hey!" I yelled at Todd, and hurled a bottle of motor oil at the window to get his attention. The bottle cracked, leaving a slick trail of fluid down the window and splattered on the floor. "I said which way out of here, boy?"

Todd didn't raise up, but lifted his hand and pointed in the direction of the back store room. "Dude! It's that way. One emergency exit and another door that leads out by the dumpster."

"Are they locked?"

"I . . . I don't think so. Maybe. Naw . . . One of them is always locked. But the warning siren will go off as soon as you open the door."

Good. Hopefully, the door was wired with an alarm. Maybe a patrol car, if one was available, would come to investigate. I didn't feel guilty about leaving Todd at all. He wasn't hurt. He'd be all right until somebody could get to him. Then again, as soon as I opened that door and the alarm sounded, Denny and Darryl would know that I wasn't coming out the front door. No direct assault. And with the alarm blaring, no element of surprise. No sneak attack. Made me wish that I *did* have that big red *S* on my chest that Jess saw there. I could use some superhuman strength right now. A dose of invincibility, rather than this overwhelming feeling of fear and frustration.

"You got a car, Todd?"

"Huh?"

"A car. Some wheels?" I snapped my fingers at him. Focus, Todd. Focus!

"Yeah . . . It's out back."

"Gimme your keys."

"What for?"

"I'm gonna go on a joyride," I said sarcastically. "What do you think what for?"

"Dude, I just got that car."

"Dude, I don't care. Gimme your keys. Now!"

Todd's hand reached and shoved the keys through the money-exchange slot.

"Not one scratch," he warned, shouting out to me. "You bring it back to me in perfect condition or I swear, man, I'm suing the Codell County Police Department."

"Take a number," I muttered, turning my attention back to the window.

Denny was struggling with Jess, trying to get her into his truck. Just like I thought, she wasn't making it easy for him. I couldn't help but grin.

"Give 'em hell, girl!" Slow them down just long enough for me to get to them. She was probably the reason why Denny didn't have better aim. He couldn't take on me and her at the same time. I don't know of many who could. Even Ms. Ramsay had been known to give up when it came to trying to handle me and Jess.

Careful not to slip on the mess that I'd made with the motor oil (and thirty weight leaves an awful mess when smeared over a tile floor mixed with shattered glass), I darted down the aisle and went back through the storeroom—the very same storeroom where all of this began.

A tiny, condemning voice in the back of my mind insisted that if I hadn't gone foraging, if I hadn't left Jess alone, she probably wouldn't be at Denny's mercy right now. I don't know what I could have done when Denny and Darryl came in to stick up the place. I certainly wouldn't have let them just walk out of here with her, if I could have done anything to stop it.

Stop it! Stop it! Stop it!

I held onto the last words of my swan dive into self-pity and turned the mental energy around. This was no time for self-recriminations. I had to keep my mind clear . . . focused. Jess was counting on me. She needed me. She wouldn't be able to hold off Denny for long. The clock was ticking. Every minute I spent wondering what I should have done was keeping me from doing what I needed to do. And what I needed to do was get out there and get my woman back.

Though the back storeroom was crowded with boxes

and crates, cleaning materials and trash that hadn't made it to the dumpster, the narrow corridor leading to the emergency door was clear. The sign painted in red above the door and on the push handle running the width of the door read, EMERGENCY EXIT. ALARM WILL SOUND. I looked around for the other door. It wasn't as easy to spot, not painted or marked. It wasn't more than a crack in the wall. There was a ladder propped up against it.

Shoving it out of the way, I yanked on the handle. Nearly falling back, off balance with the force of my tug, I was thankful for small favors. I was pretty sure that somewhere, in the training manual for employees, they were taught that the door should remain locked at all times. I'd take this infraction of the rule if it meant getting to the Jess.

I came out on the east side of the building, back by the dumpster and the water and air station. I didn't have to guess whether or not Denny had taken off yet. By the echoes of Jess's curses filling the air, I knew that he hadn't. I edged around the building, keeping close to the wall as I peered out to reassess the situation.

My gaze swept over the area. Now that I was out here, time to come up with a plan. There wasn't much cover to approach Denny. In one sense, I was no better off than I was when I was inside the store. Maybe a smidge better. At least no one was shooting at me. Not yet. As soon as I stepped out into the open, that would soon change. I only had a small window of opportunity to get to Denny while he had his hands full with Jess.

The door to the passenger side was wide open, but Jess wasn't going in. She had her feet planted on either side of the frame, bracing her hands against the hood. Denny was trying to push her inside from the back. She bucked him, using every trick in the book that I'd taught her to keep from getting into the truck with him . . . and some that I hadn't taught her.

He wrapped his arm around her waist. She wriggled out of his grasp. He grabbed her arm; but she twisted it out of the hold, yelling at him to keep him off balance. The rain didn't help matters much either, making her body slick. I imagined it was like trying to catch a large, flopping fish. A fish with no intention of being netted.

"Let go of me! Take your hands off of me. I'm not going anywhere with you!" Jess screeched at him.

Denny paused, his shoulders heaving as if he was trying to catch his breath. For a moment, I thought he might be considering letting her go. If he had a lick of sense he would. Or maybe the last time Jess head-butted him, she'd knocked all of the good sense out of him.

I watched, anger and fear gripping my gut when Denny pointed the gun, point blank, at Jess's temple. He said something to her. Something that took all of the fight out of her. She slid into the seat of the truck, looking back through the rear window. I don't know if she saw me.

"Hang on, Jess!" I said aloud, moving quickly but cautiously beyond the wall. By then, the truck's engine had started, backfiring a couple of times. Enough to make me flinch. No shame in that. I'd already been shot at twice. A plume of blue-gray smoke poured from the tailpipe, obscuring the truck as it pulled away from the gas pumps.

I followed behind as much as I could, automatically committing the make, model, and license plates to memory. Out of town boys. Good. That made it even better. I intended to get as many folks as I could involved with tracking them down, including agencies from Mississippi, Louisiana, or Timbuktu if I had to. They weren't going to get far.

I gave them just enough of a head start to make them think they'd gotten off clean before I leaped into my own Jeep and reached for my radio to call in to the station.

"No! No! No!"

Denny wasn't as bad a shot as I'd originally thought. I guess there was no way he could miss at that close range. The radio and the computer system that we'd just had installed—the Mobile Command Data Center—were all shot to pieces. Several hundreds of thousands of dollars' worth of equipment. Gone!

Somehow, I had to get word to the dispatcher. My cell phone was no good. Battery was dead. Time to for Plan B. Or was I up to Plan C by now? There had to be a phone in the store somewhere behind the counter, if Todd had gathered his wits about him enough to let me in. I slammed the door to the Jeep, and would have gone back inside if it weren't for the sound of a ringing phone.

Couldn't have been mine. Jess's phone! She'd left it in her purse when she went into the store and now it was ringing, calling attention to itself. I reached for Jess's purse, hesitating for a fraction of a second.

Deep down in my subconscious mind, my damaged psyche was acting up on me. I have this thing about reaching into a woman's purse. Trauma, some people call it. Probably has something to do with the time my sister beat me within an inch of my life when I was thirteen years old and she was sixteen. I'd gone into her purse looking for a pack of gum and pulled out her birth control pills that she'd gotten from an older friend. I knew she'd had them for a while. True to the nature of a bratty young brother, I was biding my time, waiting for the most effective moment to reveal that she had them. That time happened to be right in front of our folks, who didn't know she was on the pill. Got her grounded for the rest of her natural days.

I didn't want to go into Jess's purse. Not that I was still scared of birth control pills or still scared of my sister, Maia. The sneaking suspicion that I was invading Jess's privacy crept into the back of my mind. I pushed the thought aside. I had to invade her privacy to save her life. Though I'm sure several proponents of minimalist government would disagree with me.

Reaching for her purse, I rummaged through it until I found the small silver phone. It was still ringing.

I flipped it open and said without explanation, "Call back later."

The number on the LCD screen was familiar. Jess's mom. Grimacing, I knew she was going to call back, probably yell at me for hanging up on her. It couldn't be helped. This was the only way I could hang up the phone and dial out immediately. I didn't bother with 9-1-1. Why go through one extra dispatcher? I dialed on a line I knew would be picked up immediately by one of my officers. Besides, by the look of the power level indicator on Jess's phone, she didn't have much time left either.

"Codell County Police Department." The response was prompt. It was answered on the second ring.

"Walker." I recognized the voice.

"Chief?"

"Yeah, it's me. Listen up, Walker. I don't have much time. I need backup out here at that convenience store across from Motel 6. And I need it now. Who can you send?"

Walker picked up the tension in my voice, but didn't let it rattle her. She was a professional, keeping her tone crisp and unemotional as she said, "Edmonds is patrolling that side of town. I'm dispatching him right now."

I heard her fingers on the keyboard, tapping out a message that would display on the Mobile Command Data Center computer in Edmonds's truck.

"Armed robbery," I said, speaking quickly as I jogged to the rear of the store in search of Todd's car. "Two males. Caucasian. Average height. Slim build. Late teens driving an early model Ford truck. Painted out with gray primer. Louisiana plates. Last seen driving north toward the I-10 exchange. Got that?"

"Got it, Chief. And Edmonds has just responded. He's on his way right now. ETA twenty minutes. Where should Edmonds meet you, Chief?" Walker asked.

"Don't worry about me. Tell Edmonds there's a clerk here at the store. Make sure he gets a statement, collects as much evidence as he can, including the tape from the surveillance cameras. I'm going after the ones who took . . . the hostage. I'll be driving a yellow Pontiac Vibe."

"Yes, sir. Be careful, Chief."

Her words were garbled, filled with static, and fading out. Jess's cell phone battery was starting to give up the ghost.

I raised my voice, hoping that she could hear me. "Send anybody else you can. Contact the Coast Guard and see if you can divert a copter."

"I'll do what I can, Chief."

She was gonna have to do better than *try*. "Walker?"

"Yeah, Chief."

"The hostage . . . It's Jess. They took her."

I wanted it out there. Up front. Out in the open. No doubt about my intentions. I wasn't going to stop chasing them until I got her back. Not that I wouldn't do the same for any hostage. This wasn't just any hostage. This was Jess. Anyone within a hundred miles of listening distance knew what that meant.

Silence on the other end of the line. Silence for the span of a heartbeat. Was it the silence of disapproval? The first time I'd taken off to go after Jess, my actions weren't exactly looked upon with good favor. My so-called defection had, for all intents and purposes, cost me my job. I didn't have anything else to lose—except Jess. I wasn't going to lose her.

And then her voice came back, gritty with determination. "You've got that air support, Chief, if I have to strap on a couple of paper fans and flap out there myself."

I adjusted the seat, sliding it back, to make up for Todd's shorter leg reach. As soon as I cranked up the engine, the MP3 player kicked in, blaring out music from the speakers. From the volume and intensity of the music, I wondered if Todd's car wasn't just one giant boom box on wheels.

"What's that, Chief?" Walker's voice sounded tinny, far away, as I gunned the engine. "I didn't copy."

She probably couldn't hear me over the squeal of tires as I peeled out of the parking lot after them. Jess probably had a good ten or fifteen minutes' head start on me. I'd have to push this buggy if I was going to catch them.

I wish I hadn't laid down my gun and shield back at the office. If I'd had them, maybe I could have done more to keep them from getting away from me.

Chapter Thirty

The River

What is done is done. It cannot ever be undone. As time continues on its charted course, I mimic its direction. Ever onward. I can only do what is in my nature to do. Throughout the ages, all manner of man has tried to turn me against my nature. Structures of steel and stone to contain me. Gouges deep within the earth to direct me.

If anyone had bothered to ask, I would have answered. Those who are at peace with the function and purpose of time will embrace it, rather than rail and race against it. Those who are at peace with my nature will accept. Those who do not, will regret.

Chapter Thirty-One

Jess

There are a few times in my life when I could truly say that I wish I'd never . . . Even making the decision so long ago to push Mal toward Shelby didn't compare to this. Being with these two turned out to be one of those rare, regrettable times.

As my mind flashed back to how this all began, I found myself wishing that I'd never set foot in that convenience store. From the time these idiots dragged me into the truck from the time we had clawed our way out again, I was filled with useless wishing. Mama used to say that if wishes were horses, beggars would ride. *Lordy!* What I wouldn't have given for a way to ride out of this mess. I knew the memory of how terrifying our escape had been would haunt me forever.

I remember how the coldness of the water had literally taken my breath away. We'd climbed out of the truck window—me, Darryl, and Denny—struggling to keep from being swept away. Déjà vu. Didn't I just leave this party? Only, this time, there was no cottonseed processing plant in sight. No pallets. No forgotten bales of cotton. Just me, the boys, and the blackness of free-flowing water.

The current was vicious. Grabbing at me. Tearing at me. I knew from the moment that the water hit the truck that the waters were flowing much too fast. This was no slow seepage, like the night the water crept up into my kitchen. This wasn't the kind of flood that takes you by slow degrees, allowing you to mark its rise over time. This was water on a mission. A flow of Biblical proportions. Flash flood.

The flood waters caught us broadside, dragging us along Fulsome Road for several yards before the truck snagged on something, allowing us time to get out.

Kick! Kick! Kick!

I wriggled out of the window, trying to put some distance between me and the truck before it worked itself loose and was carried further downstream. The moment the water hit me, I felt as if I'd been dunked in a cooler of ice water, freezing and burning at the same time. I wanted to cry out, but knew that I couldn't. I couldn't! For once in my life, I'd better keep my big mouth shut. If I opened it this time, I would die. So, I held my breath, despite the squeezing of my lungs, and kept working my legs.

From the way Denny shot away from the truck, working his arms and moving his legs, I could tell that he was a strong swimmer. He was probably the type who would be on the swim team in high school . . . if he'd bothered finishing high school.

Darryl wasn't so strong of a swimmer. He had no technique at all. But what he lacked in experience, he made up for in enthusiasm. His long, lean legs moved back and forth in a scissor kick. Left. Right. Left. Right. It didn't take him long at all to pick up the rhythm. I guess the threat of drowning forces you to became a fast learner. At least we were all working together.

Even with the three of us pulling together, the tug of the current was stronger than all of us. We were aiming for the surface. It couldn't have been more than five feet above us. So hard to tell. The water was murky. Filled with debris and churned-up mud. Broken tree branches. Garbage pails. Whole two-by-fours from cracker-box houses torn asunder from the force of the flood. Five feet may as well have been five miles for all the good it did us.

The water carried us along, parallel to the surface. Not much time left. My legs were starting to cramp, and I was starting to feel lightheaded, taking away from my concentration and my effort. Somehow, I had to find a reserve of strength. I was the one bringing up the rear. If I couldn't hold up my end, I'd either drag us all down or be forced to let go so that Denny and Darryl would have a chance to make it out.

Now, ain't that a bitch? Where was the justice in the world? They'd kidnapped me, stuck a gun to my head, shot at my man, and I was going to have to be the noble one in order to save us all? I was going to have to sacrifice myself so that they'd live? The thought of the unfairness of it all made me mad. My anger gave me reserves of strength that I didn't know I had, if only for a while.

Kick, girl! Kick! Kick! Kick for your life! I closed my eyes, sending up a prayer for sustained strength. *Kick, Jess! Kick!*

When we finally broke the surface, I was still kicking. Popping out of the water like a bob on a fishing line. Somehow, miracle of miracles, Denny and Darryl were still with me. Denny was cursing, spitting out water. Darryl was blubbering, grappling with his brother by wrapping his arms around his neck. Now that he was up and could draw precious air into his lungs, he was starting to panic again.

"Get off me!" Denny shouted as Darryl's frantic flailing threatened to take us all down again.

"Darryl!" I called out to the boy, trying to get his attention. "Cut it out! Let him go! Let him go, or we'll all drown! Relax. It's gonna be all right."

Yelling at him wasn't getting anywhere. I changed my tone, trying to make it assuring. Still, he wasn't listening. I doubted he could hear my instructions over the sound of his own panic-stricken wails.

Denny wasn't helping much either. Once Darryl had forced his head underwater, he'd started fighting for his life. Never mind that this was his baby brother. Never mind that, moments before, we were all working together to get out of this. Primitive survival instinct had completely taken hold of Denny. He was going to kick, claw, and fight against this new threat.

"Oh, for Pete's sake!"

Was I the only one with any sense in this trio? I flung my arm around Darryl's neck, putting him in a choke hold with the crook of my elbow. I went for Darryl because he was the weaker swimmer. On his own, I figured Denny stood a better chance of making it out of the water.

I didn't really intend to squeeze the life from Darryl, but I needed to take some of the fight out of him. Amazing how much energy he still had, even after all we'd been through. Pulling as hard as I could, I flipped him over on his back, resting his body against my breasts. My injured arm was draped across his chest. The less I had to use it, the better.

Instinctively, Darryl reached up and grabbed on to my arm, kicking his legs out, trying to pull my arm from around his neck.

"Cut it out!" I snapped. "I'm trying to save your fool neck. Keep kicking your legs, boy. Kick if you want to live."

The water was still pushing us along at a good clip. But

as long as our heads were above water, where we could breath, I didn't have to fight as hard. One thing was for certain, we had to stay afloat. On the surface, it would be easier for a rescue team to spot us.

Denny moved alongside me, moving his arms and legs in a breast stroke that would have put Mark Spitz to shame, until he passed me.

"Where do you think you're going?!" I shouted at him. He'd better not be trying to leave us. This was his brother that I was hauling. If I wanted to get selfish about it, I could let him go. Let his big brother worry about him while I saved my own skin.

"Over there!" he pointed.

Craning my neck around, I saw where Denny was headed.

Trees! Thank the Lord! Oak trees, hundreds of years old and fully grown, were planted firmly into the ground. A line of trees was planted along the roadside, as much for beauty as for function. Shade. Soil erosion control. Who knew the intention of the original planters so many years ago.

Deeply rooted in the ground, those majestic, solid-trunked beauties weren't going anywhere for a while. And, if I could summon the strength to make it to them, neither would I. I'd plant my tired, wet butt on one of those branches, and cling there like a kudzu vine.

Denny reached the trees first. He grabbed onto a low-hanging branch, and held his hand out to me.

"Come on! Come on!" he urged. "Don't stop now."

I swam to him, arm outstretched. Denny clamped onto my wrist, pulling me up to the branch alongside him. Without a second thought, I made him let go of me.

"Grab hold of Darryl. Get him out first."

I had to make sure that the kid was taken care of. It was the teacher in me, seeing first to the needs of kids before my own needs. I wriggled around until I was behind Darryl, grabbed him by the belt, and hauled him out of the water. Denny pulled on his arms, making sure that he had a firm grip on the tree branch before reaching for me.

I took it, allowing him to pull me up, then maneuvered to another branch, above theirs and on the opposite side of the tree.

"What? This branch ain't good enough for you?" Denny sneered.

"I don't think it can hold our combined weight," I said patiently, even though I'd had just about enough of him.

The branch was wide enough for me to sit on with my back against the trunk of the tree. My legs straddled the branch, dangling my feet into water that only reached my ankles.

"Thank God!" I said aloud, closing my eyes. My chest heaved as I struggled to catch my breath. Beneath me, the water flowed on, still presenting a threat to our safety. But at my back, the tree trunk was solid and unyielding. The base of the tree was solid, at least four feet at its widest. I couldn't even wrap my arms around it. Good. Knowing that it was solidly built gave me a sense of security I hadn't felt since . . . since . . . well, since Mal had put his arms around me and carried me into his home.

Mal! Where was he? Why hadn't he come by now?

Putting my hands to my face, I succumbed to the fear and stress of the ordeal and cried. I don't know if the boys could see me or hear me. I didn't care. I'd earned this moment.

"Cut out all of that blubberin', bitch! I'm trying to think!" Denny spat.

"Lady, are y-y-you al-all right up there?" That was Darryl. Bless his heart. He sounded concerned for me.

"Jess," I corrected.

"What did you say?" Denny called up.

"I said Jess. My name is Jessica Ramsay." My tone was hard as I corrected him. That was my name. Not lady. Not bitch. I am Jess Ramsay, and I am alive! "And I'm all right. Thanks for asking."

Give me a medal of valor. I didn't even sound sarcastic when I thanked him.

"S-so . . . What do we do now, D-D-Denny?" Darryl's teeth chattered as he addressed his brother. In the water, the cold had numbed us so that after a while, we didn't feel it.

I hugged my arms close to my chest and rolled my eyes. Why was he still looking to that moron for guidance? I was the one who'd warned them not to go down this road. I was the one who'd gotten them out of the truck. And after we'd broken the surface, I was the one who'd kept Darryl from dragging Denny down again. Not that I was looking for fanfare or a parade. A simple thank you would have been polite. I should have known better than to expect gratitude from these two. What I did expect, however, was for them to let the one equipped with a brain do the thinking. That would be me.

"We wait here for a while," Denny said decisively. "Catch our breath . . . and then—"

"And then what?" I interrupted, half turning my head to listen. I couldn't see them without completely reorienting my body.

"We see about getting the hell out of here."

"And just how do you propose we do that?" I wasn't curious. My question sprang from pure incredulity. I couldn't believe this! Where did he think he was going to go?

"There's gotta be a boat around here somewhere. Yeah. A boat. Maybe a few more miles up the road and then we can jet out of here before the cops can track us."

False hope. He was giving his brother false hope. Or maybe he was that touched in the head that he actually believed that.

"I hope by 'we' you mean you and your brother," I said stubbornly. "I'm not moving from this spot. Not until I'm picked up by a rescue team." I crossed my legs at the ankles, effectively locking myself to the tree branch.

I raised my hands, reaching up for a slender branch to hang onto. One part of my brain wanted to pull down a switch and swat Denny with it. Maybe if he'd had a few more green switches slapped against his bare bottom and legs, he wouldn't have turned out so rotten.

"We can't stay here," Denny insisted. "What if the water rises? What if this tree falls over?"

"I don't know about what if. I know what *will* happen if you're talking about getting back in that water again," I returned. "I know we're dead. That's a stone-cold fact. We won't have the strength to swim out like we did. We were lucky. I don't trust my luck or you to get us out alive. The best thing for us to do is wait here to be picked up."

Wrong choice of words. It didn't phase Denny that I'd expressed my lack of confidence in his ability. What did bother him was the fact that he'd survived near drowning just to be picked up and taken to jail. And for what? A measly hundred bucks.

"Picked up. You mean by your cop boyfriend?" he returned. "You want us to wait here so he can pick us up and send us to county? You gotta to be out of your freakin' mind!"

"Maybe she's right, Duh-Denny. Huh? Th-think about it. We can't get back in there. And maybe you tuh-took c-c-care of her boyfriend at the stuh-stuh-store. He wuh-won't be g-g-going any wuh-wuh-wuh-where."

"Make no mistake about it. Mal will come after you,"

I said, with all the certainty in the world. "But maybe another rescue boat will get here before he does."

Now it was my turn to offer up false hope. "We could be rescued by the Red Cross or some other rescue effort. Volunteers. What do they care that you held up a store?"

"You trying to tell me that you won't start flapping your lips as soon as someone comes? You won't tell them that I took you from that store? You won't say a word about me shooting at your cop friend?"

"No," I lied, and not very convincingly. "I won't say anything if it means it'll save our lives."

"You don't trust me? Well, I don't trust you, Jess!"

The way he said my name, so full of venom, really ticked me off. What did he mean he didn't trust me? I had my chance to leave his butt to save myself. But I didn't. I should have. I could have. Some of their dumbness must have rubbed off on me. By sticking by them, I certainly wasn't using the good sense given to me.

I shifted around, wrapping my arms around the tree trunk, and leaned out to look at him.

"You don't trust me?! Then why'd you bring me along!" I screeched at him. "If you want to risk your own stupid neck, fine! I don't give a flying flip. But I'm not gonna let you keep me in the middle of your mess. Go your own way, if you have a mind to. I'm not going. I'm staying right here."

"You don't tell me what you will or won't do. You'll do exactly what I tell you to do!" Denny yelled back, pointing at me.

"Or what?!" I challenged.

Automatically, Denny went reaching for his gun. He slapped at his waistband and wound up grabbing at cloth and skin. Gone. Somehow, he'd lost it.

In the frantic flurry to get out of the truck as we sank, I didn't bother to mention that one small piece of debris

that I saw sinking back to the ground as we swam away. I
didn't even make a swipe for it as it swirled past. I'd let it
go, knowing that it was better off rusting at the bottom
of the river than stuck in Denny's pants waiting to be
drawn again.

Let's see what a big-time kidnapper he was gonna be
now, now that he didn't have a gun to stick in my face. I
wish I'd had a camera to capture the way he looked after
he realized that he'd lost that damned gun. His face crumpled, his mouth turned down, and his lower lip trembled.
Was he gonna cry? Was the big, bad convenience-store
stick-up man gonna bawl like a baby because he'd lost his
pop gun?

He'd relied on it to intimidate, to force others to do
what he wanted them to do. Without it, how was he
gonna get anyone to listen to him? He'd lost his power
and his control.

Shaking my head, I turned my back on him, muttering, "Yeah, that's what I thought. You can't do nothing
to me. Not a blessed thing."

All he had to do was sit tight and wait for someone to
find us. Nothing complicated about that plan. Fool-
proof. Only, Denny was no fool. He was worse than a
fool. He was a boy—a boy trapped in a man's body, with
none of the benefits of a full-grown man's experience.
Denny had all of the drawbacks of being too young. Impatience. Imprudence. And now that I'd belittled him,
I'd brought to the surface his sense of impotence.

When I heard a splash in the water, I thought he dove
back in to go looking for the gun.

"Denny, no! Let it go."

"Denny!"

Both me and Darryl were yelling. Darryl tried hanging from the branch and easing his legs into the water.

"Where do you think you're going?" I snapped. "Get

your ass back up there and stay there!" I didn't risk my life, dragging him all the way over there, just to see him throw it away for his brain-damaged brother. "Do you hear me, Darryl? You stay up in that tree. No matter what."

"Wh-where is he? Where's muh-muh-my brother?" Darryl's head swiveled back and forth, looking for him.

"I don't know. Did he fall in?"

"He j-j-jumped."

"He jumped?"

Denny hadn't gone too far. He eased around the trunk of the tree, coming up on my blind side. I felt him clamp onto my leg, trying to dislodge me.

"What do you think you're doing?!" I yelled, swatting at him. It wasn't easy. I was using my injured arm to try to hang on to the tree. I couldn't swing too hard, or I risked falling into the water myself.

"We're gonna find that boat. We're gettin' out of here before your boyfriend comes. You said yourself that he wasn't gonna stop until he finds us. You think I'm gonna wait here until he shows?"

"You don't need me," I insisted. "You go on."

"Nuh-uh. You're insurance."

"You're crazy!"

"Get out of that tree, or I'll break your leg!" he threatened, tugging at me.

"No!"

"I said get out of there!" Denny reached up, grabbed me by my blouse and yanked hard. In I went.

"Denny!" Darryl shouted. "L-let her guh-go! Cuh-cuh-cuh-cut it out, muh-man!"

"Stay out of this, Darryl! You want to go to county? You want to be locked up? That's what's gonna happen if we stay here, bro. She's just stallin' for time. She knows these back roads. She's gonna show us how to get out of here, or I'll snap her neck!"

He had me pressed back against the tree, his hands encircling my neck. I don't know which was worst, being afraid of what uncaring, unfeeling nature was trying to do to me or that I was going to go at the hands of this teenaged homicidal maniac.

He shook me to emphasize his point, slamming my head back against the tree until I saw stars.

"Take your hands off of me!" When I clawed at his hands, trying to pry them from my throat, Denny brought his face to within inches of mine, his teeth bared as he hissed.

"Useless. You're useless! I should have done you back at the store when I had the chance. Maybe made your cop boyfriend watch before I popped a cap in you, that clerk, and then him."

He pressed closer, and I could feel an intense hatred boiling inside of him. For a moment, I thought he was gonna make good his threat, even without his gun. His aggression wasn't about sex. It was all about dominance and control. Jeez! And I thought Mal was a control freak.

"S-stop it, Duh-Denny. I w-w-won't let you hurt her."

Another splash in the water. Darryl! He'd ignored my warning and jumped in.

"Darryl!" I croaked, trying to twist my head to see him.

I saw him bobbing in the water, his hands clawing for the tree. Yet panic, inexperience, and fatigue were taking their toll on him. His fingers couldn't get a grip on the water-slick bark. Without us there watching out for him, helping him, he didn't have a chance. Darryl's head went under, fingers grasping at empty air.

A few seconds was all it took before there was no sign of him. I couldn't see him. Couldn't hear him. No splashing. No thrashing. No cries for help as he'd done after we'd escaped from the truck. Had he been pulled completely under?

"See what you've done!" I railed at Denny, pounding at him with all earnestness now. "He's gonna die, and its all your fault!"

Denny's response was to release my throat and back away from me.

"Darryl!" He sucked in a deep breath and dove his head under the water.

Massaging my neck where his fingers had dug in, I breathed deeply myself. I'd had just about enough of these two. Current or no current, I had to get away from them or they were going to be the death of me. I just knew it! I wasn't ashamed to admit that was my first impulse. Get away before they dragged me under, too. Then, I thought about Darryl and how he'd been misled by Denny. He'd relied on his brother to watch out for him, and his brother had failed. Who else was there? Me. Just me. And as afraid as I was, I'd have to be a sorry human being if I didn't do something to help.

"Darryl!"

Trying to cling to the oak tree, keeping it between me and the pull of the current, I put my head under water as well. I stayed under as long as I could, and swam as far as I dared. If I swam too far, I'd risk not being able to get back.

Kicking hard, I came up for air and called out for Darryl again. Nothing. He was gone. Gone! And there was nothing I could do about it.

Moments later, Denny popped up, too. On his face was a look of murderous fury. I had no doubt that if he'd had his gun, he would have used it. He would have shot me and never blinked an eye.

"You!" he said, his voice ragged. All of the hatred of his pitiful existence compressed into that one word.

"No!" I was denying. He was blaming me for his own stupidity. Denny was focusing all of his frustration into a single beam, boring through me, pinning me to the spot.

Shaking my head, I tried to back away from him. Yet, where could I go? What could I do? I tried to skirt around him, putting the oak tree between us. But Denny was a strong swimmer; and I was flopping around with one good arm.

He reached out, grabbed a handful of my hair and pulled my head underwater. The sound of rushing water filled my ears. The water burned as it shot up my nose. My first instinct was to panic and flail against him. Reaching up, I clawed at his hands. Denny yanked back, drawing me back enough for me to sputter and gasp.

"See how you like it!" He raged at me. "This is for Darryl!"

Down I went again! Longer this time. I couldn't count the seconds. I could only count the throb of my own heartbeats and wonder which one would be my last.

Once more, he allowed me access to the surface, leaning his face into mine to whisper a final taunt. "This is for what you done to him!"

Chapter Thirty-Two

Mal

"Do what you can!" I yelled into the handheld radio, communicating to the pilot in the rescue copter hovering above the water. "Take 'em away!"

The whirring of the blades sent water spraying in all directions, obscuring the limp body dangling from the harness.

Edmonds climbed out of the water and stood on top of the levee wall. Lifting his hands, he gave visual confirmation and permission for the pilot to take off. As soon as it was safe for him to do so, he bent low and sprinted toward the left side where I stood impatiently waiting for him.

"You think he's gonna make it?" I asked.

He held a tennis shoe in his hand, then tossed it with disgust back into the water.

"I dunno." Edmonds shrugged his wide shoulders, made even bulkier by the bright orange life vest that he wore. "There wasn't much I could do for him while we were in the water."

"I'm sure you did everything you could, Eddie," I assured him.

My eyes scanned the water, made relatively calmer now that the helicopter was gone. "Just like I'm doing everything I can to find Jess. Somewhere out there that bastard Denny has her. And I don't care if I have to dredge the entire state of Mississippi, I'm not gonna rest until I've found them."

"You sure that kid was one of the ones who held up the convenience store, Mal? I mean, he fits the description you gave Walker when you called into the station . . . and he's in the vicinity, but—"

"Yeah. I'm sure." I cut him off, heading back to our vehicles parked on the far side of the levee . . . the side where the water had receded. How could I forget? Acid washed jeans. Purple Abercrombie & Fitch T-shirt. High-topped sneakers with purple shoe laces. No doubt in my mind that he was one of them. He was Darryl, the one with the stutter. I knew it was him. So, why did Edmonds have his doubts?

"Mal," Edmonds said, reaching out and putting his hand on my shoulder to stop me. "Something you should know . . ."

"What is it?"

"That kid . . . well, while I was hooking him up in the harness, he was kinda muttering. Hallucinating."

"And?"

"He asked about her . . . about Jess, I mean . . . something about not let anything hurt her. That doesn't sound like the trigger-happy fool you reported."

"He's not the one I'm worried about, Eddie," I admitted. "It's that other lunatic."

It was Denny. He was the loose cannon. Literally. He was the one taking shots at me like it was personal.

"Don't worry. We'll find them. We've got your officers upstream and down combing the area."

My officers. That's what he'd said. Had he forgotten? They weren't my officers anymore.

"Russell Colby's officers," I corrected.

As the mayor of Codell County, Russell had exercised his right to replace me. He was my friend; I couldn't blame him. At the moment, I didn't like him very much. But, I still couldn't blame him. He was doing his job to protect the public.

Helluva thing, though. By taking away my badge, he was preventing me from doing the very same thing. I couldn't do my job. Then again, maybe he'd done me a favor by relieving me. As long as I wasn't the chief of police for Codell County, I was just an ordinary citizen. A run-of-the-mill vigilante, running around half-cocked, and half out of my mind with worry. Nothing to stop me after I'd caught up with Denny. Make no mistake about that. I was going to get him. With that badge figuratively pinned to my chest, there might have been a shield between me and Denny.

Edmonds canted toward his vehicle, indicating that I should follow him. He popped open one side of the silver utility box stretched across the bed of his truck, reaching for a towel. As he dried himself off and tossed his vest in the back, he continued to assure me. "We should have more boat patrollers here within the hour, Mal."

"Thanks, Eddie. I appreciate it. I'm sure Jess appreciates it, too."

Eddie looked away, ignored the fact that my voice had cracked. Strain. Emotion. Fatigue. All of that was acting on me, making me lose my cool and my perspective.

"Mal," he started. But I held up my hand to stop him. What more could he say to me?

"Everybody and anybody who can break loose will be here. I promise you that. We're all behind you, Chief."

He pushed aside a spare life vest and revealed a small metal lock box.

"All of us." Edmonds reached inside the utility box and picked up another box, about the size of a tool chest. Without a word, he shoved it into my hands.

"What's this?" I asked.

"You *know* what it is," he insisted, even as I flipped open the lid.

"How'd you get this, Eddie?" My badge and gun. "Did Russell Colby give these to you?"

"A present from Walker." Edmonds grinned at me. "She gave it to me before I headed out."

"I can't take this. I'm not . . . uh . . . that is . . ." I faltered, holding the box out to him.

"Why not?!" Edmonds demanded.

"Because I don't work for Codell County PD anymore. Don't you get it? Haven't you heard? They fired me!"

"Not the way I heard it," Edmonds retorted. "The way I heard it, they were just offering you an extended vacation."

I gave him a look that told him exactly what they could do with that extended vacation.

Edmonds got the hint. His laughter rang out over the water as he grabbed the badge and ID out of the metal box and slapped it into the palm of my hand.

"Consider it this way, Chief. This wouldn't be the first time you let the job cut your vacation short."

I couldn't help it. I started laughing, too, and grinning at him like an idiot. I couldn't count the number of times that I'd made plans, only to have them cut short. A cruise to the Bahamas was cut short by an untimely break from the county jail. An all-expense-paid suite at a Biloxi resort was given to my sister because I had to work security at a strike by union workers at a nearby food-processing plant. Somebody had to be there to protect the picket line crossers. No skiing in Colorado. No camping in Yosemite. No stock-car clinic in Daytona. I wasn't just talking vacations of the two-week variety. But the interruptions included days when I needed to get away, if only for a few hours.

Shelby always gave me hell for it, complaining that there was no way we could get close as long as the job came between us. She had no idea just how crowded it was between us. Between the job and Jess, me and Shelby never really stood a chance. Or maybe she did know. Which was why she wound up with that Riley Evans.

"So, Chief," Edmonds made sure to stress the word. "How far down you think he floated before we fished him out?"

"Hard to tell. I tried to take off after them as soon as I could. I didn't want to lose them. But I did. I lost sight of them before the turnoff to Fulsome Road."

"You think they could have turned down there?"

"Noooo," I said confidently. "Jess knows that it's underwater. They wouldn't be crazy enough to go there, would they?"

Edmonds narrowed his eyes. He turned his head, following the direction of the water. "I don't know. You said that other kid was a lunatic. Was he crazy enough to try it?"

"Yeah. He was just that crazy." I climbed back into Todd's car and cranked up the engine.

"You're going after them." It wasn't a question coming from Edmonds. It was a statement of fact.

"Did you have any doubt that I would?" I asked, lifting my eyebrows.

"No, sirree. I didn't. If you're going down there, you'll never make it in that, Mal," Edmonds warned me.

Todd's car sat too low to the ground. The moment I ran into something bigger than a mud puddle, I'd stall out.

Edmonds climbed into his truck, a Ford Super Duty modified by an aftermarket lift kit. Its frame was sitting a good two and half feet above the wheels. Coupled with oversize tires and a powerful V-10 engine, it was perfect for moving through high water. The Beast, as Edmonds called it, could go where most vehicles couldn't. And Edmonds didn't mind testing the limits of his new toy either. In fact, I think he was getting a thrill sloshing through the countryside. He leaned over and opened the door for me.

"Get in, Chief." He gave me the order.

"Nuh-uh. Move over. Let me drive."

Edmonds made a rude noise in the back of his throat. "Oh, hell naw, Chief. No offense. But in the state that you're in, you think I'm gonna let you drive my truck? You must be crazier than the looney-toon that we're after."

I climbed into the truck, grabbing on to the frame and planting my foot on the chrome extra step. You know a truck's way too damned big when you gotta use a step ladder to get in. Todd's car looked like a Hot Wheels toy car in comparison.

"Buckle up, Chief!" Edmonds said, yelling over the roar of the engine. "It's gonna be a bumpy ride."

Edmonds took a moment to check in to the station, giving them our current location, and calling for a flatbed tow truck to get Todd's car back to him before stepping on the gas and heading back out to the main road.

I reached out and flipped the switch to activate the lights and siren, ignoring the fact that earlier I'd asked Walker to relay that ten-forty code to anyone joining me out here.

"What did you do that for?" Edmonds asked, his

expression puzzled. "I thought you told us that you wanted silent running."

"I know, Eddie. I changed my mind."

My hands reached out, bracing against the dashboard as if I could propel us forward faster by pushing. "I know who snatched her, what kind of man he was. Only she knows the hell that she's going through. I want her to hear us coming. I want her hear us so that she knows we didn't leave her out there alone. I don't want her to give up hope."

Edmonds shook his head, pursed his lips. "I've known Jess Ramsay since the tenth grade, Chief. You know as well as I do that she's no quitter. She's got more spirit than anybody has a right to have. She won't give up."

"I hope you're right, Eddie. I hope to God you're right."

"I just hope that she doesn't use all of that sass and piss that guy off and push him."

"That's more like the Jess I know," I said ruefully. Nobody could find hot buttons quicker than Jess.

He slowed down just enough to keep from tipping us over when we took the turn-off to Fulsome Road. From the deep ruts in the road, I could tell that someone had passed by here. Not too long ago, either. I rolled down the window, concentrating on the tracks, making sure that they didn't turn off the road to cut through the thick underbrush.

Without my having to ask him to, Edmonds took his foot off the gas, easing to a slow coast. Though it was daylight, Edmonds kept his headlights on.

Fulsome Road was perfect for those who liked their privacy. It was a two-lane dirt path with aspirations of becoming a road—only a cut through to allow passage through underdeveloped land. Sometimes, the overgrown brush grew so thick that people on surrounding

could feel him giving me that look . . . that same look that Jess gave me when I'd tracked mud into her house two days ago when her mom had sent me out there to get her.

Had it really been two days? Hard to believe. I closed my eyes, rubbing them until they creaked. Only two days. Seemed like an eternity.

Edmonds shifted gears, turning the truck's nose so that we followed the water's flow. The oversized tires continued to roll, but seemed sluggish and unwieldy as we churned up more mud.

"You're not gonna get stuck, are you?" I asked him.

"We'd better not!" Edmonds exclaimed. "It's not as if we can call a tow truck to haul us out."

We rode in silence another quarter mile up the road. Every now and then, Edmonds let out a low whistle. The water was still pretty high, covering the rooftops of a few shacks that remained standing, lining the water's edge.

"Hey, ain't that Bull Pearson's dog?" Edmonds pointed out the window.

Floating on what appeared to be part of a picket fence, the mutt that had menaced me when we'd gone to help Bull clear out of his house was riding the river waves like a California surfer. Her long pink tongue hung out of her mouth. That stump of a tail was switching back and forth. At the sight of us, she started to bark—long and loud.

What Bull ever did to deserve that much loyalty and dedication, I'll never know. Her barks echoed across the water, still protecting Bull Pearson's property, even though there was no sign of the property or Bull. I could still hear her, long after she was swept down the water, out of sight.

Chapter Thirty-Three

Jess

"Open your eyes!"

A stinging slap against my face. Then another. I tasted salty blood in my mouth as I cracked open my eyes. My ribs hurt. Something was digging into my stomach. I tried to shift, to take the pressure off until I realized that I was draped across a tree limb, my arms and legs dangled on either side. Denny sat on the limb beside me, glaring at me.

"Get up," he ordered. When I didn't move right away, he grabbed me by my hair, tugging until tears sprang to my eyes again. "I said get up!"

The first thing I was gonna do when I got the chance was to walk into the first barber shop I could find and get it all shaved off. Every inch of it. Forget vanity. The price for being cute was too high.

"Why don't you just leave me alone! What do you want from me?"

Wrong tone to take with him. As I sat up, resting my back against the tree trunk, Denny's hand shot out, gripping my throat. Reaching up, I tried to pry Denny's finger's lose but couldn't get enough leverage. He had me pressed against the oak tree, trying to strangle the life from me.

"I want you to know what Darryl felt like before he died," he said simply. "I'm gonna make you suffer like he did."

"You don't want to do this, Denny," I pleaded with him.

"You're gonna pay for what you did to Darryl," he vowed. His eyes cut to the water below us. Had he pulled me out only to push me in again?

Denny wasn't listening to me. He was long past reason. He was all about hate and revenge and punishment. Punishment for something that wasn't my fault. As twisted as he was, there was no arguing with him.

"Fine!" I conceded. "Make me pay . . . but make me do it on dry land," I snapped.

"You think I'm playin' with you? You think this is some kinda joke? Lady, don't you know that I could snap your neck right here, right now?"

"I get it, Denny. You want me dead. But do you want to die? Is that what you want? If we don't get out of here, we are going to die. Look, Denny. I'm sorry about your brother. If I could have done anything to save him, I would have. You know it's true. Why else would I bother trying to warn us about turning down that road? Why else would I have tried so hard to get us all out of that truck? Nothing is more precious to me than young lives. I'm a teacher, for God's sake. You think I'd want a child to get hurt?"

The fingers relaxed, if only partially. I had his attention. He was listening, if not completely convinced.

"Let's get out of here, Denny," I whispered. "I . . . I just want to go home . . ."

Tears sprang to my eyes. They weren't crocodile tears. They were real. There was nothing I wanted more than to go home. All I could think about was climbing into my bed, pulling the covers over my head, and hoping that when I woke up, all of this would have been a nightmare. A terrible, terrible nightmare. Except the part about me and Mal. My being able to love him openly, without having to hide my feelings, was the stuff my most pleasant dreams were made of.

"He . . . He was just a kid," Denny said, dropping his hand from my neck. "Stupid kid . . . always following me around. What did he have to do that for, lady? Huh? Why'd he have to do that?"

Denny drew up his knees, hugged them to his chest, rocking slightly back and forth.

"I don't know," I said softly. I wanted to reach out to him, to let him know that despite everything he'd put me through, I was still capable of sympathy and understanding. He was a kid. An angry, confused kid.

Slowly, cautiously, I lifted my hand, letting it hover near his face so that he'd see I wasn't a threat to him.

"He shouldn't have done that!" Denny wailed.

I flinched at the rise of his voice, but didn't stop reaching out to him until I'd placed my hand gently on his shoulder.

"I'm sorry," I said simply. The words were true. There was no reason for them not to be. It was always a tragedy when a life was taken. "I'm sorry Darryl's gone."

"It shoulda been me," Denny muttered.

Uh-oh! I knew where that conversation was going. Nowhere but down. The way Denny was looking at the water, contemplating his brother's drowning, if the next words out of his mouth were "suicide" or "taking his own life," it wouldn't have surprised me at all. Surprised, no. Dismayed, yes. I wasn't going to let him do it.

"Denny," I said, using my most strict teacher's voice. "Listen to me."

When he didn't look at me, my tone went harsher, "Denny!"

He turned vacant, flat eyes to me. "It shoulda been me, Jess."

Jess. He'd called me Jess! Was that a good sign or a bad sign? I didn't know and didn't have time to ponder it.

"Listen to me, Denny. Darryl is gone. And I'm so sorry about that. But you're still here. *We're* still here. Whether you believe or not, there's a reason for us being spared."

"You trying to tell me that there's a good reason for my brother dying like that?"

He was angry again. Good. As long as there was a spark of life in him, I was gonna continue to fan it to keep it alive. I would fight equally as hard for his life as I would my own.

"Yes," I said, filled with conviction. "There's a reason for everything that happens to us."

"You tell me why!" he raged at me.

"I don't know why," I confessed.

"Then you don't know anything! You're just like everybody else . . . full of talk but not sayin' nothing."

"You have all the answers, Denny?" I turned the microscope of self-examination back on him.

He turned away, his face sullen.

"Well?" I prompted. "Do you?"

"No."

"Then don't you think it's worth it to live long enough to try to find out some of them?" I insisted.

"It's too hard," he protested.

"What's hard?"

"Everything." He shrugged helplessly. "Trying to live . . . It's too hard."

"That's why you need someone to help you, Denny. You need help."

"I ain't crazy!" His body stiffened at the suggestion. "You're trying to tell me I need a head doctor."

"No . . . No, that's not what I'm saying at all."

I was losing him again. He was shutting down on me. Shutting me out. I could tell in the stiffness in his back and the hardened set of his jaw. His eyes, so full of pain and mistrust, darted from my face down to the water again.

"It doesn't have to be a psychiatrist. It could be a minister . . . or a teacher . . . or a crisis counselor . . . or even a friend."

"I don't have any friends."

Risking his anger again, I slid closer to Denny. "That's a choice you make, Denny," I told him. "People choose to go through life alone. You don't have to make that choice."

Denny didn't shy away from me when I moved even closer. He looked up at me, his expression on the brink of tears, as I put my arms around his shoulder.

"So, what's it gonna be, Denny?" I asked.

Tentatively, he rested against me, laying his head on my shoulder. For the moment, it looked as though I had a new friend. I put my hand on his head, cradling him against me, murmuring words of comfort.

Chapter Thirty-Four
Mal

"Don't hurt him!"

That's what Jess had the nerve to scream at us—me and Edmonds—as we pulled that trigger-happy fool out of the water. We'd hauled Denny out, tugging on the life vest that we'd strapped on him before helping him from the tree and into the rescue boat. He didn't make it easy for us to save his miserable life. He kicked and flailed and twisted every step of the way, splashing that nasty runoff water in our faces.

As soon as we'd cleared the water, I shoved Denny in the small of his back, sending him sprawling. He lay on his stomach, face down in the mud. My knee was in his back, keeping him pinned as I pulled his arm behind him and snapped the first cuff around his wrist. For a wiry thing, he still had some spunk in him. He'd almost wrenched his arm out of my grasp before I got him under control by jerking his arm back with a bit more force.

"Ouch! Hey, man! You're tearing my arm off!"

"Do yourself a favor and exercise your right to keep your mouth shut," Edmonds advised, leaning with his

hands on his knees to address the boy. Denny bucked
and kicked out, nearly dislodging me. He raised up on
his hands, got his feet under him, too. He looked like a
sprinter, getting ready to take off from the starting block.
He might have gotten a few steps if Edmonds hadn't
jumped back, drawing his own weapon and pointing at
him.

"Down on the ground!" he barked. "Put your face in
the dirt, boy! Down! I said get down!"

Out of the corner of my eye, I saw Roderick climb out
of the squad car, preparing to offer backup if we needed
it. I waved him off as Jess yelled out, "No! He's not
armed. He doesn't have a gun."

That was a mixed bit of news. We'd searched him for
the weapon. It would make our case easier against him
if he still had it. On the other hand, one less thing for
me to worry about if I knew he wasn't armed.

She stood beside Edmonds's truck, struggling against
the twins, Melvin and Kelvin, as they tried to wrap a blanket over her shoulder. Jarvis Darby, who'd joined the
search team, picked up the blanket from the ground,
clucking his tongue in disapproval, and put it around
her shoulder. The twins and Jarvis. Felt like old-home
week. They'd been with me when we'd rescued Jess the
first time. Then she'd shown a lot more gratitude.

Her change in attitude completely stunned me. What
the hell was she saying? I knew she wasn't defending
him, was she? I stopped, midway between cuffing Denny
and reading him his rights, long enough to glare at her.

"Eddie," she entreated, turning to him when she saw
no sympathy or leeway coming from me. "Put your gun
away. You don't need it." She took a step toward us, but
the twin stepped in front of her, blocking her path.

"Get out of my way!" She threw the blanket off and
tried to dart around Jarvis. He was too big. She collided

with his chest and bounced back. When she couldn't get around that wall of man, she peered around his arm and continued to yell.

"Let him go! You're hurting him!" she called out as a response to Denny's writhing in the dirt and complaining.

"Hey, man! I'm suing. Police brutality! I want a lawyer."

Hurt him? I was only a step away from wrapping my hands around his neck and throttling him. He'd shot at me. Kidnapped Jess. Made me tramp through the mud and the wet and the weeds. Had me so worried about Jess's safety that I thought I was gonna have a coronary.

And then we'd found them, snuggling together in that tree like a couple of lovebirds. What kind of bullcrap was that? Give me five minutes alone with him. Just five minutes. He didn't know what a hurtin' was yet.

I finished reading him his rights, making sure that everything was by the book. This was one worm that wasn't gonna wriggle off the proverbial legal hook. Edmonds stood on one side of Denny. I stood on the other side. Gripping Denny's arms above the elbows, we dragged him to his feet toward the squad car waiting to take him to jail.

"Watch your head," I said automatically, putting my hand on top of his before shoving him into the backseat. Then I slammed the door shut.

Denny started yelling at me again, obscenities and threats.

"You settle down in there!" I gritted, slamming my hand on the hood of the squad car, and cutting loose with a few obscenities of my own. I was wet, hungry, exhausted, and had run out of patience a long time ago. I wasn't gonna put up with any more of his crap. I didn't have to. I had my badge back and my gun and plenty of good reasons to flash both.

"Easy, Chief," Roderick said in quiet warning.

"Don't worry, Roderick," I assured him. "I'm cool.

Got it all under control." There would be no repeat performance of what had happened with Myles. I stood too much to lose.

When I looked back at Jess, she was standing there, her hands on her hips, giving me that look of disapproval. For a hot minute, I didn't even care. All that mattered was that she was safe. Let her glower at me all she wanted to. It wouldn't be the first time that she'd been pissed at me. And I was guessing that it wouldn't be the last time either.

When I walked up to her, she lifted her chin. She was seething with anger, could barely wait for me to say something to get an opportunity to tear into me. I wasn't going to give her that satisfaction. I let her stand there for a few minutes while I gestured for the twins, Jarvis, and Edmonds to follow me.

"Roderick is gonna take our friend Denny back there and offer him the full hospitality of the Codell County Police Department," I said.

"Me and Kelvin are gonna go up the water a ways and see if there are any more odd birds to be plucked out of the trees," Melvin said.

"I'll hang with you," Jarvis offered. "We'll radio back in if we find anyone."

That only left me, Jess, and Edmonds as the twins and Jarvis pushed their boat far enough into the water to start the outboard motor.

"Give us a lift back, Edmonds?" I asked.

"Nuh-uh," Edmonds said, tossing me the keys to his truck.

"What's this for?" I asked. Was Edmonds offering to let me drive? Not his precious truck.

"Looks like you and Jess have got some things to talk about. And I don't want to be anywhere near you when the fur starts to fly." He clapped a radio into my hand, squeezed my shoulder and said with all sympathy, "Good luck, Chief. And may the best stubborn mule win."

He whistled shrilly between his teeth, getting Roderick's attention. "Hold up there, partner." He lifted his hand as if hailing a cab. Edmonds jogged past Jess. He stopped in front of her, speaking to her for a moment. He glanced back once over his shoulder at me, his expression unreadable. Then, without another word, climbed into the squad car.

Jess and I both watched them go, less than ten feet between us. It may as well have been ten miles. This wasn't the kinda reunion I was expecting once I'd caught up with her. Her anger. Her coldness. Where was that coming from? Why was she being so hostile toward me? Why was she so quick to side with Denny against me?

I walked toward her, trying hard not to be angry. I didn't understand. But I wanted to understand. I wanted desperately to know what was going on inside that head of hers. Jess and me, we'd always had a connection. An unexplainable bond. I might not have always agreed with what she was feeling or thinking, but at least I could say I understood it. I'd always understood where she was coming from. Not now. This . . . This was something completely foreign to me. I had to do something . . . anything . . . or bust wide open from the unbearableness of this distance between us.

Fumbling with Edmonds's keys, I opened the lockbox and took out a first aid kit. It took some jiggling of the latch and wrangling to let down the tailgate. The latch was encrusted with mud. After swiping off most of the mud and matted grass, I patted my hand on it, indicating that she should sit down.

Wrapped in the blanket, Jess leaned against the tailgate. I put my hands around her waist and lifted her onto it. She still wouldn't meet my gaze head on.

"You got a nasty cut on your lip," I said, taking out cotton balls and a small bottle of hydrogen peroxide.

She reached up, gingerly touching the spot. "Oh." Her tone was distracted, as if she didn't even notice.

"How'd it happen, Jess?" I asked. I'd had my suspicions, but I wanted to hear it from her. When she didn't respond, I pressed. "Did Denny do this to you? Did he hit you?"

I wanted to sound all business. Just a cop on the job. But I could feel my professionalism slipping a notch.

"He didn't mean it," she said. "It was an accident. A stupid accident."

"An accident? What was he doing? Swatting at a fly?"

"He was upset," she insisted. "He'd just lost his brother."

"That didn't give him any right to put his hands on you, Jess." I dabbed at the cut, trying to be gentle. She shied away from me, complaining that it stung.

"Sorry," I murmured. But when she turned her head away, and I saw the raw bruises on her neck, I lost all sympathy. All sense of perspective. There were claw marks all over her neck, and huge mottled bruises.

"Jess!" I gripped her chin, tilting it up to get a better look. "That son of a bitch . . . You gonna tell me that this was an accident, too?"

"Don't, Mal!" she pleaded with me, gripping my forearms.

"Don't what!" I snapped. My eyes cut to her bared arms, exposed as the blanket fell away. More bruises. Denny had really worked her over.

"Don't go after him," she said wearily. "It's over. It's all over. Just let him go."

"I don't get you, Jess. What's the matter with you? He tried to kill you."

"But he didn't. He had an opportunity. Plenty of

them. And plenty of rage inside of him. And confusion. And sorrow."

"You feel sorry for him, don't you?"

"More than that, Mal," she confessed. "What I feel for Denny goes deeper than pity."

That said it all for me. Maybe I didn't understand her as well as I thought I did. Why would she side with the man who tried to kill her? I was the one who'd jeopardized my career for her. I was the one who loved her beyond compare. More than I thought I ever could—risking my life and the lives of people who worked with me to get her back. Was it all for nothing? Maybe the love we shared wasn't as strong as I'd thought. Slowly, deliberately, I readjusted her blanket.

"Come on, Jess. Let me take you to the hospital . . . get you checked out."

Denny had hurt her, had physically abused her, that much was obvious. What else had he done to her? What, if anything, had he done to her that I couldn't see?

"I'm all right, Mal," Jess said wearily. "I don't want to go to the hospital. I just want to go home."

"You need to be examined by a doctor, Jess. I'm gonna have to insist on that."

"He didn't rape me, Mal, if that's what you're worried about," she snapped, drawing the blanket around her, as if it were a shield. "He could have, but he didn't. He had a chance to kill me, but he didn't. He kept me out of the water. Kept me from dying. You're making up charges against him."

"Did I say anything about rape?"

"You didn't have to! I know you, Mal. I know what goes on in that suspicious brain of yours!" She thumped me against my forehead.

"And I thought I knew you!" I retorted. "I guess I

don't know you at all, for you to start acting like that bully was some kind of savior. You're just—"

I stopped in midsentence, struck by an idea so wild that for a moment, I thought I'd lost my mind. It couldn't happen. Not to Jess. Not strong-willed, sharp-minded Jess. But here she was, standing here in front of me, pure nonsense spewing from her mouth.

"Jess," I said gently, sitting next to her on the tailgate. I spoke slowly, calmly. "Jess, I know you've been through a lot these past few days."

"And?" she said, her tone still belligerent.

"I know that you're tired and hungry and scared. You've got every right to be."

"What's your point to this conversation, Mal?"

"Jess, baby," I said, putting my arm around her shoulder and drawing her close to me. She stiffened, as if she didn't want me to touch her. Still, I didn't release her. I wasn't going to let her go. Not like this. We weren't simply arguing. We were fighting. At least, I was fighting. Fighting hard to save our relationship. Our love. Because if I couldn't convince her that what I was about to tell her was true, it would be the end of us.

"Listen, okay. Just listen to what I'm gonna say to you. All right? Will you do that for me? All you have to do is listen."

"I'm listening," she said, though her tone told me that she wasn't prepared to believe me yet. She wasn't willing to believe that anything I could tell her was true, even if I told her that the world was round. Somehow, I had to regain her trust.

"You know I'd never hurt you," I said. "Never deliberately, intentionally hurt you. Have I ever hurt you?"

"N-no," she replied hesitantly. I could tell that she was thinking back. There were plenty of times that we'd wounded each other. But those were hurt feelings. And she'd given me just as many hurts as I'd given her. On that account, we were even.

"I'd cut off my own hands before I ever put a hand to you, Jessica Ramsay."

"I know that, law man," she said. Jess sighed and rested her head on my shoulder. I swear, I almost jumped three feet into the air. I didn't. I was careful not to do anything to startle or confuse her. I needed her thinking. Thinking clearly.

"You're a smart woman, Jess. You've got more book sense, more common sense than anyone I know. I want you to think now. Have you ever heard of a condition called the Stockholm syndrome?"

"The Stockholm syndrome?" she repeated.

"Yeah," I said, waiting for her to respond.

Jess closed her eyes. I felt her shoulders start to shake as realization swept over her. She was crying. My woman was crying. I let her, comforting her as best I could without trying to stop her. Whatever was inside her, whatever it was poisoning her spirit, I wanted it out of her.

"That's it, Jess," I murmured. "Let it all out. Lean on me, baby. I'm here now. I'm here."

"Stockholm syndrome! You think I'm suffering from the Stockholm syndrome? You're trying to say that I'm nutty as a fruitcake!" she reached out and punched me in the middle of my chest, then leaned into me to sniffle against my shoulder.

"No, Jess. That's not what I'm saying at all. It's not a mental defect. It's a . . . a . . . a type of coping mechanism." I struggled for the right words even as I marveled at the strength of her punch. "People who are threatened, held against their will, are placed under a lot of stress. It's something the mind does to protect you. It's a proven, documented fact. People who undergo the type of trauma you've experienced, they . . . well . . . They form this strange bond with their captors. They start to identify with them . . . even want to support them."

"You said I was too smart for that. So, how does a smart woman like me wind up with a messed up mind like that?"

"You're not messed up!" I insisted. "But to get over what happened to you, you are gonna need some help. Professional help."

I didn't understand why she started to laugh. Laughed so hard that she doubled over. First she was crying. Then she was laughing hysterically. I guess that was good for her emotionally. I wasn't really sure. It wasn't my job to play pop psychologist. I left that job to Jess.

"What's so funny?" I asked.

"Professional help," she replied, gasping and wiping at her eyes. "It's what I told Denny that he needed. He was so distraught at the loss of his brother. For a moment, I thought that he might be suicidal."

His brother. The younger kid. I'd almost forgotten about him. What was his name?

"If it makes you feel any better, we found him."

"Darryl? You found Denny's brother? Was he . . . was he . . . dead?" She could hardly bring herself to ask me.

"He was alive when Edmonds pulled him from the water near the Bramfort levee. He tried to perform CPR on him. We had a chopper take him to the county hospital. Last report I received, his condition was serious, but stable."

"Oh, Mal!" she exclaimed, flinging her arms around my neck. "Thank you!"

"What are you thanking me for? I was only doing my job."

"Forget the job!" she exclaimed. "I'm not talking about the job. I'm talking about you, you wonderful, wonderful man, you!"

She squeezed me tighter, pressing her body against mine. We stood there for several moments without moving, without speaking, simply letting the emotions take us where it would.

"I'm so sorry, Mal." Jess pressed her cheek against my chest and sobbed. "So, so sorry."

"For what?" I asked, lifting her chin and staring into her eyes. "What are you crying for now?"

Was it because of Denny? Was she apologizing for the way she'd shown concern for the man who'd threatened and kidnapped her? I understood why she'd done it. I'd already explained to her what that kind of trauma could do to a person. The Stockholm syndrome was as good as any reason I could find for her behavior.

Then again, that level of empathy she'd shown for those two was typical of Jess. She was always watching out for someone else, even when on the surface it didn't appear as if they'd deserved it. I was a living witness. She'd done it for that woman Brooke and her brood, fearing and suffering for the safety of that little boy Carter as if he were her own.

She'd shown me the same kindness, taking care of me when I'd hurt her time and time again. I knew how it must have been for her, day after day, year after year, watching me with Shelby when we both knew, deep in our hearts, that she and I belonged together. We were meant for each other.

"You don't have anything to apologize for," I insisted. "Everything's all right now."

"Take me home," she whispered wearily, clinging tightly to me. "I just want to go home."

I didn't make her ask me again.

Chapter Thirty-Five

Jess

Mal helped me up, lifting me into Edmonds's truck. I settled into the butter-soft leather interior but couldn't get comfortable. It seemed as though I'd been wet and cold and scared for such a long time.

Hold on a minute! I blinked in realization. I felt that way because I *had* been. I'd started out Monday morning mopping water that had seeped in my house and hadn't been completely dry since then. Here it was, Thursday and I was still soaking wet. That had to be some kind of record.

I leaned my head back against the headrest, breathing deeply, trying to restore my sense of perspective. Even though I felt like one giant sack of wrinkly prune flesh after being in the water for so long, I knew that I was going to be all right.

A sense of peace settled over me as soon as I heard Mal open the door. Something about familiar sights and sounds and smells, from knowing the fact that I was now in the care of a man who loved me above his own life, calmed me, even in the face of our surroundings.

No, the rain had not abated. And who knew how high

the river had yet to rise. Out there, away from the con-
fines of this truck, there were those who were just as
scared and as weary as I was. I sent out a prayer for them,
hoping that each one of them had their own special kind
of Mal to watch out for them.

Mal opened the door and climbed into the driver's
seat, but didn't start the engine right away. I could feel
him looking at me, but I didn't open my eyes. I couldn't.
I was too tired. Every bone in my body ached. My body
had turned into one giant muscle cramp. I shifted again,
this time groaning out loud at my discomfort.

"Are you all right, Jess?" Mal asked softly, his voice so
filled with tender concern that I thought I was going to
cry again. I didn't trust myself to speak. The lump in
my throat hurt too much. All I could do was shake my
head from side to side, clutching the blanket so tightly
that I thought my nails would rip it to shreds.

"Come here, baby," Mal said, putting his arm around
my shoulder and drawing me closer to him.

"Hold on to me, Mal," I whispered hoarsely. "Just hold
me. Don't let me go."

"I won't," he promised. "I swear I won't."

He was squeezing tightly, so much so that I heard my
ribs squeaking. "*Oomph.*" My voice was muffled against
his chest. "Okay, too tight."

I felt Mal's laughter rumble in his chest. Sort of like
the storms we'd experienced these past few days. Only,
this time I was safe, held within the shelter of his arms.

I knew that he meant it, too. I felt it in the desperate
way he entwined his fingers in my hair, pressing his forehead against mine. Face to face, he confronted me.

"Don't you ever, ever, ever scare me like that again,
woman. You hear me?"

"You were scared?" Not Mal. Not the man who'd

braved bullets and near drowning and the wrath of Mama's scoldings.

"Yeah," he admitted. "Of course I was. I thought I'd lost you."

"Never!" I declared, shaking him. "You can't lose me, Mal. Don't you know that by now?"

It was true. I'd waited too long for him. Nothing was going to stop me from being with Mal. Nothing. Not my best friend. Not a couple of teenaged thugs. Not a raging river. Not even my own foolish pride. As I sat there holding him, loving him, I wondered how I could have ever doubted him. It was my own fault that I'd pushed him to Shelby. I should have trusted my feelings for him and his commitment to me.

"You never did answer my question, you know," Mal said.

I shook my head uncomprehensively. "What question, Mal?"

"Seemed to me that a few days ago I asked you to marry me, Jess Ramsay. You never gave me an answer."

"You were serious about that?"

"I know it was hard to take me seriously, me standing there as naked as the day I was born," he began.

"It's not a question of taking you seriously," I quickly contradicted him. "It was a question of being able to concentrate on your words long enough to focus. You know you have the cutest little birthmark right *there!*" My hand slid over his thigh, caressing the sensitive area.

Mal scooted away from me and pushed me back to my side of the truck seat.

"Hey, none of that now! I'm cutting you off until you give me an answer, woman. Which will it be? Celibacy or ceremony?"

"Oh . . . gee . . . such a tough choice . . ."

"Jess," his voice was filled with warning.